BITTER REMEDY

BY THE SAME AUTHOR

The Dogs of Rome
The Fatal Touch
The Namesake
The Memory Key

BITTER REMEDY

CONOR FITZGERALD

BLOOMSBURY
LONDON · NEW DELHI · NEW YORK · SYDNEY

First published in Great Britain 2014

Bloomsbury Publishing Plc
50 Bedford Square
London
WC1B 3DP

www.bloomsbury.com

Bloomsbury is a trademark of Bloomsbury Publishing Plc

Bloomsbury Publishing, London, New Delhi, New York and Sydney

A CIP catalogue record for this book is available from the British Library

ISBN 978 1 4088 5345 0

10 9 8 7 6 5 4 3 2 1

Typeset by Hewer Text UK Ltd, Edinburgh
Printed and bound in Great Britain by CPI Group (UK) Ltd, Croydon CR0 4YY

PROLOGUE

Everything slithered. Trillions of spores filled her lungs, eyes, nose, and throat. They settled in Alina's stomach and chest, where gas and nausea and hunger waged war. At first, she tried to measure time through her memory of how long a day lasted. Then she tried measuring the hours by when she went to sleep and woke up. After an indeterminate period, she was no longer able to tell sleep from wakefulness. Sometimes she touched her eyes to see if they were open or closed.

Then she tried screaming as a unit of measurement. Every now and then, she would open her throat and shout for help at the top of her voice. When it came out as a croak or a whisper or a whimper, she knew very little time had passed since she last tried it; when it came out loud and raw and full of desperation, she knew some time had passed, but the sound of her own terror horrified her, and she began to wonder if it was really her doing all that shouting.

She tried to recall stories from her childhood, her travels, even the violent men. A slap or a punch now would be familiar and welcome. Male violence would mean she was alive. One time she woke up and the room was full of swirling colours, and she felt a sudden uplift of joy. But then she realized there was nothing but colours. There were no objects to which they might attach themselves. They floated like those she used to conjure up in the classroom by pushing her knuckles hard into her closed eyes. Behind them was only darkness. They were not even proper colours, more ideas of what colours might be.

Even so, she wanted to give some sort of geometrical form to them. Sometimes the yellow-green lights behind her eyeballs would resolve themselves into boxes or triangles. She could make red circles, yellow spirals, hexagons in green. She imagined an invisible demon sculpting pieces of black coal into twisted forms. Sometimes they appeared all too vividly, going far beyond mere geometrical shapes. Aborted babies, smashed faces, smiling men with black lips floated by her. Harry Potter was there, too.

Alina prayed. Not only for rescue, but preventatively, in case she died and failed to notice, and found herself unprepared on the other side.

The colours had gone. She was unsure if she was standing or lying, or perhaps seated on the ground. She put out her palms, and felt wall. Or was it floor? She pushed and felt her arms ache. She turned round and heard the squelch and pop of fungus under her spine. Lying then. She stood up and drew in the blackness though her eyes, nose, and mouth. Total, except for a tiny sliver of greyness that floated into the side of her right eye. She waited, expecting it to float into the middle and then up to the far corner of her right eye like the other optical effects had done, but it stayed there. Cautiously, she turned her head towards it, and it was gone. She tilted her head back, ready to scream again, no matter how futile and quiet the action might be, but stopped because the grey was visible again. She began to walk towards it, and it remained more or less where it was. She touched wall, vertical this time. The rectangle was gone, but reappeared as she stood back. She slid her hands up the wall, and felt it slope away from her. She felt around with her fingers, and realized it was an indentation of some sort. Overcome with a sudden wild urge that filled her with momentary strength, she jumped, stretching her fingers in the direction of where she estimated the hint of light might be. She banged her face and fell back almost senseless to the ground, but the tip of her forefinger was tingling. She had felt air.

1

CATERINA MATTIOLA let herself into the apartment, closing the door softly behind her. As soon as she entered, she knew he wasn't there. Not only his top-floor apartment, but the entire building was empty. The entire neighbourhood, for that matter. Alec had chosen to live in a new-build apartment put up by a construction company that had run out of money, or had been accused of recycling crime money, or had been embezzling public money.

'It's complicated,' he had told her once. Complicated or not, the construction company had vanished, leaving the apartment block above and a line of unfinished houses below, and the site office selling them had closed.

So now he lived, alone, the only inhabitant in a tall tower block, which stood on an isolated piece of ground that had been partly cemented over, but was now returning to nature. The vista from his living room window was, on first impact, expansive. There was the blue top of the IKEA sign and, beyond that, smooth green hills, now turning orange as the sun set, rolling all the way up to the nature reserve of Veio, where she had gone twice on school trips to see the remains of the Etruscan temples. It had seemed so far away then, well outside the city, but Rome's suburbs were moving northwards and Alec Blume was in the vanguard, his apartment overlooking the lands soon to be conquered. But then the eye was drawn downwards to the narrowness of the abandoned rows of houses and the narrow roads leading nowhere, and it became clear that the outward expansion had been halted.

'Alec?' She called his name, though it was clear he was not home. The sound of her own voice made her uneasy, and if he had actually answered, if any sound came back, she might have screamed.

She looked at the room. He had bought himself a large television. The few pieces of furniture were all from IKEA, presumably the one she could see out the window.

The first bedroom off the narrow corridor was filled with crates and boxes, which seemed to contain mostly books. She recognized them as the art volumes that had once belonged to his parents, but he had yet to put up any shelves and she was not sure the low-ceiling apartment could ever accommodate them. The next bedroom, the larger one, was his. A bed with three legs and a headboard fitted on backwards had been propped up vertically against the wall, an Allen key still sticking out of it. The frame included two wooden slats, splintered and split as if an angry someone had stamped on them several times. On the floor was a mattress made up with sheets and a grey-and-white chequered duvet. Beside it, on the floor, was a blue plastic reading light. On the pillow lay a copy of the book he was reading. *Austerlitz*. His neatly folded clothes were stacked on the windowsill, on an ironing board, and on an incongruous coffee table that he must have assembled in there because it was too wide to fit through the door. A sad pile of unpaired socks sat in the corner.

The bathroom was long and thin, the far end curving outward slightly in a semicircle, creating a slight outward bulge that was visible as a ripple on the brickwork on the outside of the building, presumably for decorative effect. The effect inside was to give the room the shape of a coffin, the toilet and shower sitting where the upturned face would be, the bath and hand basin playing the part of the arms, the floor and washing machine where she was, the feet. The medicine cabinet contained mouthwash, an unopened razor, and nothing else. She imagined him simply sweeping everything else into a plastic bag.

This was only her second time in his tower, as she thought of it. The first time she had been in a far more hostile mood, having kicked him out of her apartment just a few weeks before when he had proved himself incapable of being a caring father both for the child they had made together and for her son, Elia, whose dead father seemed to be a matter of complete indifference to Blume. As she was leaving that first time, he had pressed his house keys into her hands, but she had thrown them back at him, saying she was done with caring for him. She was past caring, she had told him.

But then, one day, he had left them on her desk in the police station, and when she had grabbed them and marched into his office to throw them back in his face, she found he was not there. Later that day, she learned he had taken an 'indefinite leave of absence'. For several days all the talk, the whispers when she drew near, had been about the Commissioner Blume's *crisi di nervi*.

Two days later, she swept the keys angrily into her handbag before going home. A week after that she had phoned him, and he had sounded . . . Fine was not the word. Definitely not fine, but he had lost none of his ability to infuriate her, which, after her anger subsided, she had found comforting. He was all right. That is what he had told her, too.

'I am taking a break. I have been told to take a break, to avoid a breakdown, so that is what I am doing.'

'Who told you?'

'The doctors.'

'Doctors, plural?'

'You always need a second opinion with those bastards. And a third.'

'I am glad you are seeing someone. Listen to them.'

'One of them told me I should do something that is the opposite of what I am. I had to ask him what he meant, and he said I should try to be open-minded. And to learn how to relax.'

'Sounds like good advice.'

'Sounds like an insult.'

'Take it as a challenge.'

'You can't fucking challenge someone to relax,' he said in what she recognized as a return to form, and the conversation had ended shortly after.

She allowed two weeks of silence to pass, then called him again, but he was not answering his phone. So, in spite of all her promises to herself, and without quite realizing what she was doing, she had left Alessia and Elia with her mother and come all the way out here.

The kitchen was separated from the living room by a breakfast bar. He had bought himself a 1950s-style diner stool with a red plastic cushion, but it seemed unlikely that he ever ate there, seeing as the bar top was taken up by an outsized printer and photocopier, a laptop, notebooks, stationery, and papers, arranged neatly enough. In the fridge, she found a carton of milk and smelled it. It had gone off, but only by a few days. A lump of cheese sat like an unused bar of soap on the middle shelf. Three bottles of Nastro Azzurro beer lay on their sides, which angered and dismayed her, and sent her searching through the rubbish bags to see how many empties he had left, but she found only a closed bag bulging with wastepaper and cardboard. He must have taken the bottles out with the rest of the waste before he left. Alcoholics like to hide their empties.

She turned her attention to the paper and printouts, expecting to find case files. He would sometimes look at old files and point out mistakes that had been made, and he liked to bring home profiles of victims, perpetrators, charts showing connections between suspects. But, apart from a printout of an IKEA brochure showing different shelving solutions and, oddly enough, a Wikipedia entry on herbal teas and a colourful catalogue on Bach Flowers, there was nothing.

She tore open the bag containing the wastepaper. It consisted mostly of pizza boxes, which he had conscientiously ripped up into small pieces, along with a few torn sheets of A4 paper printed on both sides; she took them out, spread them on the floor, and looked at them, working out their order. Two intact ones had to do with SIULP, the police union, and pension rights. Another page, stained with tomato sauce from a pizza and missing its top half, was something about a villa:

> . . . is sadly dilapidated but remains a handsome and ample building whose stone façade contains only a few faint streaks of the milk-and-lime red paint that had once made it stand out so clearly against the green garden that surrounds it.

'What villa, Alec? What are you doing?'

> The gardens are now more famous than either the building or the family that once lived there, and when people talk about the 'villa', the gardens are what they mean. They outclassed the villa even in its heyday, as well as the three generations of the family, which failed to see that building the

8

family mansion in the flatlands below a fortified hill town meant they could never dominate. By the time the great-grandson realized the mistake and had bought the highest house in the town, the historical centre of the town itself had become depopulated.

The microcosmic qualities of the gardens are exceptional. This patch of ground lying flat all year under an unrelenting sun and surrounded by stinking marshes and mosquitoes manages nonetheless, thanks to the exceptionally cool underground waters, to host Alpine flowers as well as Mediterranean plants. The garden has its own icy river, rising in a deep underground spring and forming a lake before it allows the water to flow out into the brown marshes outside. The villa even has its own mountain, which is just high enough to generate a unique weather system for this blessed patch of land by causing the rising moisture from the marshes and the nearby sea to form clouds that pile up and cool down against the black slate cliff face that makes up the western prospect of the mountain, which also casts a cool shadow over one-third of the grounds and half the villa. As night falls, the clouds move up a little, burst, and water everything below.

On top of this mountain sits the town of . . .

She turned over the torn page, and found only a few more lines of text from the bottom half.

The land is marshy in places, silty in others, clayey here, and acidy there. Springy turf, thick mud, soft grass, bright red dust, and fine-grained pH-perfect soil alternate so that almost any kind of plant will find perfect conditions, but no invasive species can traverse the boundaries of the soil types.

Outside the window the hills had now turned purple and grey as the sun dipped below the horizon. The lights of the shopping centre, the IKEA car park, and the motorway were shining like beacons of distant hope, and she badly wanted to get out of this ghostly apartment block before it got dark.

It seemed Alec Blume was taking a holiday. Well, good for him. As for her, she had two children to look after, one of them his.

2

STANDING IN the middle of a carefully designed maze of privet and jasmine bushes, well-tended but not grown high enough to function as a labyrinth for anyone but the smallest children, Alec Blume was nonetheless disoriented. He felt his dark trousers, heavy shoes, dark blue shirt, and beige jacket were too heavy for the soft green vegetation around him. He remained still, listening for the sounds of the other people he had expected to find, but hearing only the whisper of insects flitting between the pool and the plant stalks, and the fat buzz of a bee landing on a yellow floret. Had he mistaken the day?

One thing was certain: the villa made its own sounds. They could be mistaken for individual human sounds, for whimpers and throaty rasps and faraway cries, but not for the comfortable, generalized hubbub of visitors gathering at the beginning of a course, the sound of a teacher greeting them. Evidently he had come to the wrong part of the garden.

Although sweating now, with the hives on his chest smarting, it made him shiver to turn his back on the empty windows of the villa, which he imagined watching him. He turned round again, and it seemed as if the whole building had shuddered and taken a lurch in his direction. Something seemed to be moving in the corner of his left eye. He turned round again, this time with more resolution, ignoring the sensation of shimmering from behind, the hints of voices and muffled curses, and the sense of danger. These were precisely the sensations that he had come here to cure. He swallowed a Doxepin to stop the itching, and dismissed the sounds, so that even if someone in the villa had been screaming at that precise moment, he would have dismissed the sound as too faint, and he continued walking away, shoving a Lyrica pill under his tongue to calm his frayed nerves.

With the help of directions from a gnarled gardener who had disconcertingly sprung from a bush as he was passing, he found his group on the far side of the garden, behind the gate lodge he had parked in front of, but then ignored, presuming, for no particular reason, that the villa was the appointed meeting place. They were all looking in his direction, waiting for him, and, politely, he waved and quickened his pace a little, though none of them waved back. When he drew close, a slender young woman in blue jeans and a soft yellow cotton shirt with a paisley motif, folded her arms and shook her head in what seemed an exaggeration of amazed disappointment, given that he was only a few minutes late. The others in the group seemed to be regarding both him and, oddly, the young woman with some hostility.

'You didn't get my email?' she accused as soon as he was within earshot.

'No email,' said Blume, pausing to register his surprise and catch his breath.

'Is that your car out front?'

He wiped the sweat from his forehead and nodded.

'Guest parking is down the road. You go around the corner, and then turn left. It was signposted. That courtyard is ours. It's not for guests.'

'Nothing is for guests,' said a young man, a leather satchel slung across his body, wooden beads on his wrists, an observation which made his girlfriend giggle and a middle-aged woman stamp her foot and say, 'Exactly.'

Blume spread his hands seeking explanation.

'You would have come round the side of the gate lodge and found us immediately in the spice garden, where we were scheduled to meet, instead of wandering around the gardens on your own like that, and getting lost. Were you at the villa?'

'Near it,' admitted Blume, smiling at the young woman. 'Anyhow, a gardener, a small brown man in dirty clothes, showed me the way, and here I am.'

'My father, you mean,' she said.

'Oh. I didn't mean to . . .' But he never got to finish his apology, because now the young man with the satchel had had enough.

He made a fist of his right hand and attacked the palm of his left with it. 'This is total bullshit. We came all the way out here to the arse-side of nowhere . . .' He glanced over at his tanned girlfriend who giggled again at his wit.

'I thought I had cancelled all the bookings. Do you have more than one email?'

'Silvana, that's your name isn't it? Well, listen to me, Silvana,' said the young man, 'are you trying to tell us,' he swept his arm to include his sniggering girlfriend, the middle-aged woman, and Blume, 'that we are at fault for daring to have more than one email?'

To avoid watching the flush of embarrassment that was spreading upwards from the soft spot in the centre of Silvana's throat, Blume plucked a leaf and rubbed it between his fingers.

'It's just I probably sent the cancellation notice to the address you signed up from . . . I'm sorry. The Polizia Provinciale came the other day. I have a problem with ASL health and safety permits. I sent out an email immediately cancelling, just after they left.'

'Only in Italy,' said the young man, who indeed looked as if he had travelled to many places in the world, picking up a bead or a talisman to decorate his body in each one.

At last the older woman spoke up. 'I expect you shall be refunding our travelling expenses.'

'And maybe something for the sheer waste of fucking time. And false advertising,' said the young man. 'Isn't that illegal? Maybe we should report you to the police.'

Blume, now intent on smelling his fingers, glanced up at the word 'police'. I have thyme on my hands, he thought in English, then surprised himself by laughing out loud at his own private joke. 'I would be surprised if they gave much thought to your complaint,' he said, earning a grateful glance from Silvana.

'Oh, we have an expert,' said the young man with a shake of his curls.

Blume extracted a nasal spray, shot a jet up his nose, and snorted rudely with the back of his nose and throat.

'*Ma vaffanculo*,' said the young man. He turned to his girlfriend. 'Let's get out of here.'

'I don't think I would have enjoyed spending three days with that couple anyhow,' said the middle-aged woman, once the young couple was out of hearing range. 'So, Silvana, about the refund for fuel? I came down from Milan for this.'

'Milan? That's very far,' said Silvana.

'You say that like you doubt my word,' said the woman. She repeated the concept to Blume. 'She says that like she doubts my word.'

'I am inclined to believe you are Milanese,' he told her.

She peered at him suspiciously, seeking irony. Then, as the sound of the young man angrily revving his engine in the car park reached them, she said, 'Three hundred and thirty euros. Toll charges and fuel, down here and now the trip all the way back.'

Silvana blinked. 'I'll need to ask my father for that. Do you mind waiting?'

The woman sighed. 'We've waited this long, what's another few minutes?'

This last was addressed to Blume, who, however, had turned his back on her and was wandering aimlessly back into the garden. He did not need a refund, and he certainly did not need company.

Silvana found him a quarter of an hour later outside the crumbling villa at a point where the wooden stays keeping the wall up were overgrown with sprays of white and pink flowers. He had his hands pressed on the small of his back and was staring upwards to the boarded windows on the third floor, as if looking for something. He did not seem to notice her come up behind him, and she was afraid she might startle him, but when he turned round, he seemed completely unsurprised to see her there.

She held out a wad of banknotes. 'Your refund.'

'I don't need a refund.'

'I did send emails, you know.'

'I'm sure you did,' he said.

'Are you sure you don't want the money?'

'Quite sure.' He waved his hand at the crumbling mansion. 'So this is the villa we were supposed to be staying in?' When she nodded, he continued, 'I'm no expert, but it seems to me you'd need to spend a few hundred thousand to fix it up, and thousands per year in maintenance. How were you expecting a weekend course on Bach Flower Remedies to pay for that?'

'I am not trying to fix up the whole house, just a section of it.'

'It looks like a dangerous place. I can see why they did not give you permission to hold classes in it.'

'The classes would have been back at the lodge. The sleeping quarters were supposed to be in the villa.'

'Then I definitely see why you got no permissions. Hardly any of the windows even have glass in them. Creepy place to sleep, if you don't mind my saying.'

'It was not here. At the back of the villa, where it is structurally solid, we did a conversion. You're not supposed to be here.'

He looked at her, seeking clarification.

'You ignored the striped tape cordoning the area off. This side of the house is unsafe. Did you not see the sign saying this is off-limits?'

'Actually . . .' He seemed on the point of explaining himself, and then simply shrugged. 'Sorry. I'll go back now.'

He had authority and was wearing it lightly. She had naturally used the formal 'Lei' with him, but was surprised, and a little put out, when he used it back at her.

'Come round the other side, and I'll show you. But use "tu" with me, please.'

'With pleasure. As long as you do the same with me.'

'Of course, Mr . . . ? I have your name on my computer, but I am afraid I can't remember it.'

'Alec. Alec Blume.'

'Oh!'

'You seem surprised?'

'No. I remembered the unusual name. I thought you would be more foreign.' She led him round to the front. 'The main door is still boarded up.'

'Where is the part where the course participants were supposed to be staying?'

'I told you, at the rear. Basically opposite where we are now.'

'Shall we go round and see?'

'Why?'

'No reason,' said Blume. 'I just want to see what I am missing.'

'I don't really feel like gazing upon my failure,' said Silvana.

'I could go round myself, I suppose.'

'No. I'll come with you. Just stay outside the plastic tape, or what's left of it. You don't want a piece of masonry falling on you. We have to keep a wide berth, make a detour through the garden, and the path is not direct, as you'll see. It's sort of like having to creep up on the building from behind.'

The villa walls were plastered with yellow warning signs. *Pericolo Crollo. Vietato ingresso ai non addetti. Non Entrare.* They walked off to the right, following a D-shaped path that led them into the garden away from, then back to the building. On their way, Blume stopped to drink from a fountain, once sculpted but now so weather-worn that the stone seemed to have melted.

'Is the water all right here?'

'Of course!' said Silvana.

'You can't always be sure,' said Blume. 'I was visiting a tomb recently in Rome. The graveyard has hoses and fountains for the flowers, you know? And there was a man there drinking from it. I didn't like the idea, drinking water that comes up from graves.'

'This is a garden, not a graveyard.'

'True. The land outside the gardens is marshy, I suppose I was worried about that.'

'I have lived here all my life and drunk the same water,' said Silvana. 'And there's nothing wrong with me.'

As they reached the back of the building, where, indeed, the walls were straighter, and no windows were missing, she said, 'You can smell the damp here.'

'Like mushrooms,' he said. 'I find it soothing.'

'Unless it's in a bedroom,' said Silvana. 'OK, so here you have a walled garden coming out from the back of the villa, a perfect square. In fact, the area is precisely the same as the villa itself. In 1870, they added sheds, stables, and storerooms on this side, and, well, you'll see in a minute, this is where we did the conversions. So strictly speaking, the intended living quarters were not in the villa. Through this gate here . . .'

They came into an enclosed courtyard. The central area was filled with prolific weeds, most taller than humans.

'The former owners . . .'

'The Romanelli family,' said Blume.

'You did your homework,' she said. 'The Romanellis, maybe because they did not have that many guests, converted the stables into storerooms and this courtyard into a vegetable garden.'

'As if they didn't have enough garden already,' said Blume. He pointed to the far side, 'Are those steps leading down to a basement?'

'Presumably.'

'So three floors, plus an entire basement. They built big in those days,' he said.

She fished a key out of her jeans, unlocked a door next to them. 'This is one of the converted stables.' She switched on a halogen light. The fresh plaster was peeling and blackening already. Corrugated tubes were sticking out of the walls.

'The wiring is not finished either,' she said sadly. 'We did up ten rooms like this. We had a *geometra* check for structural integrity, we got all the necessary permits, or almost all of them, the Region even made us sign a rider to our lease specifying that these improvement works would revert to public ownership in the event of a sale, even though that's already part of the agreement.'

'I don't follow.'

'My father and I. We have a concession for the villa and the gardens, but it is owned by the Regional government. In the old days, you would get the concession practically in perpetuity and hand it down generation to generation, but these are tough economic times. The Region could even decide to repossess and sell the place. We get right of first refusal, and we would get a decent discount, but we're still talking in terms of millions for the house and gardens.' She pointed to the empty room. 'Do you like those hexagonal tiles?'

'Very much.'

'You would not believe how much it cost to restore them. More than all the plastering and new wiring put together. They refused me the licence at the last moment. An inspector said it was not fit for temporary habitation, which of course it wasn't because we did not want to invest any more until we were sure we could get the licence. We tried to explain it to him, but he would not listen. Anyhow, if you don't mind . . .'

'What?'

'Can we leave now? It's all a bit depressing for me.'

'Oh, of course. I am sorry,' said Blume. 'You were doing a great job with those rooms. Funny isn't it, the way the former stables and your gate lodge turn out to be far more habitable than the building to which they were meant as accessories.'

They returned to the courtyard.

'Well, I suppose I'd better be getting back to Rome,' he said.

'That's where you're from?'

'Yes. It's a pity this didn't work out for you. Maybe next time, you'll have more luck. I hope they give you a licence, and you get this place done up.'

Together they contemplated the crumbling masonry, the rotten shutters.

'Come on,' said Silvana, 'I'll show you the way back. It's harder than it looks to find your way. You tend to use the house as a landmark, but the paths follow a different logic. By the way, this section of the garden closest to the villa is the least looked after, because, well, my father says he'd need another three people to keep the whole place in order.'

'I'm sorry for my description of him. I meant no offence.'

'That's all right. You were not to know.'

'He does a fine job,' said Blume, pausing to admire a tangle of high-growth weeds.

'Only by avoiding this area. The seeds from those plants get everywhere.'

Blume turned his admiration of the white-topped plants into a critical frown. 'Must be a nuisance,' he said. 'How about fire, to control them?'

'Some weeds love fire. They thrive on it. The seeds need heat to pop open. And it's illegal and dangerous, too, especially near the villa.'

They walked on in a comfortable silence. She pointed to an unkempt patch of weeds, one of the last before her father's landscaping efforts reasserted themselves. 'You see those really tall plants?'

He nodded.

'Most of them belong to the carrot family.'

'Really?'

'Yes, really,' she said. 'They thrive on damp soil. There is a river running below this villa. That's probably why the Romanellis were always sick and left here. Damp. Mould, mildew. The walls in the villa are sponges.'

'Big carrots.'

'What?'

'If those are carrots, they must be giant carrots.'

For the first time that day, Silvana felt she could laugh. 'The carrot family, also called the apiaceae, includes all sorts of other things: parsnips, fennel, hedge parsley, celery. If you smell or taste them, you'll see what I mean.'

Blume pulled off a handful of curved seeds and smelled them. 'You're right. Parsley, or . . .'

'Angelica. That's called garden angelica – I think. The seeds are used as flavouring in candies and cakes . . .'

Blume popped a handful into his mouth, and chewed for a bit. 'Can't say I'd want that in a cake. Too much like . . . parsnip or horseradish. That's it. Horseradish. Excuse me . . .' He spat out a few remaining seeds and fingered his teeth. 'Bitter! Well, I suppose I should be going.'

'I'll accompany you.'

They walked back towards the gate lodge, and she explained the layout and how he had turned straight into the main gate ignoring the sign for parking ahead. 'Not that it matters, of course. The car park behind the spice garden, well, it's larger but its main advantage, I suppose, is we don't get people parking outside our house.'

'Spice garden? That sounds interesting.'

'We were standing on the edge of it just now with the other guests. If you had used the right entrance, you'd have walked through it.'

'I can't get anything right.' He pulled out his car key and bleeped open the door. 'You know, I wouldn't have been a good customer anyway. I don't really believe in Bach Flowers, herbs, and all that sort of stuff.'

'But you were open enough to give it a chance.'

'I suppose,' said Blume, rubbing his upper arm, then scratching his chest.

'You seem anxious. Valerian is very good for that. I have some in the lodge. We live upstairs. Downstairs is my herb centre. Come on, I'll give you a free sample. Are you itching, too?'

'Bit of an itch. I have pills though.'

'I have a balm that works miracles! You never asked me for any refund. It's the least I can do.'

She entered the gate lodge. It was a long building, with two floors, but so low that a tall man could probably jump and grab the windowsill of the upper floor, which he noticed was accessible from an external staircase. Inside, in a far more successful version of the efforts in the stables behind the villa, they had cleared out the old agricultural equipment and whitewashed the lower part, which was divided into three rooms. The central section was a herbal store and laboratory, and he was quite impressed by the sanded floors, baskets, flowers, spot lighting, tasteful books, and the scent of dried and fresh herbs. One of the smaller spaces contained a large oak table. Beside it was a disused potter's wheel and an old Singer sewing machine. Keys, rusty and unused, hung on the wall.

It should have felt pleasant and cool, but he felt suddenly constricted, and found himself hurrying outside again in search of more air. He drew a breath, which stopped halfway before he was finished. He drew another, which stopped a quarter of the way, and the one after that was even shorter. He coughed, then winced, then coughed some more, and, as he reached the outdoors, called back to Silvana, still searching for the balm, 'I don't suppose I could trouble you for a bit of water? Those seeds seem to be burning my mouth.'

She appeared on the doorstep, holding a jar of ointment. 'Burning? They shouldn't burn.'

'Something is definitely burning my mouth and throat – and chest. It's sort of a soapy taste.'

She looked at the pointless ointment in her hand, then at him.

'What sort of weird cakes . . .'

'Cakes?'

'You said the seeds were used to flavour cakes.' He stopped talking. His tongue felt too big for his mouth. He started fumbling at his shirt, which was soaked in sweat. On the third button, his finger slipped and he ripped it open. 'Water.' It was a command, not a request.

Silvana went running back inside, calling for her father. She filled a pitcher of water and brought it out to Blume, who was sitting slumped against his car now, breathing heavily. In the minutes since she had left him, he had turned deathly white.

'Papà!' she screamed. Blume grabbed the pitcher and poured the water into his mouth and over his face, then groaned and stretched out on his side.

'Papà!' Then she remembered her phone. She had left it in the store. She ran in, found it, fumbled with the keypad, and finally managed to call him. He answered almost immediately. 'Papà, there's a man here . . . no, listen, this is serious. He's eaten something poisonous. *I* don't know. It was . . . he just took a handful.'

'Some sort of carrot,' said Blume. 'Call an ambulance, please.'

Silvana collected herself. 'I am sorry . . . My father's calling an ambulance. Look, there he is now!'

'The ambulance?'

'No, my father.' She seemed to turn away from him as she said this, and then suddenly her face was right up in front of him, and her voice was bellowing and loud. Everything felt chubby, like in a Botero painting, and his stomach heaved. A sensation of enormous pressure filled his chest, as if there were a vastness of air in it and the only escape was through a thin tube that could block or burst at any moment. And there was a lot of pain. The air in his chest seemed to be expanding, forming an echo chamber in which he could feel his heart, thumping out of rhythm with his breathing, which, he realized, was coming in short rasps. Not red jumping pain like when a dentists drills into a nerve, but grey and spreading. He no longer felt his legs, but a new type of ache had spread to his arms. Usually an ache was a deep but dull sensation, a promise of pain to come, but this one had all the panicky urgency of a cramp. And now his bowels, too . . . A bony man, dark brown, soil embedded in the wrinkles of his wide forehead, a smell of earth from his clothes, was shouting something – then whispering, it seemed. Blume retched. The burning was intolerable, but he was afraid to scream in case his throat ripped itself open.

'Cicuta possibly. I can't think of anything else. It wasn't a giant hogweed, was it? . . . Marshy there . . . Too far south, even for this garden.'

Blume tried to prop himself up, but found he could hardly lift his face from the ground. He focused his energy on speaking. 'What is happening?'

A man's voice, southern-accented, friendly, answered. 'I can't be sure, but my daughter thinks you just ate hemlock.' It was the man with the chestnut face, the gardener, who seemed to see something amusing in all this. Blume sort of saw it, too; but was it possible to laugh at your own impending death? An image of Caterina came into his mind, and their baby daughter, Alessia, nine months old. Caterina threw him out of her life, but had named their child after him. He should leave a message for them, but none came to mind.

Five minutes later, the gardener, showing far greater strength than Blume could ever have imagined, dragged and pushed him into a dilapidated Fiat Uno.

'An ambulance will take too long. I'll get you to the clinic in town instead. Silvana is calling ahead.'

Blume was too big for the back seat and lay huddled up in foetal position, knees in chest. 'Far?' was all he managed to say.

'Just up the hill,' assured the old gardener.

Blume recalled plenty of gear grinding as they drove slowly up the winding road. With each hairpin turn, the car seemed to get slower, but to compensate, his mind was racing, his thoughts flying.

3

I T WAS Alina who, all those years ago, had discovered the free
tickets to Hogwarts University of Magic in London. The offer
was right there, flashing inside a pink star on the screen in front of
them. Nadia was sceptical. This was her default mode; in part because
life so far had taught her to be so, in part because she felt it was her
role, being a year older than Alina. But Alina's zeal was infectious,
and the best of it was that the offer was for two people. Nadia had
introduced Alina to the Harry Potter movies and books, and was
pleased to see her friend as enthusiastic about the adventures as she
was, so it seemed unkind to be sceptical.

But however many times they clicked on the flashing message,
they found out no more about the University, but plenty about
the need for credit cards. Following these links, they soon found
themselves in a world of non-stop pop-up gambling sites, and clicks
to close these down led them eventually to images of women giving
blow jobs, sometimes with the same star flashing just where mouth
met cock, but just as often uncensored. Nadia tried to be grown
up and casual about the pictures, and Alina made a great show of
laughing at them, while all the time grimly persisting with the mouse
clicks, convinced that she would eventually hit the enchanted link

that would show them how to enrol in the Hogwarts University in magical London. The dream lasted two days, until Alina's brother, Michael, scoffingly introduced them to the concept of spam and online scams.

That was all a lifetime ago. Years passed, Harry Potter was replaced by reality stars and boy bands and Alina left school to become a hairdresser. But apart from three Saturday afternoons sweeping up hair from the floor of the beauty salon at the north end of Bulevardul Oituz, she did not go far. And yet, she had not quite let go of the dream of London, or at least somewhere that was not the town of Onesti in the snow, a place whose greatest claim to fame was a gymnast from sometime long ago in the previous century and the Rafo refinery, where Michael had failed to get a job.

Nadia stayed on in school a little while longer, but she was never going to take the final exams. Her father had long ago vanished 'abroad'. All that remained of him in her mind was the memory of a smell of oil, though he had not worked in the factory or been a mechanic.

Nadia had once had an older brother, of whom she also had little memory. Apparently at the age of fifteen he had been crushed by a reversing cement mixer. He lived on in agony for three months before dying, and her father – she had to work out the chronology herself – had left 1 month later.

Her mother, who had kept her figure and for whom alcohol had a thinning rather than a fattening effect, suddenly lost all her teeth. They came out one by one over three weeks. Saliva and blood was everywhere in the bathroom, even in the kitchen, along with crushed tissues lying around the house that Nadia dared not open.

On the day her last teeth fell out, a front tooth and a molar, Nadia's mother howled and yelped like a tortured dog. Her gaping mouth with black gums spoke unintelligible angry words. The following day she was silent and motionless, and so she remained for three years.

In the meantime, Alina and Nadia had been deliberately hanging out with the wrong sort of people. Older boys, men even, who would buy them beer, snacks, take them for drives. The older men were always the same, but the turnover among the younger ones was fast. Some tearaway aged sixteen would arrive, get into trouble, hang around a year, and then he'd be gone, off on his adventures in Europe, England, Italy, France, Germany. The girls, too, came and went, and one night, drunk, sitting in the back of someone's car, Nadia turned to Alina, or Alina turned to Nadia — neither of them could ever say for certain who it had been — and said, 'We have been here too long.'

One of the ways out was through the wife of a man who worked as a city clerk, handing out building permits. Olga was her name. It was not easy to get a meeting with her husband, let alone Olga. When they did, it was in a bar outside the town-planning department, and he demanded a fee before telling them that he was not sure if they would be lucky enough to get a meeting with his wife.

No one liked Olga, even those who had never met her, but all agreed that she made things happen, moved people on, arranged contacts, knew people abroad, and, it was said, spoke six languages. There was talk about Milan, possibly a Vidal Sassoon Academy, but the details were vague and the trip would be a roundabout one.

They heard nothing for months. Olga's husband refused to speak to them, refused even to acknowledge Nadia when one day she tried to waylay him as he left the office. A day later, the two of them turned up, but so did two men, who threatened them.

And then, on the day the clocks went back, Olga got in contact. She phoned both of them, and invited them round for tea in her house, which was outside the city. She sent a man to pick them up. Olga's house was brand new, so new it still smelled of cement and new carpet, and it was stiflingly warm. They had salami and pickles, cakes, tea, coffee, a few liquors. Nadia and Alina were not the only girls there. The mood became quite raucous, and they all left in high spirits. Olga winked at the girls a lot, and many jokes at the expense of men were whispered. The girls giggled, and Olga laughed uproariously. She asked them about passports, cash, and, in detail, about their family situations, even though she seemed surprisingly well informed already. On their third visit, Olga offered them nothing to eat or drink, cracked no jokes about men or anything else, and told them she had made arrangements for the New Year. They were to be ready by then.

Nadia's mother did not even bestir herself from her bed when, a few days before Christmas, Nadia announced that she was leaving. On 2 January, *Anul Nou*, she left Romania and her toothless, useless mother.

Looking back, Nadia could not quite remember at which point she had allowed herself to be properly deluded. She had walked into the trap with her eyes open. She wondered about Alina, who really spoke as if she were going to work with Vidal Sassoon in person. Their friendship seemed as deep as ever, deeper even now that they knew they were going away together, but somehow their conversations about the future skated along the surface of things. Neither of them seemed to want to be the first to confide her fears, to admit that she knew what they were getting into, because then they would have to back out, and what would be left?

Alina's ignorance may have helped. She did not even notice that the coach that was supposed to take them on the first leg of their journey to Italy was headed east. As they crossed the Moldova border, Olga cheerfully told them and the six other girls, one of them no older than fifteen, that they were going to Odessa, where they would catch a boat.

Alina put up her hand, which is something she had never done in the classroom, and said, 'Excuse me?'

'What is it, my pretty thing?'

'Nadia and I, we're going to Italy. We've paid the fare.'

'Ah, yes,' said Olga. 'But you didn't pay very much, did you? You don't think that was nearly enough to get a plane all the way to . . . where was it, Rome?'

'Milan.'

'Oh, Milan. I envy you. It's a great city. But I am afraid it will be a long journey. We'll be stopping off before we reach it.'

'Where?' asked Alina.

'Ports of call. I don't suppose you can name them, can you?'

Geography had never been Alina's strong point. Nor had much else. She shook her head, brushing Nadia's face with her red hair.

'Odessa, Istanbul – perhaps we'll stay a day or two there. Thessalonica, probably, but it might even be Athens! Then a short ride across to Patras and a ferry to Bari. Don't worry. I have your passport here.' Olga patted her massive bust as if it was filled with all the passports she had taken off the girls, and the girls before them and the girls before them.

They rattled their way across the uneven roads of Moldova. They somehow managed to fall asleep and missed the border crossing into the Ukraine, but Olga handled everything. No one even came on board to check.

Finally, Odessa. Nadia had not expected it to have so many impressive boulevards and trees. Banks, luxury hotels, boutiques, prosperous people everywhere. The buildings looked like they belonged in France or Italy. She nudged Alina awake.

'This place is like Milan. Maybe we could stay here.'

Alina stared grumpily out the window, just as the coach, its wheels making a plopping sound on the cobblestone road, passed a row of boarded-up shops. 'You've never been to Milan, how would you know,' she said crossly, and tried to fall asleep, using Nadia as her pillow.

Nadia shrugged viciously, causing her friend's lazy head to hit the broken armrest between them. 'At least I knew Milan wasn't in the Ukraine.'

The coach pulled into a parking area and stopped beside a lump of slate with 1941–1945 inscribed in it. The air below them glinted and sparkled, and Nadia felt her heart leap with excitement and possibility.

'Look, Alina, the sea!' She grabbed her friend's hand in excitement. Maybe it was going to be a great adventure after all.

4

'TIME IS muscle,' said a voice. 'Good morning.'

Blume opened his eyes. He felt a bit nauseous. Above all, he felt frightened. The person who had spoken was a man with a bright round face which seemed unreasonably cheerful, and wisps of white hair.

'It's a phrase we doctors use,' said the man. 'You need to thank the gardener, Greco, with the pretty daughter who came here with you. If it hadn't been for him, we might have wasted time listening to your nonsense. Silvana, that's her name, the poor girl you say poisoned you. How can you say a thing like that?'

'Not deliberately.'

'You were never poisoned, Mr . . . Blume? Is that how you pronounce it, rhymes with boum-boum? The name was on your driver licence. Tell me, what's your profession, Mr Blume?'

'Why?'

'For your prognosis. If you work in an asbestos factory or a steel mill, it's going to have an effect on your health. If you spend the day seated or standing, if your job is stressful or not: it makes all the difference.'

'I understand,' said Blume.

'So what are you?'

'A tax accountant.'

'Really?'

'Is that so interesting?'

'Well, it is for me, because the one I have, well, he forgot to deduct his own fees from my taxable income. Can you imagine?'

Blume could not. He was bothered by the fact the room was small yet contained an echo.

'But obviously your practice is in . . . ?'

'Rome. Can you lower your voice, please?'

'I am speaking in a normal tone. You appear to have an overstimulated auditory sense. That's interesting.' He dropped his voice to a whisper. 'I am Doctor Bernardini. You are in a semi-private clinic for now. Breakfast?'

'What time is it?'

'Half past seven. Here, I brought you this.' The doctor reached behind him and produced a tray holding a small carton of apricot juice, two slices of melba toast, a plastic knife and a capsule of sugar-free strawberry jam.

'No coffee?'

'The nuns don't really go in for coffee, and it's probably best not. Avoid stimulants for the next few days.' He watched as Blume munched his way through the dry bread. 'You seem fine. So, how *do* you pronounce your name?'

'Blume.'

'It does rhyme with *Boum!* Do you know the song?' asked the doctor. 'No? By Charles Trenet?' He stood back from the bed to give himself some space. 'I'll need to raise my voice a little for this.'

'For what?'

The doctor sang:

> *'La pendule fait tic-tac-tic-tic*
> *Les oiseaux du lac pic-pac-pic-pic*
> *Glou-glou-glou font tous les dindons . . .*

They almost ruined it for me by using it in a biscuit commercial. You should eat fewer biscuits. Do you take prescription drugs, Mr Blume?'

'No, not really.'

> *'Mais . . . BOUM!*
> *Quand notre cœur fait BOUM!*
> *Tout avec lui dit BOUM*
> *Et c'est l'amour qui s'éveille.'*

The doctor stopped, his face flushed with pleasure. 'I first learned that in primary school. Some time ago, now. I have always loved Trenet, Brel, Brassens, Gainsbourg. An area where the ubiquitous rhythms of English have yet to penetrate. So no drugs, but herbal poisoning? I am not sure I can possibly believe that.'

'I ate these seeds . . .'

'And you almost had a heart attack, but didn't,' finished the doctor for him. 'Pure coincidence. This is how I see it: the burning sensation in your mouth set off a panic attack causing acute arrhythmia, but it was your own panic that did it, not the seeds, whatever they were. We could have wasted valuable time looking for poisons if we had listened to you. But Greco kept insisting it was not the plant you ate.'

'How could he be so damned certain?'

'Too fast, he said. The symptoms hit you too fast. Also, he knows a lot about the plants in those gardens. Greco's quite the expert. A bit of a loner, but . . . lovely gardens. The highlight of our little town, I suppose. Usually worth a visit, though . . .' The red face turned even redder and the doctor giggled. 'What a stupid thing for me to have said. My wife will find that hilarious when I tell her. She loves it when I make a *faux pas*. Here am I telling you to visit the gardens, and you have just come from there with definite signs of a heart attack.'

The doctor's words sank into him like a heavy gas. 'I've had a heart attack?'

'No! A panic attack! God, I am so sorry. Another gaffe. I am so gauche!' Bernardini gave Blume a knowing wink. 'You seem to have reacted poorly to our extraordinary gardens. An allergic reaction. I see you have hives, too. Were they there before?'

'Yes.'

'Well, nothing to worry about then. A bit of a panic.

> *C'est un jardin extraordinaire,*
> *Il y a des canards qui parlent anglais*
> *Je leur donne du pain ils remuent leur derrière*
> *En m'disant 'Thank you very much Monsieur Trenet . . .'*

'I did not panic.'

'*Au contraire, Monsieur Boum!* Yes, you did,' sang Bernardini without breaking the rhythm of his song.

> '*Il fallait bien trouver dans cette grande ville perverse*
> *Une gentille amourette un petit flirt de vingt ans.*'

He stopped and looked thoughtful. 'You have angina. We both know that. And now your body panicked. For me, that is the same thing. Do you consider your body separate from your mind? Cartesian extremism, if so. How do you explain tears? Or laughter? That feeling of fear in the stomach, the evacuation of the bowels in cases of extreme danger, the loss of appetite from sorrow?'

'I'm sorry, was that a question?'

'Just remember, panic can kill, too. But you are still here and talking to me. All in all, it could have been worse. You are too young. You have no business having a heart attack at your age.'

'You said it wasn't a heart attack.'

'Not this time,' said Bernardini shaking his head grimly. 'What about your parents?'

'Both dead.'

'Ah-hah.' The doctor looked pleased, then mortified. 'I am terribly sorry. I didn't mean it like that.'

'Not from heart attacks,' said Blume, driving home his advantage.

'Hmm, *chose curieuse*. Are you sure?'

'Of how my parents died? Quite sure.'

'An accident?'

If being shot as innocent bystanders in a bank raid qualified as an accident, thought Blume. If a double homicide could be described using a word that would make the doctor think of a car crash, then, yes, it was an accident. Blume nodded.

'Too bad. *C'est-à-dire* a tragedy. What about your wife, girlfriend?'

'What about her?'

'Don't you want her here by your bedside? Who do you want me to call?'

'I am not married.'

'No one then?'

Blume closed his eyes, and fell immediately into a world of swirling colours, prismic, intense, and dark, like the gleaming rainbow on an oil slick. A two-hour drive would take him back to Caterina, still on maternity leave. She was probably holding Alessia right now, breastfeeding her. They had induced the birth a month early, because the pregnancy had caused hepatosis in the mother. Caterina scratched herself till she bled as her liver failed and her blood filled with bile. At one point, she phoned Blume, who had not seen her in two months, and screamed down the phone at him, as if the poison coursing through her were all his fault, which it was. That meant that he somehow gained the right to accompany her the following morning to Fratebenefratelli hospital on the Tiber island, where they broke her waters. The Tiber was swollen and lapping against the hospital walls just below the window. Blume saw two rats swimming upstream, against the current. The cure for foetal hepatosis, a nurse explained, was childbirth. As soon as the baby was out, the disease vanished as if it had never been.

Alessia came out weighing 3.8 kilos, and everyone joked that it was a good job they called her out early. Perhaps the dates had been slightly miscalculated. She did not look like a child ripped untimely from the womb, though she was very red and in the middle of her head was a huge area of softness like bread taken out too early that seemed to pulse and he was afraid to touch. Even the nurses said they had rarely seen a fontanelle so open, and the doctor came and took a look at it and handed Alessia back to her mother with the assurance that all was perfectly as it should be.

'You had a stroke, didn't you?' Dr Bernardini interrupted his thoughts.

'A panic attack, according to you.'

'No, I meant before now. I have been watching you. We need to get you into a larger hospital. A real one. You are now in Casa di Cura Madonna della Misericordia. We're too small to have a hospital.'

Blume folded his arms, and scowled at the doctor. 'I don't know what you've been seeing, Doctor, but I did not have a stroke.'

'Lift up both arms.'

'Fuck off. *You* lift up both arms.'

To his surprise, the doctor did. '*Et voila!* Look, Blume, may I ask an awkward question? Have you consumed certain illegal drugs?'

Blume looked suitably disgusted at the suggestion.

'All right, so I return to this question of prescribed drugs, perhaps improperly renewed?'

'I hardly even drink any more,' said Blume.

'No? That was going to be my next conjecture.'

Blume looked around at the flaking green paint on the walls, at the wheeled table with a piece of equipment that looked like it might have had a purpose in the mid–1950s, then glanced back quickly at the friendly red face.

'Nystagmus,' said the doctor. 'No one noticed that?'

'First I have heard of it,' said Blume, glancing over to the corner of the room where a minor commotion seemed to be unfolding between two colourful – no, nothing. It was just a mop and the way the sunlight gleamed on the steel table leg. The mop seemed to sway a little as he watched it. 'What is it?'

'Your left eye tends to wander. Do you experience dizziness?'

'Not as a rule, no. Wander where?'

'To the side and back again, slowly, like it's scanning for something. Nice and smooth, with the occasional saccadic jerk. It's quite noticeable. It's as if you're looking for something to the side, then you snap out of it and focus your attention on whatever is before you.'

'This is a bad thing?'

'Well, I see it as a medical issue,' said Bernardini. 'For others, it might give the impression that you're not quite paying attention, or don't quite trust them or the people around them. For all I know you have always had it. But, looking at you now, seeing this, and considering the way your bottom lip curves down a little strangely on your left – I would say you are recovering from a stroke.'

'A transient ischaemic attack,' said Blume quietly, as if afraid someone might overhear. 'It's not the same as a stroke.'

'How long ago?'

'Five weeks.'

'How long were you in hospital?'

'Two days,' said Blume, his voice low with shame.

'What brought you in?'

'I was shaving . . .'

'And your arm grew heavy?'

'No. My arm is and was perfectly fine.'

'Sorry, I shouldn't have interrupted.'

'Interrupted what? There is no story. I looked into the mirror, and there was this sort of tragic-comic mask looking back at me. I checked in, but it was all over already. I came here . . .'

'To hide from someone?'

'I beg your pardon?' said Blume.

'Sorry, there I go leaping to conclusions again. You came here to get quite better. Relax, get some exercise done, go back to Rome, looking perfectly normal, and perhaps a little fitter, apart from the nystagmus, which you may have always had. Admirable. What about your clients?'

'What clients?'

'You're a tax accountant, remember?'

'Oh, them. That's all taken care of. I have a junior partner . . . Alessia. Yes, quite right. I was trying to relax. Herbal remedies, flowers. And look what it did to me.'

'You ate a poisonous plant.'

'So it *was* poisonous.'

'Perhaps it was not. If I ask you to go to the hospital, you won't, will you?'

Blume avoided the doctor's eyes.

'This is a clinic. We specialize in urology, really. That is to say, a urologist whose brother's a bishop has managed to persuade some nuns to run what is essentially a private practice . . .'

'A friend of yours, I gather.'

'A cousin, actually. The point is, here is no good. Will you allow me to make a few guesses and then a suggestion?'

Blume propped himself up on his pillows. 'Sure.'

'You are reluctant to go to hospital,' Bernardini paused to see if Blume would object. 'I see. *J'ai raison*. About that. Well, that's good inasmuch as it suggests you are feeling strong enough to resist good advice. But I will say at this point that you might simply drop down dead.'

'As might you,' said Blume.

'As might I,' agreed Bernardini, rubbing his hands in what seemed like eager anticipation of the moment. 'I am also guessing that there is someone back in Rome you would prefer not to see, or be seen by. So my suggestion is that if you are planning to stay here in town for a few days, let me check up on you.'

'No need. I can leave immediately. This very moment, in fact.'

'No, Commissioner, that is not what I meant.'

Blume sat back and regarded Bernardini levelly, allowing the silence between them to lengthen.

'*Putain!* I just called you Commissioner, didn't I? Blume is not a common name. I looked up your medical records.'

'As any conscientious doctor would do.'

'So not a tax accountant after all.'

'No. I am on leave.'

'You work in the murder squad?'

'*Squadra mobile*, yes.'

'It must be stressful. That would explain your poor health and cagey manner.'

'Also explains the Nisi . . . that thing that makes my eyes watch out what's going on nearby.'

'Nystagmus. Except you better hope your enemies come at you from the left. Are you here about the missing girl?'

'What missing girl?'

'Ah!' He winked and ran his thumb down his cheek. 'I understand.'

'No *ah*! No, you don't. I know nothing of any missing girl, Dottore.'

'Call me Bruno.'

'OK, Bruno. One thing, I'd prefer it if you didn't mention to anyone . . .'

'About the girl?'

'No, I just said . . .'

'About your mini-stroke?'

'Not that either. Just that I am a cop. It raises some expectations, lowers many more.'

'Oh, of course!'

'You already have, haven't you?'

'No! I have said nothing. *Rien.*'

Blume could see he had, but it made no difference. His five days of relaxation, during which time he had planned not to let anyone know what he did for a living, were not going to happen.

5

Niki Solito, up and about earlier than he liked, blew his nose long and hard into a snow-white cotton handkerchief. He folded it and its contents and placed them carefully in his left pocket. From his right pocket, he drew out a second handkerchief, this one a pale green, and dabbed his damp forehead. He folded and put away this handkerchief, too, double-checking it had gone into the correct pocket. He sat down, breathing heavily, on a rickety chair outside the gate lodge where he had expected to find Silvana, on what would have been the second morning of her Bach Flowers lessons. She would take it out on him, of course. She always did. She would blame him for the cancellation, say he had always been dead set against the idea, whereas in fact he had just never seen the point. Money was not a problem.

He dropped his satchel onto the ground before him, opened it, and lifted out a small pile of freshly laundered handkerchiefs, which he placed on his lap. He then dug his hand back in and pulled out the black leather insulin kitbag. Inside there, he knew, everything was in place. He did not need that. Pulling it out had been an act of confusion, and he calmed himself by checking that everything was in its place. His hand moved over the Exo grip on his DB380m, a pistol small enough to fit in the palm of a hand and remain invisible. He had small hands, and elegant fingers, and the weapon suited him just fine, though it gave him no comfort. It was part of his repertoire. It was expected of him.

Silvana was not in her herbal store, but, typically, had left it open. No one was around to steal anyhow, which was part of the problem with Silvana's business plan. Besides, nothing in the store was worth stealing. Certainly there would be no money. But it was the principle of the thing that annoyed him. The world was full of thieves and criminals and an unattended store should be locked. He had just seen an unknown car, a green Alfa Romeo driving away from the parking area next to the gate. Albanians and gypsies drove Alfa Romeos. He did not really object to his future wife working. Hadn't he and her father allowed her to do that economics and commerce course in Rome at the Luiss Guido Carli? And when she came back, they could see she was different. She learned little enough about economics or running a business, but she came back filled with knowledge of a different type. The knowledge of a woman who had explored . . . well. And still he did not object. That was her right, just as it was his with the occasional dancer, but her attitude towards him had hardened, too. Her father, of course, pretended that everything was as before. It was not even possible to allude to the fact that maybe his daughter had enjoyed some other men.

She had returned with a degree a year ago, then set about using his money to prove that she was perfectly capable of running her own business. A business that failed before it opened. But that was fine. He would subsidize her all her life, if needs be.

'Domenico!' he called, not hiding the irritation in his voice. He was always formal with Silvana's father, paying the old man more respect than was his due. Domenico Greco was his name, Signor Greco, when he first knew him. *Qualsiasi cosa che volete voi, Signor Greco. Proprio qualsiasi.* That was then. Now he liked to undermine it by also using the old man's diminutive, Mimmo.

'Mimmo!' It was like calling a dog. Only one that did not come. He waited, his temper rising, as all he heard was the sound of hundreds of birds chattering and insects humming. He called again, and got no answer. The old man had a mobile phone but only answered it if his daughter called. If Niki needed to speak to him, he had to call Silvana who would call him, or come down to the garden and shout.

He set off across the garden, forced to double the actual distance by the playful path that wended in and out around bushes too thick or thorny to push through, even when they only came up to his waist. Besides, he didn't want to mess up his trousers, which had a thin chalk-stripe motif so subtle as to be invisible, yet emphasized, he felt, the length and slimness of his legs.

He found the old man bent over some scrabbly soil, scraping with a hoe around some weird plant with blue leaves. He glanced up as Niki arrived, then continued with his work, clearly finding the vegetable more interesting than his potential son-in-law.

'You're sweating, Niki. Another attack?'

As always when he was close to the old man, Niki felt slightly impeded. He could be contemptuous at a distance, but up close it became harder. 'They are not "attacks".'

Domenico put aside his hoe. 'Whatever you want to call them, you are very white.'

Niki stared back. Anyone would look white compared with the old man, shrunken and brown as a chestnut, constantly caked in soil. 'Where's Silvana?'

'She went to Madonna della Misericordia,' said Domenico. 'You just missed her.'

'The clinic? Why? What's wrong with her?'

'Nothing wrong with her. She's visiting a person.'

'Who's this person?'

'Someone from her course who fell ill.'

'Her delusional flower course? I thought she had cancelled it.'

'Some fools turned up nevertheless,' said Mimmo. 'And this particular one seems to have eaten some conium seeds. That's my guess.'

'When was all this?'

'Yesterday, around this time.'

'Why am I only hearing about this now? Why didn't you say anything last night?'

Mimmo resumed his hoeing. 'Last night we were talking about your Romanian. I didn't see the relevance. But now I am beginning to wonder.'

'Wait, Silvana is visiting this *stronzo*? Is that his car I saw leaving?'

'Yes . . .' Mimmo gave a vicious neat twist to the handle and the blade of the hoe bit into the roots of a delicate-looking plant. 'Ground ivy. And yes, that's his car.'

Niki pulled out a handkerchief and blew his nose, though it was dry. In fact, he was suddenly very thirsty. 'So who the fuck does this guy think he is? And why is Silvana not answering my calls?'

Mimmo spread his grimy hands. 'You know how it is. She thinks mobile phones damage the brain. She leaves it at home or in the store.'

'Runs in the family.'

Mimmo stopped gardening and pushed his hands into the small of his back. 'Here's the thing. The man lying in the hospital bed is a cop.'

Niki searched the hard brown face for meaning, but got none.

'And here's another thing, he was pretending not to be.'

'Undercover?'

Mimmo shrugged. 'Not very deep undercover. Dr Bernardini found out simply by checking his medical records.'

'And how do you know?'

'Were you listening, Niki? I just said Dr Bernardini. Bruno Bernardini. You know the individual to whom I am referring. By now the whole town will know all about it.' 'So,' continued Domenico, 'my assumption is that the man was simply looking for a break from his identity. After all, it must be quite a burden waking up every morning and knowing you're a cop. And that is all I know, really. Unless you have something to add?'

'Why would I have anything to add? I am only finding out about this now, for God's sake,' said Niki. 'It's just a coincidence.'

Domenico forked a leaf between two fingers and examined its underside, and shook his head at what he saw there. 'A coincidence requires the occurrence of two events. So what is the other?'

'There *is* no other event. It was just an expression.'

'But there is another event, Niki, isn't there?' Domenico ripped the leaf from its stem and massaged it into his palms. 'That girl that's vanished from your club. I was thinking of that. The Romanian girl.'

A look of pain passed across Niki's face. 'You think I'd call in a policeman from Rome for that?'

'You reported it to the Carabinieri here.'

'I had to. I was covering my ass in case she turns up dead somewhere.'

'Will she?'

'Jesus, I hope not.'

'You liked this girl, Alina.' It was a statement or a challenge, rather than a question.

'Maybe you've been standing in the sun too long, Mimmo.'

'Mind how you talk to me, Niki.'

'Think about it. When did this cop book his course? Months ago? Alina went missing three weeks ago as of Friday. And "missing" is probably not the term. She upped and went.'

'What about her friend, Nadia: could she have called in the police?'

The sun was behind the old man's head, putting Niki at a disadvantage. He could not see the expression on the face in front of him, but he knew his own registered stupid surprise. 'You think because I'm in this garden all day I don't know about the goings-on in your club? Remember who got you started. You're my business, Niki. Your business is my business.'

'All I am saying is that this policeman must have booked before Alina went missing.'

'Alina. Listen to yourself. Alina. Little Romanian whore, fucks off somewhere, and you're still sweating and slithering around my daughter. Alina. Of course I checked. This cop booked on 17 April. The same day, as it happens, that you reported Alina missing. That was the coincidence you could have been referring to, if you were so stupid as not to check.'

'Why would I have called up a policeman in Rome – me?'

'What about that other bitch, Nadia? Maybe she got worried about her little friend.'

'How would Nadia know about a policeman in Rome, Mimmo?' Niki tipped light cologne into a handkerchief, and dabbed at his throat and neck.

'Sweating, Niki. Have you had your insulin?'

'I hate this garden. All the plants use up all the air.'

'That's not how plants work, Niki.'

'It's how your plants do.' He folded away his handkerchief. 'This is a stupid conversation. Neither you nor I called in the policeman.'

'I know I didn't,' said Domenico. 'I can't imagine you did either. Unless you were thinking of events from far longer ago than the disappearance of your latest piece of fluff.'

The two men eyed each other steadily. When Niki spoke, his voice was a whisper. 'One of the agreements was that we would never talk about that.'

'Exactly. So have you kept your word?'

'Of course. Why would I ever say anything? And who would I tell?'

'One of your whores, maybe, when you're high?' said Domenico.

Niki retrieved his handkerchief and dabbed spittle off his lips. 'If I want to get high,' he said, 'I just forget to inject insulin.' He balled the handkerchief and stuck it into a pocket on his trousers. 'You don't own me any more.'

'You're supposed to marry Silvana, isn't that the idea? Frankly, I'd like to get a better son-in-law than you, but seeing as this is how we're doing things, why don't you just hurry up and get it over with?'

'I don't think she's ready. She still sees me as too old.'

'So your strategy is to wait several more years until you're younger?'

'Until she's older. Until I'm less of an uncle to her,' said Niki.

Domenico placed his leathery hand on the younger man's shoulder. 'We mustn't argue. I just have a bad feeling about this. I'm going to check out that policeman. You check out that Nadia at the club and anyone else. Just in case.'

'There is only one other person who could know anything about back then,' said Niki.

'Silvana? She knows nothing. She was a child.'

'She has had a long time to think about it.'

'Hurry up and marry her, we can close the circle for good.'

'She doesn't want me. We should never have let her do that course in Rome. She came back changed.'

'She'll have met younger and more handsome men than you, Niki. Almost everyone she met, probably. But don't worry. I know how to bring her round, and I've taught her the value of money. She'll see you as a good catch, if a safe one.'

'I think she met someone in Rome.'

Domenico laughed. It sounded genuine. He followed it up with a hard squeeze on Niki's shoulder. 'Silvana is no fool. She knows what she wants. So maybe you give her a bit of room, just like she gives you room. Meanwhile, do what you need to do with this policeman.'

Niki frowned to show he wasn't following.

'When you have a rotten tooth in your mouth, Niki, you can do one of two things. Either you pull it out, or you fill it with gold.' Domenico shouldered his hoe. 'I'm going back to the lodge. I suggest you go to the clinic, talk to Silvana. Maybe take a look at the visitor, who'll probably be gone tomorrow.' When Niki didn't follow immediately, he added, 'Are you coming?'

'In a moment,' said Niki, pulling out a phone.

Mimmo nodded and left. Niki waited till he was out of sight, then put his phone back in his pocket, unzipped his fly, and aimed a stream of piss at the blue cabbage, a little act of sacrilege he would have enjoyed more if he had not been alarmed by the Coca-Cola colour of his urine dripping from the leaf.

6

SILVANA CLUTCHED a child's exercise book with a flower motif against her breast. 'You think I am foolish,' she said.

He thought that the way she had pulled her auburn hair back into a ponytail suited her extremely well, and he thought she was young, and he thought she was very kind to be visiting him in hospital, and kinder still to have driven up his car and brought his suitcase all the way into the room where he now lay. 'Not at all. I was willing to let you become my teacher, remember?'

'You hadn't met me.' She looked at him appraisingly. 'You don't seem the type who'd go in for Bach Flowers therapy.'

'No. I am not. But it was either that or yoga or religion. And I am not flexible enough for the other two. But thank you for the suitcase. Where did you get my car keys?'

'From the doctor. He came down with them and asked me to drive it up, so you could have your suitcase too. Wasn't that kind of him?'

'It was kind of you,' Blume conceded.

'The keys are in your suitcase now. Your car is almost as dilapidated as my father's Fiat.'

'I like my car.'

'It does not look loved.'

'It's complicated,' said Blume. 'We have had a long-term relation-ship.'

Silvana laid the exercise book at the foot of the bed, then made to sit down next to it. 'Do you mind?'

Blume magnanimously waved at his own feet, and she sat down on the bed, ignoring the chair next to him.

'I'm not sure about remembering how to love,' said Blume as he felt the toes of his left foot sink almost imperceptibly a millimetre beneath the weight of her leg. She probably did not even realize that was his foot down there. 'More remembering how to talk, drive, and tie my shoelaces.' Now he was being self-pitying. And confes-sional. And gruffly facetious. It was impossible to talk to a woman so young and . . .

Silvana blushed, leaned forward, and laid her hand on his knee for a moment. 'You poor man. Why is no one visiting you?' As she sat back, his foot beneath the blankets became a little more pleasantly trapped beneath her weight.

'You are,' he gave her leg a gentle nudge with his foot as he said 'you'.

'I mean others. Even a colleague from work?'

'I would have to tell them first. Anyhow, I'll be out the day after tomorrow.'

'We'll ask Doctor Bernardini if it's OK for you to take an infusion of agrimony and perhaps some crab apple. I am sure he'll say yes. I can make them up for you.'

'What do they do?'

'Agrimony is a *lovely* yellow flower. Its yellow is . . . oh, it's difficult to describe the exact hue and tone, delicate, pale, yet deep and strong and pronounced. Yellow like . . .'

'A banana?' offered Blume.

She gave him an absent-minded smile, as if she had hardly heard him, her mind being too busy searching for a suitable simile. Eventually she smiled, and said, 'The sun: early morning in the winter. Yes, that's it.'

Blume playfully flexed his toes. She stayed where she was.

'It cures mental torment and it's especially good for people who like to put a brave face on it, but are suffering inside,' said Silvana.

'I'm not putting a brave face on it.'

'Oh, but you're suffering inside! And yet, I can see you don't really believe in any of this.'

'Any of what?'

'Herbs, Bach Flowers, star signs, the essential goodness of people.'

Blume shook his head in exaggerated weariness. 'I am now of an age where everything confirms my prejudices.'

'I might surprise you.'

Silvana, he decided, would be lovely just to watch. Ideally, from behind a pane of perfectly clear and completely soundproof glass, because when it came to conversation, he felt his insides cringe in embarrassment. Then, again, no one else was there. No one would ever see him pretending to take her seriously, nodding at her wise little pronouncements, looking impressed at her poetic flourishes. He might feel a bit humiliated deep inside, but he felt a lot of things deep inside that he managed to suppress.

She was perched, sideways, on the end of his bed, below his feet. Her head was turned towards him, her neck was graceful and smooth, her breasts beneath the thin material of the dark blue dress were, well, big. And firm and upright and he could see the outline of the nipples.

'Surprise me then.'

'Are you Aquarius?'

'Did I include my birthdate on the form?'

'I am taking that as a yes.'

'And I am remembering I put my tax code down, which would also give you my birthdate.'

'I did not look at your birthdate.'

He told her he believed her, and lay back on his pillow. Silvana was saying nice things about him again, which was not as delightful as it might be, because he could not help but imagine Caterina listening to this conversation; she would use it against him for life. He imagined her imitating Silvana's silvery voice. *Oh, but Alec! You're so DEEP and BRAVE and INTERESTING.* To which Caterina, about halfway in age between Silvana and himself, would then add in her own hoarse, deep, Roman, and slightly masculine voice, and so *OLD and THICK and WITLESS.* Nystagmic Blume, Alec with the Roving Eye. He shook Caterina's mocking voice out of his mind. She wasn't there. He could allow Silvana to find him endlessly fascinating for a few moments while no one was looking or listening.

She smiled at him, stood up, and smoothed the blue dress against her body. He realized she might be leaving.

'What about the crab apples?' he asked. 'What do they do?'

Silvana's skin tone was too dark for her to redden, but he imagined she was blushing. She looked away for a moment, then back at him. 'Crab apples, Alec, are for self-hatred.'

His name in her mouth was quite something. He felt himself beginning to blush, and resorted to banter. 'Crab apples make you hate yourself?'

'No! They are for people who . . . oh, you were joking!'

At least her comprehension could get that far. He probed a little further. 'You believe in this stuff?'

'Oh yes. It doesn't seem likely, but you'd be surprised. There is another cure I'd recommend for you: rock water.'

'What does that cure?'

'Self-repression and rigidity.'

'You think you know me pretty well, don't you?' He knew as soon as he had said it, he had struck too aggressive a note.

Silvana lowered her head, causing her hair to fall over her eyes, and stood there penitent. He felt like a monster.

They started speaking at the same time.

'I'm sorry, I didn't mean . . .'

'I'm sorry. It was presumptuous . . .'

'Sorry, I'm interrupting . . .'

'No, no – you go first. Speak.' He put in an authoritative note, otherwise the mortifying to-and-fro might never end.

'The books I read . . . I am always on the lookout for personality clues.'

'I'm not saying you were wrong about me,' said Blume, happy that the conversation had returned to him and his complex personality, 'but some of these cures . . . I mean "rock water". What is that about? Water basically, right? Same as in that plastic bottle beside me.'

'Water, yes, but fresh from a spring, preferably without a shrine or any human construct.'

'Does your father believe in any of this stuff?'

'No. He laughs at it. Except when it comes to the question of the holy water.'

Blume gave her his best sceptical look.

'What's that look supposed to mean?'

'Scepticism,' said Blume.

'Then stop looking at . . .'

'That's involuntary. A problem with my eye.'

'Oh, sorry. I didn't realize you couldn't help yourself.'

'Just tell me about the holy water.'

'Surely you've heard of it? It is, or was, one of the most famous things about the gardens.'

'Not me,' he said in a tone that clearly indicated he was uninterested, but she missed the cue.

'OK, well, the Romanelli gardens . . .'

He interrupted her. 'Why don't you sit down again?' Blume glanced at the foot of his bed, but, disappointingly, she pulled up a plastic chair. She crossed her legs and anxiously clasped her right ankle with her left hand, and allowed her sandal, a complicated affair with lattice work and even jewels of some sort, to hang loose from her heel.

'Dr Bernardini told me you were a policeman? From Rome?'

'I think Bernardini might need reminding of patient-doctor privilege.'

Silvana's surprise was such that her almond eyes turned momentarily circular. 'Why? Is it a secret?'

'No, not a secret,' said Blume.

'Actually, I asked him not to say anything to anyone else, because I thought maybe you would not want people to know. Perhaps I was wrong?'

'No, no, that's good, though,' said Blume.

'Maybe you won't mention to my fiancé, Niki, that you're a policeman?'

'Why not?' said Blume sharply. He hadn't wanted to break the mood, but her comment had caught his attention. Now he felt a different more familiar type of arousal, more intellectual and aggressive than the soft sexual feelings he had been inappropriately luxuriating in until now. 'What's he got to hide?'

She looked at him, fright written all over her lovely features, and he began to relent. 'I didn't understand your comment about not telling Niki, though it's unlikely I'll be meeting him.'

'I phrased it badly,' she said. 'Are you leaving so soon?'

'Yes. Though the doctor wants me here for a few days.'

'Do you have to listen to him? Wouldn't you be better off back home? Bernardini is a very nice man, but whatever made you sick is gone now.'

'I agree,' said Blume. 'You still haven't told me about Niki.'

'He runs a nightclub and a discotheque.'

'Uh-huh. And?'

'Well, you know.' She clasped her ankle again and stared at the floor.

'Drugs?'

'And girls,' she said, staring at her manicured toes. 'Not quite pole dancers, but the ones who get up on those flashing platforms, topless and that sort of thing? East European girls. Fifty- and hundred-euro bills stuffed into their panties . . . maybe they sleep with some clients?'

'This is your fiancé?'

She nodded sadly. 'He works in an environment where – people in his situation . . . dealings with the authorities, the police can be complicated. He would be angry with me if he thought I spent so long talking to you knowing you were a policeman.'

'Well, don't tell him you knew, then,' said Blume.

Her face brightened. 'I hadn't thought of that!'

'I am not sure I like the sound of Niki,' said Blume.

She stood up to go. 'Your car is in the car park, and maybe you'll pop in and say goodbye to me before you go back to Rome – when did you say – the day after tomorrow?'

'Maybe, or the day after. Soon. Here, let me accompany you.'

He peeled a monitor off his chest, it was attached to a switched-off machine anyway, and started to clamber out of bed.

'Don't be silly! You can't get out of bed like that! I'll see myself out. I've arranged to meet Niki outside. He's giving me a lift home.'

'I need to see how I feel,' said Blume. 'If I can't make it across the room, I'm hardly likely to be able to drive.'

He stood up, paused, and leant down to allow the blood in his head to catch up with the unexpected movement. He was in a hospital gown, which was unbecoming. The machine that he thought had been switched off started beeping, like in one of those American TV shows, except without the team of fast-talking, quick-walking, joke-cracking medics rushing in to save him.

'I feel fine,' he said. 'I just realized, I haven't eaten either. I think I had better put that thing back on my chest to stop the beeping. Look out the door and tell me if the mad Dr Bernardini or some evil nun is on the way.'

Silvana opened the door, then swung it half-shut again, just as Blume regained his bed. Her voice sounded a little shaky. 'No, but Niki is.'

'Niki is what?'

'Coming up the corridor,' said Silvana. 'Play nice. Ignore him if he says things that offend you.'

'I am not easily offended,' said Blume.

'Oh yes, you are,' said Silvana. 'It's sort of your most noticeable characteristic.'

'*Ma vaffanculo*. You don't even know me.'

'See? Don't let him provoke you about being a policeman.'

'If he even tries . . .'

'Or about not acting the policeman.'

'Huh?'

'If he says anything about you not knowing your job. Not caring. He might do that, too.'

'Why are you with the bastard?'

She sighed. 'I wish I knew.'

7

O N THE ferry across the Black Sea to Istanbul, Olga kept poking her big dyed head into the cabin and checking if the girls were all right. She told them to go up on deck if they were feeling seasick. She even offered to buy sandwiches and Coca-Colas for anyone who wanted. The two youngest girls did, and went giggling out of the room together, and, like two ducklings, followed Olga's large backside as it waddled its way down the corridor.

'Istanbul,' said Nadia. 'You know what's going to happen there, Alina, don't you?'

'We're going to stay a few days, then we move on.'

'That could happen. What about sex with a Turk, do you think you could do that? Turks are Muslims.'

Alina shuddered, but did not reply. A few minutes later, Nadia returned to the attack. 'You're very pale. Apparently they like redhead pale girls. And blondes. Ukrainians in particular.'

'How come you're the expert? Have you made this trip before?'

'No, but I've heard things. The police are in on it, too. And if we ever go home, they'll just say we were asking for it.'

Alina looked defiant. 'Not everyone . . . I know some girls end up in dance clubs and bars and worse, but a lot end up in domestic service and doing ordinary stuff, too.'

It was a relief to hear Alina hint at what might lie ahead. Nadia was beginning to fear her friend really had no idea, which made her feel guilty, as if she were the corrupting influence. Guilty and lonely. 'Listen, I have been thinking about this, Alina. We're going to stick together, right?'

Alina slipped her arms around Nadia's neck. 'Oh, please, yes.'

Nadia detached herself gently. 'I don't know how it works yet, but I am pretty sure that if they see we are close, they will separate us. Like in the factories? The bosses don't want solidarity. So maybe sometimes we are going to have to pretend not to be together, not to care. I might be wrong, but be prepared to do that.'

'What about Italy? Will we go to Italy together?'

Nadia put her arm around Alina's thin waist. 'I don't think that is up to us any more. From here on, for quite a long time, other people will be making the decisions.'

'But they could send us to Italy?'

'Of course they could. And someday we'll be free to do what we want.'

'What about the Vidal Sassoon Academy?'

'I am sure it exists, Alina. And maybe you'll be working in it someday soon. But between now and then, be prepared for some things you won't like.'

Alina turned her face into Nadia's shoulder. 'Just make sure you stay as near me as possible.'

Nadia stroked Alina's long straight hair, red in the sun, purple down here where the walls were painted green and the light came from a porthole looking out over a blue sea.

★

They spent the rest of the journey up on deck. Nadia thought it might be good idea, or at least morally rewarding, to hide from Olga and make the fat bitch worry, but Olga never came looking for them. She did not need to. She had their passports.

Nadia had had a vague idea of Istanbul being located on the southern rim of the Black Sea, and was confused as the ferry entered the Bosporus Straits, and they sat watching land glide by, with people out and about walking with their children, climbing up to round towers as if this were perfectly normal. Nor had she been expecting to see quite so many ships. At one point, they were sailing so close to the land that she considered jumping and swimming what seemed like a few metres, where she could join the picnickers and dog walkers. They rounded a point and suddenly the water stretched far and wide, and there was no question of jumping. The shrubby land and excursionists had gone and now it was all coastal city, to the left and right and straight ahead.

Alina, who had been lying with her head on Nadia's lap, apparently asleep, sensed the movement and excited hubbub of ship passengers nearing the end of their journey, opened her eyes, and sat up. She pointed leftwards across the water at the jumble of white and grey apartment blocks and dark green trees. 'Is that Istanbul?'

Nadia was not entirely sure, but said it was.

Alina was interested now, she stood up and looked westwards towards Europe. 'Also on the other side?'

'Sure.'

'I didn't know Istanbul was so big.'

Neither did Nadia. The buildings looked prosperous from here, the sun was bright, and the water sparkled. As the Fatih Sultan Mehmet Bridge came into sight, hope and happiness rushed into her lungs, pushing out the dread she had felt in the cabin below deck.

They passed under the bridge, and another one came into sight. It was as they passed below, Alina looking solemnly and reverentially up at it, that the anxiety returned with redoubled force. Nadia had never been so far from home. She was in a boat sailing down a sea in the middle of a vast city. It seemed impossible that she should ever return. She went over and embraced Alina, who had fallen silent in the presence of the bridges, and tried to play the adult soothing a child. But when Alina returned the embrace, Nadia found herself burying her face into her friend's shoulder and seeking as much comfort as she was giving.

Olga had disembarked with the other six girls and was waiting for them. Nadia felt so much like a recalcitrant student on a day trip that she had to fight the urge to apologize. They breezed through customs and were divided into two taxis. Five of the girls were bundled into one, and Olga leaned over and gave the driver instructions. The taxi drove off and was immediately lost amidst the chaos of other taxis and vehicles of every description, from sleek German saloons to Russian trucks that smelled of home-heating oil. Then Alina, Nadia, and another girl, a wisp of a thing who seemed to be below the school-leaving age, squeezed into the back of a second taxi, sick with anticipation, longing, and dread. Olga sat in front, and, amazingly, started talking Turkish to the driver. She turned round and beamed at them.

'You all look a bit tired from the journey, but I am sure I look much worse!' She laughed, and said something to the taxi driver, perhaps a translation of her remark. The driver merely grunted.

Fatigue and sensory overload from the sights and smells of Istanbul, now twinkling as the evening drew in, and, more than anything else, the constant unremitting noise of the place caused Nadia to become detached from and almost indifferent to all the many things that happened next.

A man with fingers that smelled like rotten potatoes forced open her mouth at one point and stared down her throat, then fingered her teeth. An old man with a wet moustache weighed her breasts in his hands, his whole demeanour more medical than lustful, though he was clearly saying something disgusting in Turkish, a language she already hated, to his table companions. All the time Olga stood there, nodding her approval, chatting in Turkish, and, right in front of them, counting out euro banknotes.

When they had walked into the bar, Olga had sat the girls down at a table, mysteriously empty in such a crowded, small place, and ordered them sweetened drinks. She did not ask them what they wanted. The barman arrived in a filthy apron and set down warm cans of cola and hot cups of apple tea. Nadia didn't like the tea, but she was thirsty, and the wait was long, and eventually she had drunk it all. The girls were called up one by one, and they went and stood by a table with five men.

When Nadia, the second of the group to be called, was standing there, she felt so overwhelmingly tired that it occurred to her the tea might have been drugged. Some sort of docility drug. Or maybe not. For some reason, a thought that should have been inconsequential had lodged itself foremost in her mind: it seemed impossible she had travelled all this way to such a strange place to end up in such a small bar. It was smaller than the bar beneath her apartment in Onesti. For some reason, this one thought dominated, prevailing even over fear and disgust.

It was hard even to say who the boss at the table was. They all looked like weak men, but that could not be the case. The one man who had impressed her so far had been the barman who brought them the tea, the glasses small beside his huge hands. When he had arrived at their table, she saw he was young, and strong, and she wondered if she could ask him simply to throw Olga and the men at the table out. Maybe if she could speak the language, she would have said something. But half an hour later, two policemen with 'Polis' in huge letters written in white on red across their shoulders came in, and the men at the table did not even change the tone, speed, or loudness of their incomprehensible chatter. Nadia looked up and considered, just considered, running over to them. She caught the barman looking right at her, and she knew he was reading her thoughts as clearly as if they were written on the wall behind.

At a some point, Nadia realized that the young girl was gone. Alina was still there. She had not seen her walk off or be taken away. Olga showed no sign of having noticed anything. Nadia would later learn that the girl, a scrawny little thing in a polyester yellow skirt, had been transferred to a man who wanted no more than a housemaid for his wife. Sitting there in the bar, the fate of the girl had been decided, and she was whisked off to another part of the black market to learn that abuse and exploitation of young women was not always sexual.

The district in which Nadia found herself was called Aksaray, where one could get by for days without speaking any Turkish. Russian or Romanian were the languages of the pimps and night-club owners and many of the women. Turkish was useful for some clients, but even more spoke English. She soon learned to identify the actual English and Americans from the Germans, French, Italians, and Spanish who used English. If she couldn't understand a word of what they were saying, English was their first language.

Willingness to accept what was happening was not enough. The gang that ran the girls had to teach them a lesson anyhow, and the preferred tactic was sudden, inexplicable violence. Alina stopped speaking that night and did not start again for six months until the randomized beatings finally became rarer, and the violence was concentrated on the newcomers. For the first few days, she had tried to demonstrate to their pimp, Tamer, that she was willing, though her eyes said otherwise, but that was not the point. It was not even beside the point: it was, in fact, almost as bad as direct rebellion. One of the most important lessons Tamer and his crew had to teach them was that they were not allowed to be willing or unwilling, because both were simply two aspects of freedom.

At the end of that six-month period, Alina and Nadia were still together, in that they were in the same place, but contact was limited to a few passing glances, and Alina by now showed no sign of wanting to know her or anyone. The owners were Russian and two of the bouncers were Romanian, but by now they all knew not to look for help from anyone. On the contrary, the bouncers were especially to be avoided, because they could listen in to conversations and report back. Although she hated the language and the people and the food, Nadia began to learn Turkish. English she found a shapeless language, basically a set of informal phrases run together, one after the other, without any criterion. It was spoken by tourists in short trousers who had sneaked away from their wives or groups of businessmen who liked to behave as if they were fun-loving and boisterous when drinking together, but turned vicious and demanding when alone. She knew the English she heard was spoken mostly by non-native speakers, but that simply confirmed her feeling that it was a simplified language for the stupid and dishonest.

And then there were the Arabs. Though they were no worse behaved, Nadia's whole spirit continued to rebel against them. She had been brought up to despise them, along with Negros and Gypsies, and now look at her.

★

In the clubs and bars, they were all referred to as 'Natasha', regardless of their real names. Nadia, a variant of Natasha, had a name that her keepers found easy to remember, but she responded quicker to Natasha. She preferred it, because Natasha wasn't her.

Once an Arab client, overhearing the pimp call her Nadia, told her in faltering English that her name in Arabic meant wet and tender. It was the one time she refused to service a man, for which she received a beating. Three days later, one of her molars simply cracked in half and fell out, leaving a gaping hole that filled with puss. Her face swelled up so much it squeezed her eyes shut. She was surprised to be taken to the dentist, who referred her to a doctor, who prescribed antibiotics. For three weeks she did not have to do anything, and though she knew this was just their investing in an asset that gave good returns, she could not help but feel grateful.

Eventually, she and Alina were separated. There was no wrenching scene of parting. One day, Alina was led up to a man in a leather jacket, which must have made him unbearably hot. It was certainly making him smelly and bad tempered. His name was Fyodor. He pulled her onto his knee and continued his conversation, which had something to do with car imports from Italy. Then, instead of going with her into the windowless room at the back, he led her out of the club and into a compact Mercedes A class. He drove up and down several slip roads and ramps to traverse the large highway that ran through the district before crossing the Golden Horn and heading north. Alina understood that Fyodor, who was very young – only a few years older than her – was her new pimp.

Fyodor, when not wearing his leather jacket, seemed to have a great sense of humour, and appeared to listen to what the girls said, even if he did not listen very hard or for very long being more interested in his over-sized phone. But he liked to try to make them laugh, which he did by telling jokes in a mixture of Russian, Turkish, Romanian, and English, sometimes with a few Italian curse words thrown in. The punchline tended to get lost in translation, but you could always tell when he had reached it because he would peel back his thick lips to reveal gold-tipped teeth and slap the table in helpless mirth. One day, Alina thought she might even have understood the punchline, which had to do with Stalin advising Putin to paint the Kremlin blue.

Fyodor personally administered fewer beatings but he allowed the customers to be rough with the girls, so things were not much better. One day the barman put an icy beaker of vodka on a steel tray and seeing as Alina was standing there doing nothing, told her to carry it over to Fyodor. She did as she was told, and Fyodor ordered her to sit down.

He stroked his phone and then her, and started a joke about the Pope. By now she knew it in three different languages, and still didn't get it. Suddenly, turning serious, he told her in English and Turkish that if she played her cards right, she could soon buy her freedom, and he might even invest something in her to help her on her way. He set out the terms, and estimated that in 18 months, she would have paid off what he had paid to get her, plus the rent and board. He nodded encouragingly and Alina took a chance and asked about Nadia.

He listened, then told her he had no plans to 'hire' any more girls for his club, and for all he knew Nadia had been sold on. Then he reverted to Russian and she lost track of what he was saying, and she simply nodded.

'You didn't understand me, I can see.' He traced a line on the frosted glass with his index finger. 'Some persons are very bad, *rau, kötülük, порочный, cattiva gente*, you know?'

She nodded.

Fyodor pointed an accusing finger at his own chest. 'Me, no. Not so bad. They kill, you know. Arabs, Italians, Turks. Killers.'

Offering her freedom, then warning her of the dangers. She was getting wise to the tricks already, but the dangers were no less real for all that. She had heard certain names whispered: the names of people in whose employ no woman wanted to end. There were sadists and killers out there, more interested in pain than gain. People who used large banknotes to snort coke, put gold flakes in their cocktails, and would pay good money for a beautiful young face just for the pleasure of taking a box cutter to it. You were never so bad but there was somewhere worse. She hoped Nadia was OK.

8

ONLY TALL men can stride, thought Blume, watching the short, balding figure with the waxy skin approach him. The man had hurled open the door with force and violence, like a jealous lover, but then been quite fastidious about closing it. Halfway across the room, he paused to mop his forehead. Lying in his bed, Blume began to wonder if this might not be some sort of creepy doctor, because it certainly could not be Silvana's fiancé.

The man came over to Blume's bedside. '*Ehhi! Saluti*. I'm Niki. Niki Solito.' He turned round to Silvana, still lingering at the doorway, and ordered her out. 'Wait for me at the car. I'll just say hello to the commissioner here.'

Silvana bent her head down meekly. 'Don't be too long, Niki.'

When she had gone, Niki offered Blume his hand.

'So you're Silvana's fiancé?' he asked, reluctantly taking the proffered hand, which was warm and damp.

'Absolutely.' Niki affected not to notice Blume's incredulous tone. Instead, he reached into the pocket of his tight-fitting trousers and produced a small clear bottle of Amuchina disinfectant gel, which he rubbed into his hands, filling the air between them with an insulting lemony scent.

'Only because you are sick,' he explained. He put the bottle away, stood back, and grinned at him, showing teeth small and white as a child's. 'Alec Blume, Alec, Alec, Alec!' as if he and Blume were old pals meeting after too long an absence.

'Niki, Niki, Niki, Niki,' replied Blume. 'How do you spell that?'

'With a K.'

'With a K,' said Blume, manoeuvring himself to the side of the bed and sitting up. 'And your surname?' Automatically, he cast around for his notebook, which wasn't there.

'Solito.'

Blume had never owned a shirt as white as Niki's. The buttons gleamed like pearls, the massive collar shone in the dim room as if it had its own source of light. Perhaps the whiteness was exaggerated by the contrast with the triangle of sunbed-treated skin, visible down as far as the third unfastened button, where the edge of a blue and red tattoo peeked out. Niki slid his hand in and massaged his breastbone. He caught Blume's eye.

'I have a condition, but I keep myself fit.' He slipped his satchel off his shoulder. 'Very fit,' he added. 'In fact, I have come to consider my curse, which is diabetes, the real version not the one fat people get, as a blessing in disguise. Without it, I would not have taken such great care of my body!'

'Well, Niki-with-a-K, Niki with a condition, what are you doing in my room?' Blume found himself standing on the floor. Without quite realizing it, he had decided to get dressed. The first thing he pulled out of his suitcase, however, was a blister pack of Lyrica lozenges. He muscles were tensed, his eye kept wandering over to the corner of the room and seeing movements where there were none. To be on the safe side, he took three.

'Drugs?' said Niki, amiably enough.

Blume ignored him and started getting dressed.

Niki now tugged at the tail of his white shirt that billowed like a clean sail, executed an elegant *pas de valse*, put his hands on his hips and stared at Blume, his face flushed with defiance and anticipation, as if he had just been challenged on one of his strong points. 'What do you think I weigh?'

Blume peered upwards with the air of a professor disturbed from his studies, then lowered his eyes again, and did not answer.

'No, seriously. How much?'

Blume glanced at him again. Maybe 70 kilos, he reckoned, about 1.68 metres tall. Blue eyes, thinning fair hair – in his mind he was describing a suspect. 'I haven't a clue,' he said.

'Sixty-seven!' declared Niki. 'I am aiming for 62. That's my ideal weight. Yours?' He stroked his eyebrows and lifted up the side of his lip with a finger to examine an eye-tooth. Blume folded his arms like a passer-by determined not to pay for a piece of street theatre he has been watching. Seeing as he was getting no response, Niki said, 'OK, so you couldn't guess my weight. Here's an even harder one: how old do you think I am?'

He patted his stomach, and turned his insubstantial flank towards Blume. 'Go on. Guess.'

'Forty-six.'

A look of shock followed by rage passed across Niki's face, which he managed to twist into a tight smile.

'You must have looked that up.'

'Just a lucky guess.'

'People don't guess with such precise numbers. Usually you say 30–35, something like that. You don't just come out with a fixed number.'

'I do.'

'You looked it up.'

'Where, when, and, also, why the fuck would I bother doing that?'

'Because you're a policeman, pretending not to be one.'

'Listen, Niki-with-a-K.'

'Stop saying that.'

'I could call you Nicola. Is that your proper name?'

'On my birth certificate only. My mother named me after San Nicola of Bari. My father renamed me Niki in 1976, after Niki Lauda.'

'Either way, you're a saint or hero. Is that where you're from: Bari?'

Niki sat down, and stroked his throat with forefinger and thumb, then gently patted his own cheek. 'Did you know that men have better skin than women? Women over a certain age envy men their skin. They don't like to talk about it, of course.'

'Answer my question, Niki-with-a-K.'

'*Minchia*, you're a real cop, Cop, aren't you? I'm from Molfetta originally. A long time ago. There, satisfied?'

Blume shrugged.

Niki picked up his shoulder satchel, opened the flap, extracted a thin metal disc, and opened it.

'I know what you're thinking. You're thinking drugs but –' He dipped in two fingers and scooped out some white cream, 'Moisturizer. Men should not be afraid to use cosmetics where necessary. I had my eyes lasered, my teeth whitened. These are things you could do for yourself. Along with losing some weight, maybe. Women find me attractive. Women of my age find me pretty irresistible. We men, we can just keep going, can't we? We don't have to limit ourselves. They say Picasso fucked on his deathbed.'

'Silvana?' Blume could still not quite believe it.

'What about her? She's my *fidanzata*, but she recognizes my needs and rights. No man in my line of business could do otherwise, but you don't know about my line of business, or do you? Is that why you're here?'

Blume gazed at Niki's patent leather shoes, and wondered idly if they ever needed polishing, or if they were even leather to begin with. They looked plastic, and weak. He pictured himself stamping on Niki's toes. 'I know you run a discotheque, girls, probably drugs. I know you're from Bari. Anything else I should know, apart from why you are sitting here in my room right now?'

'I have interests in some organic vineyards. All told, 80 people or so depend on me for their employment.'

'Good for you. Italy needs as many restaurants and discotheques as it can get,' said Blume.

'And a tattoo studio. They did this one.' He unbuttoned his shirt exposing smooth hairless tanned skin and more of the tattoo, which turned out to be some sort of stylized Celtic beast.

'I don't need to see,' said Blume.

'Body art makes you uncomfortable?' He made his pectorals ripple.

'You're sweating, Niki.'

'Not a problem.' He slipped out a handkerchief and dried his chest. 'Just makes it glisten all the more.'

'Silvana is considerably younger than you,' said Blume.

'Do you have a problem with that?'

'No, I guess not. It's all perfectly balanced. She's younger than you, you're shorter than her.'

Niki's narrowed his eyes and lifted his lip in what was presumably an attempt at a sneer. He stood up and advanced a few paces towards Blume.

'Coming closer doesn't make you seem any bigger,' said Blume. 'My brain worked out the trick of perspective a long time ago. Also, that thing with the lip? Makes you look like a jackrabbit.'

When Niki finally spoke, it was in excessively modulated tones, as if he was trying to use his own voice to calming effect.

'My discotheque has live dancing girls. Short skirts. Often they don't have anything on below. Are you interested?'

Blume stared at his feet. His toenails needed a trim. 'Do I look like a disco-dancing type to you?'

'For the girls. They dance, you watch. They like strong men. You're a fat old *stronzo*, but you're strong.'

'You're telling me, a policeman, you run a prostitute ring?'

'You don't get it, do you? Most of those girls pay me to come in and dance. They get up there on stage, get themselves seen, get to choose from the men. They want a man with money. There are others. Young, Romanian. A Russian with tits out to here?' He mimed cupping two breasts some distance away from his own thin chest, and made a thrusting movement with his pelvis.

'Go sit down,' said Blume. 'And stop trying to provoke me.'

'You shouldn't talk to me like that. You think I don't have policemen in my clubs? Magistrates, too, and judges. They come from all over. Rieti, Terni, Pescara, Teramo, even Frosinone.'

'*Addirittura* Frosinone. Well, colour me impressed. You still haven't sat down, but that's OK, because you're leaving.'

Niki went back to the chair and stood behind it. 'Did someone call you? As a policeman, I mean. Are you here for some purpose?'

'Would it bother you if I were?' said Blume, grunting as he pulled on a pair of socks.

'Typical cop answer. You're like . . . I don't know, priests or politicians. Never a straight answer.'

'Whereas the criminal class are such candid souls.'

'At least criminals say nothing. You guys, always another question, then another. I'm trying to do a good thing here, but I need to know: did someone call you to come here?'

'No. Nobody called me here. As is now perfectly plain to the entire province, I am a policeman. I am not retired, I am on leave. I am not a private detective, and I do not work on my own or on behalf of criminals. Or even on behalf of private citizens. *Polizia di Stato*. Of the State. Not of private individuals.'

'Good. I believe you. Also because I have been checking you out. Like I said, I have a few contacts.'

Blume bent down, waited for the light-headedness this caused to abate, then tied his shoelaces. 'Niki, I could not give a fuck whether you believe me or not.' From the corner of his eye, he could see Niki lift his hands from the back of the chair and glance at them with distaste. Out came the bottle of disinfectant. Blume gave him time to finish rubbing the glistening substance into his hands. 'And they say you can't polish a turd.'

'*Ma che vuoi che faccia*. A disease-ridden policeman and God knows what else,' said Niki. 'So you're going back to Rome?'

'Are you anxious that I do?'

From his bag Niki pulled out a plastic bottle with a bright pink liquid in it. 'One of Silvana's concoctions. She's very good at them.' He sipped at it, then put it carefully away. 'Are you any good at working on your own, Blume? From what I hear, you're not so great at working with others, but it's not quite the same thing.'

'You heard this from?'

'I told you. Some contacts. I called in one or two minor favours. I simply asked a policeman and a magistrate to be a little indiscreet about you, in exchange for which I agreed not to be indiscreet about them.'

'Can I have the name of these two paragons of the law?'

'Maybe later? After you've helped me.'

'With what?'

'A girl has gone missing.'

'Yes. I have already picked up this news. Small town. Now when you say girl, you mean a woman. One of your dancers.'

Niki nodded. 'Alina.'

'So you are asking me to track down one of your missing whores? To act as the pimp's pimp.'

'I am not a pimp and she is not a whore. She's a friend.'

'A special friend, I imagine. And you reported her disappearance to the appropriate authorities?'

'I did. The local Carabinieri. One of them frequents my clubs, the other does not, but it made no difference. I am not a relative, and the person missing is an adult, and therefore can't be reported missing. But she is.'

'What about your magistrate friends?'

'What about them? They don't have jurisdiction for this area, and even if they did, they would never expose themselves by opening an investigation into the club where they go when they tell their wives – anyhow, she can't be reported missing.'

'So you think I am just the person to track her down, like a private detective?'

'I can pay you very well,' said Niki, patting his satchel, as if preparing to pull out banknotes there and then.

'Right,' said Blume. 'I was waiting for this bit.'

'Of course you were. Everyone needs money.'

'Not me. I have more than I know what to do with. An inheritance.'

'And you're still a cop? What's the sense of that?'

'It's what I do. When I think of something else, I'll do that.'

'I hear you're good.'

'Flattery. You know what this is, of course, Niki-with-a-K. It's a badly played hand. First, you're worried that I have been sent here to spy into some of what I can assume are your many creepy activities, then you come up with this missing girl thing. No doubt one of your dancers has gone missing: who wouldn't run from a job like that and a person like you? But you don't want me to look for her. You're trying to buy me off with a false mission. Have me take money, look in a different direction. Maybe get me into your club with a few girls, give me money, fuck my credibility and reputation, stop me from looking too closely at something else about you. Isn't that it? What are you hiding, Niki? Because, you see, a few minutes ago I didn't give a damn, and now I would sort of like to harm you.'

'You can try. I do nothing bad now,' said Niki. 'Taxes, maybe not all declared, not fully compliant with health and safety, I turn a blind eye to some stuff, pay a few people. Yes, drugs do get consumed on my premises; no, I do not sell them. Yes, I have been investigated in the past for this. No, not convicted.'

'Not to worry, Niki. I am on holiday,' said Blume. 'See?' He waved an arm around the room. 'This is me, on holiday, unwinding. I won't be staying. So you can take your little self, your man bag, and all your small-minded criminal fears and fuck off out of this room, and leave me in PEACE!'

Blume surprised himself by shouting the last word. He never roared like that. He had had no idea he was losing his cool until he did.

Niki clutched at his bag as if to save it from a gust of wind, and retreated to the door. 'You need different pills, Blume.'

Blume was over at the door in two strides. '*E sparisci, stronzetto,*' said Blume, swatting the door closed.

Niki's muffled voice said something, and Blume, again surprising himself with his own rage, yanked open the door. 'What did you say?'

Niki leapt back. 'I said Alina. Her name is Alina. She does exist.'

9

ALINA, TOO, was learning. Scarcely had she even registered the shock of being taken from Nadia's company to be brought to another club when, after two days in which no one even spoke to her or asked her to do anything, she was shipped onwards to a different quarter of the city.

Her new owners liked to have her on the street. They communicated to her through an intermediary hardly any older than her, who was always dressed in yellow and red, the colours of Galatasaray, and was something of a linguist. In passable Romanian, he explained to her that the Scimitar Niteclub, where her bosses worked and behind which she was accommodated in a half-finished building with cement floors, was like a stake in the ground to which she was tied by an invisible chain. 'Like a dog in garden, yes. You are a dog. A bitch in heat.'

The young man found the simile very amusing, though he must have used it before. He threw back his head and opened his mouth in mirth, displaying a row of rotting back teeth. He explained that she was expected to wander within a certain radius of 1 kilometre, but no farther. She was to bring clients back to the hostel two doors from the club, and book them into room 17. The client had to pay the 55 Turkish Liras for the room, and she was expected to use it at least three times a day. On no account was she to leave the district.

She was hardly ever left on her own. A silky, sulky Belarusian blonde went everywhere with her, until one of them was picked up. They were under instructions not to agree to threesomes. Sometimes, Alina was followed by an older dark-skinned woman whose name and nationality simply did not interest her.

Gradually, her geographical scope was extended, and the streets around the Scimitar became as familiar as the back of her hand. Being out on the streets had improved her Turkish, too. She was building up a mental map of the city, and she would have been capable of explaining to a taxi driver where she wanted to go. But taxi drivers wanted money, and while it was easy enough to get a few extra liras from clients, it was impossible to hide it anywhere. Every nook and cranny of the rooms and every part of her anatomy was subject to frequent and brutal searches day after day. One girl, who had saved quite a stash and managed to keep it hidden in a plastic bag secured by a string attached to the inside of the overflow slit on the bathroom washbasin, had had her face literally kicked in. For weeks, her face, which had been pretty and plump and gave her a well-fed and satisfied look that made many of the others dislike her, was such a mass of bruising and purple that it was impossible to say what sex she was. When the swelling went down, her face had caved in. Her cheeks now formed concave hollows and her nose had been pushed back. Her eyes lost their colour, and her lips were thin and bluish. She stopped eating, walked with a limp, and held her ribs all the time. In two months she aged 20 years. Then she disappeared.

It was a wet evening in November, the air heavy with diesel fumes and salt, when Alina found her tree. It grew on a traffic island on which she happened to find herself momentarily trapped. The road was less busy than usual, and so the cars heading towards the port were fast and the surface was slick with recent rain. Her Belarusian companion had teetered up the middle of the road, then made a hobbling high-heeled dash to the other side. Alina remained on the central divider, which was wide enough for the council to have turned it into a triangle of urban park with crab grass and a bench no one in their right mind would ever want to sit on. In the middle was a dying tree with a grey trunk that looked like it was made of cement. The traffic did not let up. Alina, bored by waiting, looked down at her golden sandals and painted toenails, and glanced at the tree. At about knee height, the smooth grey of the trunk seemed to fold over itself, like a flap of skin over a healing cut. As three heavy trucks went thundering by nose to bumper, she let her hand absently stroke the slight bulge in the bark. Her small hand found a fissure behind. Interested now, she pushed her fingers in the gap, accidentally trapping her hand for a few seconds, then with another twist, she found she could get her whole hand and wrist inside. The wood inside was bone dry. She pulled her hand out of the cavity, and almost immediately lost sight of the fissure. The traffic relented, and she skipped across the road. Her Belarusian companion was walking down the pavement towards her, muttering something obscene in Russian, the language of persecution.

Two days passed before Alina put her first money into her hidden hollow. She simply balled up 30 Turkish liras and shoved them in on the off-chance, expecting them to drop as if down a shaft into the ground. It rained solidly for three days after that, and when she came back the grey bark was slick and smooth like sealskin. But her hand quickly found the money, and it was dry. The next time she visited, it was with 50 euros, for which she had had to do something that had made her retch. This time, she brought a small plastic bag of the type they used to put hashish in. She took out the liras and put them and the euros into the bag, and the bag into the cavity. On both sides of her, the traffic flowed obliviously by.

For a while, every time she got some extra cash, she would plant it in her tree. It was only after she had received a brutal and wordless throttling, which left her gasping for air on the floor, that she realized she was making a dangerous mistake in never having been discovered holding back cash. Trying to hold onto money was brutally punished, but never even trying was a cause of suspicion. If she became the only one never caught with some illicit money, they might start following her, or simply torture the truth from her. From then on, she was careful to let them occasionally discover a few notes hidden here and there, for which she would give weak and unconvincing explanations and receive casual, unconvinced slaps, though what really hurt was that she was depriving her tree of riches. She took up some petty thieving whenever she could, swiping tips from tables, dropping her hand into jacket pockets. Sometimes she got caught, but the important thing was to mix defiance and suffer punishment in a way that made them think they were getting everything from her.

She still wanted to get to Italy. The academy might not exist and the job offer had been a sham, of course, but Italy did exist, and Milan was full of hair salons. She would find Nadia. Together they would leave for Italy as free women. They would arrive poor, but tough and ready. They would be entrepreneurs. Alina knew exactly how much was in the tree, but remained hazy about how much they would need to get away, vanish into Italy, and set up an apartment. She reckoned 6,000 euros ought to do it. After six months she had secreted 615 liras and 350 euros in the tree.

Eighteen months later, Alina had learned quite a lot of Turkish,

Russian, a lot of English, and a bit of German. No request or insult was ever completely unexpected. Slaps, punches, and kicks still hurt, but they no longer held the power to shock. She had learned that looks, age, voice, tone, education, physical strength, apparent shyness, or bluster were not reliable guides to how a customer would turn out. People with baby faces did terrible things. People with hard faces, criminal tattoos, metal studs, hairy bellies, bald heads, and little dicks also did evil things. The ones who looked like they wanted to hurt you always did; the ones who didn't look like it, often would. Her cache was now €2,100.

It was a mixture of Turkish liras, euros, and some dollars from the Arabs. Every day she looked at the exchange rates glowing in red lights at a currency exchange booth near the clubs and recalculated the value in her head. When she squirrelled away Turkish liras, she mentally converted them into euros.

Although the women were not allowed to keep money, there was always talk about their buying their way out. The main purpose of this outrageous falsehood seemed to be to give the girls false hope of freedom, and perhaps that worked with the very dumbest and the youngest. Admittedly, a lot of them were really dumb, and a lot of them were very young. But even the dumbest and the youngest learned eventually – hadn't she? The Russians told the same lie over and over again in Russian, Romanian, Turkish, English, Italian. 'You make me back the investment, you will be free woman 18 months, no problem.'

When a girl was nearing the end of the promised period, they sold her onwards again, and the new owner would tell her she had to make good the price he had paid. What Alina did not get was why they almost always sold the girl on – they could simply renege on the promise. But somehow the owners felt the need to sell, as if they were really keeping a bargain, and the bad guy was the new owner. After all else that they did, they were somehow still ashamed of this lie.

Sometimes, a girl did simply get 'freed', which meant abandonment, without shelter or food. Sometimes an offer would come through for a ticket home, or a trip onwards to an oil state. Very occasionally, a girl would become a home help. There were stories of some vanishing into the vast plains of Anatolia to work as farmhands. There were even rumours of marriages.

More got murdered than married, of that she had no doubt. Many committed suicide. Then there were overdoses, sexual diseases. She had seen a dead girl lying in the corridor, like something floppy and lazy and thin. Alina's first reaction was annoyance. She was annoyed with the dead girl before she was afraid of her and what she signified. The fear moved in waves up and down the corridor all day, and it was as if a cold, untouchable spot remained where the body had been, but there was not much hysteria. Sobs, gasps, some mutinous mumblings but the general effect was to harden the girls' faces, as if they were trying to borrow the blank and uninterested look on the dead girl's face. Selina, she had been called. It was not until days later, as she fed her tree, that Alina found a moment to feel pity, too.

She had learned to know and not to know at the same time. She knew the job in Italy had never existed, yet she still told herself that she was working towards it. She knew as soon as she tried to use the €2,100 to go somewhere, she would probably be caught, but she liked to think that with Nadia's help they might make it. It was now two years since she had been able to talk to Nadia, but they had spotted one another three times without having a chance to speak. Nadia was still alive and still in Istanbul. Perhaps she was saving up as well. Nadia had always been the resourceful one. She had probably saved twice as much as Alina. That would make more than €4,000.

When she first asked permission, Fyodor listened to her carefully, an expectant smile on his face as he waited the punchline. As she politely explained that all she wanted to do was get back across the busy road and find Nadia, reassure her, and then come back, his face fell in disappointment. But he did not beat her or even scream at her.

She was learning things. Languages, how to read clients, which women were freer, which owners to fear most. She also learned to her surprise that a lot of women entered semi-legitimate jobs. That some women had come deliberately seeking work in the sex industry somehow surprised her, even though she probably belonged to the same category. She also learned that no matter what they said or how nicely they said it, no owner was ever going to allow you to buy your freedom until you were over 26, or had contracted a visible disease.

'We are like the old taxis.' Lyudmila, 28, who looked older but was still very popular among clients, told her. 'We do not cost so very much. The real gain comes in how far you drive it, how far it goes, how much fuel it needs, and how reliable it is. Even the best investment and the most expensive car is worth nothing in the end, but the taxi driver can make a lot of money.' Lyudmila suddenly found her own metaphor very funny and laughed throatily. Alina liked the woman. A few days later she approached her again, and asked for advice on how to find Nadia.

Lyudmila's advice was simplicity itself: walk across the busy inter-section to the other part of town, and start looking. If she got caught, they might beat her, but hadn't she been beaten before? Alina said she was afraid Nadia would have been moved since.

'It is easy to find out. What was the name of your *pezevenk* when you were together?'

'Tamer.'

'Did you have policemen as clients?'

'No. Mostly foreign tourists.'

'That's Çağdaş Tamer, then. I'll bring you there.'

'Oh, would you?'

'Sure, tomorrow, 10 o'clock.'

'Thanks, Lyudmila, I won't forget.'

'No problem. Eighty euros, yes?'

10

H E WAS closing his suitcase and checking he had his wallet as well as the car keys so kindly returned by Silvana when he saw she had left her exercise book at the end of his bed. If he hurried, he might still catch her since, presumably, she was waiting for Niki. The way he had ordered her out, like she was his to do with as he wanted, puzzled and angered him. He considered whether she might not have left this exercise book as some sort of cry for help.

A flick through the pages, as he walked across the room and out the door, showed that it contained a collection of children's stories about talking trees and animals, written in a tight precise script. She dotted the letter 'i' with little flowers. It did not seem to contain anything else. Well, maybe just leaving it was a cry for help in that she wanted him to reappear in person and give it back.

He was in the middle of the corridor when a nun floated past him, and he paused, disconcerted by the fact he could not hear her. He coughed loudly.

'Yes?'

The voice came from directly behind him, and he spun round to find another nun, this one without a wimple but wearing a blue uniform of some type, right behind him. Apologetically, he explained he was looking for the exit.

'Are you leaving us? Shouldn't you be accompanied?'

Blume did not know the answer to this. The wrinkled face smiled at him. 'Why don't you wait for the doctor to come back?'

Behind them, a door stood open. He could see part of a wall, baking golden in the warm sun. He pointed towards it.

'That's the cloister. You want to get some air and sun there? It is a lovely place.'

Blume considered the face as white as talcum powder before him. She was friendly enough, but looked like she had never seen the sun. He was expecting more advice, perhaps even an order to go back to bed.

'Is that exercise book for him?'

Blume looked at his hand in surprise.

'No, it's . . .'

But she was on her way. 'If I see the doctor, I'll tell him you're in the cloister.'

When she had gone, Blume turned around a few times to get his bearings. If the cloister was there, he had to go in the opposite direction to escape. One corner and a few steps later, he was out in the open, at the front of the clinic.

There were about 20 or so cars in the car park, which occupied a corner of the piazza. At the far end, near the gate, he spotted some movement, as of people going to their car. He looked up and down for Silvana and Niki, listening for voices and, sure enough, he heard a woman's voice raised in anger, and he recognized it as Silvana's.

Clear as a bell, Silvana's voice shouted out the word *putane*! He could hear the anger and disgust in her voice. Niki was keeping his voice down. A typical male trick. Keep your voice low as you say terrible things, make the woman sound hysterical. He had used it a few times himself.

Blume made his way quickly between the parked cars towards the voice, then spotted them standing beside a Range Rover, the purpose of which might as well have been to draw attention to Niki's small stature. He was close enough to hear them now, and still they had not seen him. Instinctively, he crouched down.

'Whores!' Silvana was shouting. 'I have put up with it, but this –!'

Niki said something.

What Blume heard at this point seemed to be a sharp intake of breath followed by a crack, and a gasp of disbelief. Dropping the exercise book, he jumped up from his hiding place just in time to see Niki make a staggering lunge at Silvana. As Blume moved towards them, she slowly turned her head in his direction. Their eyes locked and she began to weep. As for Niki, he hardly had time to register the new arrival before Blume was upon him.

Niki was still fumbling with the fastener on his satchel, when Blume's first punch hit him on the cheekbone. The other side of his face hit the car door, and as he was on the rebound, Blume hit him again, in the lower jaw. Blume pushed him back so that from a distance it might have looked as if he was trying to steady Niki, and keep him from falling. Instead, he was lining him up for a more direct punch. As the fist came straight at him, aimed directly at the tip of his nose, Niki instinctively raised the satchel to his face. The blow caused it to open and shed its contents all over the ground. The sight of a pistol, now lodged beneath the front tyre of the Range Rover, seemed to release a wild rage in Blume, who kicked him in the groin, then grabbed Niki's throat with both hands, and pressed his thumbs against his windpipe.

'Stop! No!'

The voice seemed to come from far away.

But he knew he had to obey it in a minute. Just one more squeeze, he said to himself, enjoying the squawking noise coming from beneath his hands. He pushed down. Forcing Niki backwards, bringing their lips almost to touching. Niki was flapping his hands like a little bird now, and his eyes stood out in fear.

'No!' It was Silvana again, and she sounded like she meant it. He'd let go just as soon as he had pushed Niki's head all the way to the ground. Fucker tried to pull a gun, the front of his mind was shouting, while the calmer part, where thoughts seemed more deeply embedded and arose more slowly, turned over the idea that Niki had simply been in possession of a weapon, without having made any attempt to draw on him, and that usually he was in better control of his temper.

'Blume!' A new voice, a man's. Reluctantly, he released his grip, and Niki fell back on the ground with a strange sigh, almost as of contentment.

To his surprise and disappointment, Silvana immediately flung herself down and began tending Niki, who was already gasping and making a comical hooting sound.

Blume straightened up and turned his attention to the new arrival.

'Good afternoon, Dr Bernardini. As you can see, I'm feeling much better now.'

11

That Nadia was almost broken was evident from the moment they met, but Alina could not admit it to herself until later, when she was on her return journey across town. The girl who had guided her, advised her, comforted her, played elder sister to her had become thinner, uglier, haunted and fearful that she was being watched. Nadia, Alina felt, should have been more generous with her time. After all, Alina was the one running the greater risk for having left her district.

Nadia's attention drifted and her answers were short, and she had little to tell. The life and spirit had been drained from her, and she had a few visible puncture marks on her left arm. Alina asked her if she had managed to save anything, but Nadia did not seem to understand. When Alina spoke of the two of them getting away, really away, she saw a small spark of hope and the old defiance in her friend's eyes. Then Nadia, momentarily resuming her elder-sister role, said, 'It takes money, Alina. Lots of money.'

'I have money!'

Nadia looked at her sceptically. 'I mean real money.'

And Alina realized, with sadness, that she did not want Nadia to know about the cache in the tree. Maybe she would tell her another time, but without being able to talk about the money or discuss escape, Alina found she had nothing much to say to her old friend. The conversation between them became halting and awkward, and finally they both fell silent.

After half an hour, Alina decided there was no point in staying, and declared her intention to return to her district, she leaned in to allow Nadia to embrace her, and, as she pulled back, Nadia unexpectedly said, 'How much have you put aside?'

'I never said . . .'

'But you have. You're planning to get out of the country. Where to? Greece? Italy?'

'Anywhere. Italy ideally.'

'I know a man,' said Nadia. 'A taxi driver. He would help. Maybe for 14,000 liras? €5,000.'

'For both of us?'

Nadia pulled Alina's head back against her shoulder and stroked her hair, as she used to do. 'Each.'

Alina took a taxi back to her district to save time and, she hoped, get back before her absence was noticed. But she might as well have walked and saved herself the fare. The traffic, always slow, was gridlocked. The taxi driver cursed and thumped his steering wheel, and threatened her when she announced she was getting out. He held her responsible for getting him stuck. She scrambled out of the car and thrust some money at him, a few liras more than was on the meter. 'Fuck you,' she said in parting, and eased her way between two stationary cars in the next lane.

As she walked, she heard the wail of sirens, which, she realized, were coming from the direction she was headed in. She thought nothing of it. Sirens were a common sound in Istanbul. She cut through some side streets, which were also filling up with motorists seeking to escape. The sirens kept bleating at the same pitch. They, too, must be caught in the traffic.

She was back in her quarter. Some very angry police cars, furious at the traffic for not giving way, tried to force a passage through for a fire engine. Three 'Dolphins', as the motorcycle units were known, were homing in on an area, shouting at drivers, who were uncooperative or helpless or both. Sometimes the PKK set off bombs, but she had not heard any explosions. She did not care about Kurd separatism or even bombs in Istanbul. For her, Kurds were the ones who sold heroin. If they planted bombs, too, they might have good reason. Nadia had had marks on her arms. Nadia had been dealing with Kurds.

Still indifferent to her surroundings and thinking of the impossible sum of €10,000 and the marks on Nadia's arms, she barely registered that the source of the trouble was a hotel, the Arden, which had thick black smoke billowing out of it. As she watched, the firefighters let loose with three jets, one of which seemed not to have the pressure to reach the smoking window, or perhaps they were keeping the rest of the building cool. Only now did she begin to worry.

She reached a police cordon, manned by five aggressive paramilitary police in black combat gear decorated with a red half moon and star. Whether or not it was a PKK attack, they were treating it as such and all onlookers as likely terrorists. They stood with their automatic weapons slanting downwards, just, and stared into the crowd, defying anyone to trespass into the restricted zone. But as the spectacle was not much to behold, with the smoke whiter now, already considerably less, and no flames to be seen, most pedestrians merely paused for a few moments before going about their business, or shrugging and turning back as they found their way barred.

Alina, however, stood rooted to the spot, unable to take her eyes from the scene. Had she not already been picked out by a policeman for her red hair, she would have been for the intensity of her gaze. She was transfixed, not by the hotel and its smoke, but by the coils of firefighter hosepipe snaking around her tree in the middle of the traffic island.

A policeman hoisted his automatic weapon higher on his shoulder and walked over and flashed a knowing smile at her. She stepped neatly to one side and continued to watch the tree. Now the policeman was saying something. It might have been a challenge, a warning, or an invitation. Or all three. Her Turkish was good enough now to understand most things that were said to her, especially since they mainly had to do with her body and what the speaker would like to do with it, or, if the speaker professed religion, would like to have done with it. But she was not listening. At least six people were at her tree now. Two of them were smoking. They looked as if they planned to be there for some time.

The policeman said something, and she ignored him. He stepped outside his own cordon. '*Chukumu yala.*' He made an obscene gesture with his thumb in his mouth. She stared through his invisible head at the firemen who were now looking in the tree. One of them was laughing. She could not hear it, but she could see him, his head thrown back, his mouth wide open in mute laughter. She felt tears running down her cheeks. The policeman looked at her, then stepped back behind the cordon.

Alina turned and went back to the brothel she called home.

All she could feel was a dull rage. It had completely swept away all her feelings of apprehension and fear. She spent the rest of the afternoon sitting at a bar, sipping apple tea, and feeling almost nothing. A young Georgian girl was sent to fetch her. Alina said she would be back immediately, then ordered another tea, and spent another hour till night had set in and her bladder was full.

Her absence had been noted. She had no earnings to show for the entire day. Worst of all had been the leisurely pace at which she obeyed the order to return. It might still have gone well enough for her, with only a few slaps had she begged forgiveness and promised to make it up by working all night and all the next day, but she was sullen and refused to comply. She found it hard even to hear what was being said.

It was only when she looked around and saw a few of the youngest girls had been called down that she realized she was going to be made an example of. Mikhail, the bouncer, closed the door to the club and stood there with his back to it. Fyodor, the owner, came up to her and placed his thumb under her chin and his index finger on her temple, and gently, like a doctor assessing the bruising that was yet to come, tilted her face sideways till her gaze met his. He had deep brown eyes, soft, and he was smiling down at her. Then he slipped his thumb into the hollow beneath her chin, and pushed hard against the pressure point, forcing her to stand. As soon as she did, he let go, stood back, and kicked her hard in the base of her stomach. She heard, then felt, the breath go out of her, and, as she fell forward, he hit her in the eye with an uppercut.

Fyodor grabbed her hair and dragged her around the room. He did not have to say anything, because actions speak louder than words. He forced her to her knees and undid his fly.

It was not an unusual situation. She had seen it happen to others. It was whispered that Fyodor could only really get it up in this way. She knew she should not resist, but she did. She pictured the firefighters, their mouths open in laughter, and found her mouth clamping shut. She clenched her teeth, twisted her head. Fyodor was loving it.

Alina found herself praying. She had not been brought up to pray, though her grandmother, daughter of a famously cruel atheist who let children starve, had made a point of being religious and had tried to pass it on, skipping her daughter and concentrating on the grandchildren. Alina could remember the image of the Theotokos in her grandmother's apartment. In the 'good' room, the Redeemer's face was eerily, maybe miraculously, visible in a damp patch in the wallpaper. Her grandmother worshipped the face in the wallpaper as much as the icon of the Theotokos, and maybe more. But Alina preferred the icon, which was suddenly remarkably clear in her mind, as if she had seen it yesterday. The Mother of God was slightly hunched, with her arms folded, and Alina, relenting, imitated the gesture now. Christ's mother was leaning forward, and Alina, steadying herself a little, leaned forward too on her bruised knees. Her ribs ached, her mouth was swollen, she could smell Fyodor's urine and groiny fug around her face. Her grandmother had often told her of the power of prayer and fasting. Alina there and then resolved not to eat until she was out of Istanbul. Nothing but water. And if she did not escape, she would starve to death or be put to death. He pushed pack her head, and she closed her eyes and tried to think of a prayer.

It is truly meet to bless you, O Theotokos, ever-blessed and most pure, and the Mother of our God. More honourable . . . more glorious . . . without defilement.

She apologized for not remembering the words, and prayed for guidance.

Guidance came.

When he had finished with her, Fyodor had a drink, then another, and ordered her out into the street. As she went past him, he touched her arm.

'You . . . understand why that had to happen?'

She nodded.

He seemed unsatisfied. 'You want a drink before you go out?'

She looked down at him slumped in his chair. Fyodor avoided drink most of the time because he could not hold it, and because when he started, he couldn't stop.

'You think I want to drink with you?' she said.

A look resembling hurt passed over his face, and he averted his eyes for a moment, then suddenly grabbed her arm, and pulled her towards him. 'I think you liked it. I think you . . .'

She walked out.

Alina returned to the club at two in the morning. She told the barman that Fyodor was awake and waiting for her, and he jerked his head backwards towards the stairs at the back, hardly glancing at her. But at the foot of the stairs, she veered off to the left to the storeroom and kitchen.

'Where are you going, whore?'

Her challenger was a Turk, aged about seventeen, whose distinguishing mark was the utter failure of a moustache on his upper lip.

'Mr Sholokhov wants egg and onion with yufka or anything else in the way of bread,' she told him. 'Anchovies, too.'

He glared at her, then retreated into the kitchen, 'Stay there.'

She nodded. As soon as he was gone, she went into the storeroom. She found what she was looking for immediately. She placed it on the floor behind the door. A few minutes later she took a plate of pita bread, egg, onions, and anchovies, paused to pick up the plastic tube she had got from the storeroom, and walked upstairs. Fasting and praying were fine for her grandmother; she had a better idea. At the top of the stairs, she went into the bathroom, sat on the toilet, and ate ravenously. As usual, stinking black water sat in the sink. The water did not seem to be draining, but a tide mark around the edge showed that it had been higher earlier on.

She finished her meal, and walked down the corridor. Already she could hear Fyodor's snoring. She shook the crystal contents of the tube, rhythmically, like a maraca. It was a pleasing sound.

Softly she opened the door and went over to the bed, where Fyodor was deep in an alcoholic sleep beside the young Georgian girl he had sent to fetch her earlier. Gently, Alina stroked her arm, and the girl awoke as if she had applied an electric current. Alina put two fingers to her own mouth, then touched the girl's lips.

'He wants me. I was told to come here. You must leave.'

The Georgian girl's eyes were colourless in the dark but shone with fear. Alina imagined a miniature version of the girl standing behind her own eyes, taking in details. The girl would faithfully report who it was, the time it had happened, everything. Alina would do the same in her place.

Alina realized she had spoken Turkish. She repeated it in broken Russian. The girl nodded, understanding. Fyodor snorted violently, stopped breathing for a few seconds, and twisted in his sleep.

'*Kauchmar*,' said the girl.

'You must say he sent you to get me. Alina. You understand?'

The girl did not, but she nodded.

'And that he made you leave once he had me.'

She nodded again. 'Go.'

The girl went.

Fyodor slept on his back, aiming alcohol fumes at the ceiling, his mouth as wide open as he liked hers to be. She pressed down and twisted the childproof cap on the white tube. She hoped it would be enough. Then, leaning over, she tilted the entire contents into Fyodor's gaping mouth.

She had not been completely prepared for the high pitch of his scream. Nor for the immediacy of the thrashing of his body. Most of the rest of the drain cleaner went over his face and into his eyes. From the bedside table she grabbed a bottle of vodka, and poured it over his face to get the crystals fizzing and popping. He roared 'Alina!', which was fine. It was better he knew who it was.

His screams became more pitiful and the voice higher, but he showed no signs of dying. Some of the foam from his mouth splashed on her hand, cold for a second, innocuous, then suddenly extremely hot. Fyodor was out of bed now, flailing wildly about, trying to breathe, whisper-screaming for water, bringing his hands to his eyes, then his throat. She cast libations of vodka at him. Somehow he made it over to the desk, grabbed at a chair, and, with one rip, tore the back off it, cast the pieces on the floor. He stumbled on the rug edge and fell with a thud on the floor.

If they heard this, they would think he was giving her another lesson. She thought of screaming a little herself to add to the fiction and maybe release some of the tension and excitement she felt inside, but already he was quieter. Soapy pink and white liquid was coming from his mouth. She could smell the fizzing chemicals and alcohol and underneath them a scent that reminded her of singed hair. It did not look as if he was going to die.

His voice was gone, but his muscles were still working, and he continued to kick. She watched for a while, took the pillow from the bed, and put it over his face, but he pushed her off as if she, too, were filled with feathers. Still strong, then. She grabbed a piece of wood from the splintered chair and hit at him, but she might as well have been using a matchstick against a horse. But he had given up attacking her, and was simply writhing on the floor, describing a circle with his naked hairy legs. She took another piece of splintered wood and rather than slapping at him, drove it downwards with all her force into his face. She missed completely, and the piece of wood went through his throat, without much resistance at all. The first spurt of blood went so high it shot over her shoulder, and she was in time to dodge the second, and third, which, she noticed, were followed by a foaming white liquid. After four spurts, it was all over, or at least the noise was. Fyodor still seemed to be alive, in that his chest was heaving, but his mouth was a ragged red hole filled with foam, and his eyes were an unseeing white. He no longer seemed to have eyeballs.

She sat there waiting, indifferent now, occasionally sending a thought up to the Theotokos, who sat in her imagination smiling down at her. No one came. Unexpectedly, Fyodor started rasping again. She waited till this had passed. At one point, he lifted up his index finger, like a reasonable man might do to emphasize a point in his conversation.

Fyodor had shouted her name, and the screams that followed, his screams, had been woman-like. The smashing around of furniture, the thumping and rolling were common night-time sounds. The silence afterwards was also to be expected. Everyone would be expecting a chastised and compliant Alina in the morning, or a dead Alina.

They would not be expecting this.

She found his wallet under the mattress. It had as much cash in it as she could have saved in six months. Turkish liras, euros, some dollars. Almost €1,000. It had a credit card and two ATM cards, too.

She took his phone. He had loved his phone, always stroking it, staring at it, talking into it, and making deals. The screen presented her with a 4 x 4 matrix of dots. She pictured him, sitting at the table, picking at food, then wiping his greasy fingers on a paper napkin.

He had this habit of touching the corner of his mouth, as if always worried some food might be sticking there. She couldn't resist going over and looking at his mouth now. It no longer had corners. It resembled an exploded red flower, swollen genitalia, a gash. This creature had wielded his phone with a flourish, swiping his finger down, then up, a tick mark, a V-gesture that he could manage with his thumb while holding the phone in the same hand. She tried it. Fortunately the phone gave her unlimited attempts, and after ten minutes, the matrix slid away to reveal his screensaver, a photo of tall ships on a blue sea, which she found disconcerting. Maybe Fyodor, too, had dreamed of sailing away some day. Maybe he did not want to be where he was, doing what he did.

She scrolled down through the contacts. There were not that many. Fyodor, who spent so many hours playing with the phone, had filled in names and surnames, even addresses, and added photos here and there. Except for three entries all of which began with + 333 6666, the dialling code for Turkey and Istanbul, followed by a series of digits.

The Georgian girl had left an ugly golden clutch bag. She emptied its contents on the floor and replaced them with Fyodor's keys, wallet, and phone. She let herself out, locking the door behind her, and left through the rear of the building, via an emergency push-bar door that was kept closed with two chains and a heavy padlock, to which Fyodor had the key. It led into an enclosed square courtyard full of garbage and coal dust. The gate to the street outside was also locked, but reliable old Fyodor, his face still melting in the bedroom above, had a key to that as well. She let herself out, then flung the keys into the middle of the street.

She walked straight to the first ATM, and slotted in the first of Fyodor's cards. She scrolled down the names in the phone book to where he had entered a first name without surname. She ignored the area code, and punched in the remaining five digits on the ATM panel. Planting a false name in a phone to disguise an ATM number was a trick her brother Michael had once told her about.

She got an error message. So much for Michael. She tried the same trick using the next name on the list. No good. One attempt remaining. She keyed in the last digits in reverse order. The machine wanted to know what sort of operation she needed. She pressed withdrawal, then 'Other amount'. When the transaction was complete, she did the same for the next card, reversing the five final digits on the first entry. Then she walked on to another ATM and repeated the process twice over. At the third ATM, she got a maximum-exceeded message on one card, but the first card paid out again. On the fourth ATM that card, too, was exhausted, and the Georgian girl's bag was stuffed beyond capacity. She had to slip the remaining notes into the waistband of her skirt.

The night-time blackness was now greying into early morning. She needed a taxi, and she needed to fetch Nadia and they needed to go right now. But before she could go, she needed to check up on an idea that had come to her while praying. She walked through the streets, at risk of arrest or capture, an obvious lone and vulnerable figure, yet strangely confident that, for now at least, she was untouchable. It took her 20 minutes to get to her tree, that base of which was still wet from the dripping hosepipes. She slipped her hand into the hollow. Men's hands were too big. The firefighters had been laughing simply because they were happy, just as she was. She stretched out her fingers and felt the bundle. It was still there intact. Alina pulled it out, and knew with absolute certainty that she was under the protection of a goddess.

12

THE FAINT grey light had gone. So although she had at last found a piece of furniture, from the feel of it a broken stool with one of three legs missing, that might help her climb up, she had no idea in which direction to drag it. Immediately, Alina began to wonder if the whole thing had been a dream. She ran her hand over the hard wood of the stool. It felt real. Deliberately, she ran her hand against the grain. A splinter lodged itself into the fleshy part of her palm, sending a cold shock of pain down her spine. She brought her palm up to her mouth and tried to suck it out, to no avail. The pain remained and with it, the clarity she had been looking for. The stool was invisible in the dark but real. The patch of grey must also have been real. And the gust of air? Maybe not. The light was gone now, but if it appeared again, then she would know day had come above her, and that even if she could not get out, she might at least measure out her time.

If the stool could be propped up against the wall and she could raise her head towards the patch of light, then she could, what, shout for help? Her throat was parched and closing, and she no longer had strength enough to climb. The chute, or air duct or whatever it was, would be too small. But if someone happened to be walking in the garden above just at the right moment and she made noise, she would be saved.

Nadia would surely be looking for her. Just as she had gone looking for Nadia, so Nadia would come looking for her. Nadia was good at finding good people. That was her speciality. Out of the thousands of bad people, Nadia could spot the good ones, and they were not the likeliest. She had found the taxi driver. Called him on her mobile phone, and he had not been on duty that night, yet he had left the warmth of his family and travelled across the city to help them. Two foreign prostitutes.

★

Five minutes into the taxi ride, Nadia opened the window, and said to Alina, 'If you have a phone, get rid of it now.'

Alina took out Fyodor's phone. 'Like this?' She held it out the window.

'Just drop it. If it doesn't break, it might even be better. Keep them looking hereabouts for you.'

'What about yours?'

'This is a never-used phone I have been keeping for this moment,' said Nadia.

The taxi driver, who knew he was helping them escape, had not even wanted any money. Nadia had left some anyhow, stuffed down the back seat. She called him soon after he had gone, telling him the money was not intended for his passengers, so he had better take it. Alina could hear his protests. He almost sounded angry to be so cunningly rewarded.

'Why?' was all Alina could ask about the taxi driver.

Nadia opened her arms in a helpless gesture. 'Some people are put together so well that they stay good no matter what. Maybe they have to be very stupid to stay so good. The taxi driver? He is a very devout Muslim. Now he can tell his God he saved two women.'

They were standing outside a freight area of the port. The sun was coming up over the Asian side of the city. Alina felt far from saved yet.

'You need to find a bad man trying to become good,' Nadia explained. 'That is where you can find some hope. Someone who has done a very bad thing, but wants to become good. Because someone like that knows what direction he is moving in.'

'Last night I became a killer . . .'

Nadia raised her hands to her ears. 'Don't tell me, Alina. Not now.'

'I killed a man who wasn't always . . .'

'No, Alina!'

She stopped. What had she killed? What had Fyodor been? Soft brown eyes; his almost empty contact list on the phone; the picture on his phone of the tall ships cutting the open seas; the jokes he tried to tell; and, then, the things he did. They would be finding his body soon. They might have found it already.

Nadia had resumed her senior role and taken charge of the money. Now she was showing breast and cash to two men at the heavy-duty dock security-gate, which rolled open. They stepped through and the gate rolled closed. Nadia giggled as she allowed herself to be touched by the older of the two men, and the men giggled as they received their money. Alina stood there, sick with fear and loathing. If they wanted, these two men could simply take all the money from them, and with it their freedom and their lives. They looked like weak men, but physically they were stronger. Nadia seemed to be exchanging telephone numbers with them. She pulled out another wad of notes, smiling. After a few minutes of whispering and pointing, they walked away, the elder one slapping the younger on the shoulder.

Nadia came over, slightly breathless, her eyes, which had seemed so dead the other day, now alert and shining.

'How much did you give them?' Alina felt resentment building up. That was her money. Tree money and blood money.

Nadia took off at a brisk pace towards the quayside, ignoring Alina's question. When Alina caught up, Nadia said, 'Have you ever heard of Bari?'

'No, who is he?'

'It's not a he, it's a place. A port in Italy.' She pointed towards the waterside. 'There is a ship down there carrying engine parts or chemicals or something. *Corona Apulia*. And we're going on it.' She looked at Alina critically, as if assessing the suitability of her attire, then unexpectedly said, 'A pen? I bet you don't have a pen. Neither have I. You must repeat and remember any names or numbers I say out loud.'

Nadia pulled her behind the crumbling wall of an outhouse and they stood there in silence as Nadia stared at her phone. To Alina, it felt as if they had been there for hours: long enough to grow cold, long enough to become numb, and long enough to lose hope.

The winter sun was high in the sky and they had been spotted and pointed at by several shipyard workers, though no one had come over to them yet, and still Nadia held the phone, her face screwed up with the determination not to look sick with grief at what was happening. Neither of them had spoken in 40 minutes, but it was clear everything depended on the phone ringing.

And then it did. Nadia had it at her ear before the first trill had ended. She held up a finger to Alina, reminding her to listen.

'François . . . Taymur. Taymur. OK.' She nodded at Alina, who started repeating the name to herself. 'Nitti, Salvatore. Nitti. Thank you. Yes.'

It turned out Taymur, a Lebanese, was the name of the captain of the ship. Nadia tried to boss and shove her way on board just with the name alone, but it was not enough. Two men, one in uniform, the other not, stood with their arms folded and pretended not to hear. Alina wondered why Nadia would not bribe them, and tugged on her arm. In a flash of Romanian, whispered with urgent speed and rage, Nadia told her not to let these two see any money.

'No good at all in either of them. Just say the captain's name: Taymur.'

By dint of sullen repetition and no attempt at explanation, Nadia managed to get the one in uniform bored or worried enough to call the captain, who turned out to be younger, taller, and more handsome than seemed possible for a man in charge of such an old ship manned by such dirty brutes as these two. The captain also turned out to be something of a polyglot. Maybe that and his easy-going manner had got him his job.

Now the money did its magic. Speaking in a mixture or Romanian, Turkish, and English, Nadia explained that the captain now had two extra passengers, and that they were expected by Nitti in Bari. The captain managed to look both impressed and unbelieving at the same time, but he allowed them on board, and Nadia handed over what seemed to be almost all the rest of the cash and then, with the captain watching, threw her mobile phone over the side of the ship. They had travelled but 4 kilometres and spent four-fifths of the money. It seemed unlikely they would ever make it.

And so began another sea voyage, the two of them taking turns to lie down on the bunk in a room where no one disturbed them. What Alina saw of the Adriatic and bits of Greece was through a porthole, and when she saw Italy at last, the ship was already slowing and shuddering in the water, and people were shouting and chains were clanking. The city of Bari bobbed gently up and down outside.

The ship had been docked and motionless for several hours before the captain came in. He accompanied them to the gangway and shook their hands, formally, politely, and wished them luck.

'What about customs? Immigration control?'

The captain pointed down at the water.

'*Yüzmek . . . nager . . .* swim?' asked Alina in alarm, and mimed the action with her hands close to her chin. Nadia and the captain laughed. Alina leaned over the bar. Up against the ship, risking getting squeezed between it and the wharf, a man stood in a rubber dinghy looking up at them.

'Bad turning good,' Nadia said of the captain as they climbed down a slick, stinking ladder to the dinghy. The trip to the shore cost €400. A bargain. The journey continued.

★

Alina awoke clutching the wooden stool as if it were a piece of wreckage keeping her afloat. A splinter had inserted itself into her cheek, too. She stood up. There was the grey rectangle again, gliding rightwards as she looked at it but more or less in the same position. With the last of her strength, she dragged the stool until she hit the wall. From here she could not see the patch of relative light. She leaned it against the wall and climbed up. She fell twice. On the third attempt, she managed to keep her balance, and now, at last, she could feel the air again. It smelled of mud, grass, and something very pungent, like leather, sweat, and piss. She stretched up her hand. It was a chute of some sort that receded into the wall, then turned upwards. He fingers touched something. Metal. She hooked a finger around it, then another, then a third, and pulled. The stool fell from below her feet, but now her feet found an indentation in the wall, allowing her to take most of the strain off her arms. She thrust her hand into the space and hung onto what were definitely iron bars of some sort. Even without her full body weight, her arms were tiring, and she did not have the strength to pull the rest of her body up and even if she could, it would not fit through the gap. She thought she could hear movement of some sort and shouted. Nothing replied. Tightening her grip with her left hand, she thrust her right through the gaps in the bars to find out what was behind. She splayed her fingers, feeling around. The smell was unmistakable now, and yet she could not identify it. A savage smell such as came out of her grandmother's kitchen when she was preparing hare stew.

A scuffling, then a cold, wet, familiar thing touched her outstretched hand, then something snarled and a razor-like pain pierced her fingers, the pain bringing a burst of orange behind her eyes, the brightest colour she had seen since she became locked in. With a scream she pulled away and fell backwards, her head hitting the stone floor with a sharp, final crack. Her eyes rolled back, and for a second it was like she was floating on the sea again.

Theotokos, mother of Christ, looked down, still demurely smiling, still indifferent, as Alina drew her last three breaths.

13

THE CLINIC nestled in the lowest part of the town, at the edge of a lozenge-shaped piazza called Largo Minerva, enclosed by buildings on one side and the high Roman walls with diamond-shaped brickwork in *opus reticulatum* on the other. Outside the walls, the land was too steep for any building, and the road travelled down by a series of hairpin turns till it reached Villa Romanelli. Even here, inside the walls, the gradient was so sheer that shallow steps had been cut into the pavement. Outside the walls, there was only road.

Largo Minerva was no more than a car park for the few people who did not have special permits to drive into the historical centre, which, the signs told him, started ten metres up. Everything in the town was built on a slope. A row of houses, white and clean but also crumbly and empty, repaired by European funds after one of the many earth tremors, ran up a street so steep that three doors was all it took to level the attic of the lower house with the basement of the higher.

Blume knew nothing of the history of the town. The defensive wall suggested it had once been keen to repel all comers. In that respect Monterozzo had been ultimately successful, he reflected, since he could not imagine anyone wanting to live here.

Even Dr Bernardini, who spoke fondly of the town during the half-hour conversation that followed his interruption of Blume's attack on Niki, admitted that it lacked many facilities, including a well-stocked chemist, and that many people who worked in the town, himself included, lived outside it. 'If you need some prescription drugs, you often need to wait several days,' he explained. 'So in your case it makes better sense to go back to Rome directly. I have written up a short description of what happened and the symptoms you displayed,' he said, handing Blume a piece of paper. 'Show that to your doctors, and let them decide.'

'Do I get the idea you want me to leave?'

'I certainly don't want you to come to harm while under my care,' said the doctor. 'That would be *catastrophique* for my reputation. But you need to mind yourself, too. Attacking Niki was not a good idea. Niki may not look it, but he has powerful connections and some unsavoury friends. What made you hit him anyhow?'

'Oh, nothing. *Pour encourager les autres*, maybe,' said Blume.

'*Dingue! Vous parlez français!* Wait, what "others" are you talking about?'

'Anyone else who thinks they can act – look, I don't speak French, doctor. It just sounded like a good phrase in the circumstances.'

'Will you go to Rome now?'

'I will,' promised Blume. 'I'll collect my things and be gone.'

★

He edged his car out of the car park and through the narrow arch that pierced the wall at the end of the piazza. A road sign opposite with red and white arrows on it warned him that if someone had found a good reason to travel up the hill into the town, that person would have right of way.

He drove down to a T-junction that resembled a calligraphic Y for the way the road curved away from him on either side. Anyone arriving from the left would probably be travelling slowly up the hill. The danger therefore came from the blind right, where vehicles would be travelling in fast descent. Steep curving roads had once been a source of enormous enjoyment for him as a young man, and he did not want to meet a younger version of himself now. He pulled on his orange Gucci sunglasses, a strange present from Caterina, and got ready for a drive back to Rome.

Silvana, whose exercise book he had dropped on the ground and dirtied – he would apologize to her for this when he returned it – had no business being with Niki. The K in his name because of an Austrian Formula One pilot, the baptismal name from San Nicola of Bari, who had something to do with the original Santa Claus. A gift-giver. He thought of Alessia, who would know nothing of Santa Claus for three years or so. What would that be like, being too young to understand Santa Claus? So young she had not started to believe in what she would then have to learn to disbelieve. He felt a sudden and unexpected physical longing for his child. His muscles ached slightly at the idea of holding her tightly; his brain came up with a memory of the smell of her head, but kept it tantalizingly undefined.

Maybe he would just turn up at the door and surprise them – well, Caterina at any rate. Alessia lived in a state of perpetual wonderment anyhow at all the things she saw every day. The appearance of an occasionally present father would have to compete with the thousand other marvels she was taking in from her pushchair, a sort of mobile throne in front of which the world passed and was inspected.

He swerved hard into a bend he had not quite seen coming. He also took the next curve faster than intended. The road had no hard shoulder, just a sharp drop down a rocky embankment interrupted by a ribbon of asphalt where the road doubled back on itself below and then plunged again even more precipitously. His arms felt stiff and tired, and he wished he was at the bottom of the hill already. He glanced in his rear-view mirror. No one. He could go as slow as he wished. He pressed the brake pedal, which yielded easily, and softly sunk all the way to the floor, as if the brake pads had turned into marshmallows. The engine quietened but the car gained speed.

His first instinct was to reassert control by slamming his foot against the accelerator, and it was only with an enormous effort he managed not to do so. He pumped the brake to restore some hydraulic pressure to the callipers, but all he got was a shuddering sensation and the sound of the pads scraping against the rotor. He planted his feet on the floor and negotiated a curve by swinging all the way into the other lane. It seemed easy enough but as he was coming out of it, another curve immediately presented itself while the car did its best to keep going straight. He jerked the steering wheel and felt the back wheels slide. To his right was a drop that would kill him. To the left was the opposite lane where he might meet an oncoming vehicle at any time, but it was the only option. He allowed the car to drift sideways, aiming to hit the side of the rock bluff. Too late he realized he was travelling too fast and any impact would simply bounce him across the narrow road and down the sides of the gorge, now deeper than ever to his right.

He stood on the clutch, momentarily placing the vehicle into a terrifying freewheel descent, then slammed from fourth into third gear. He heard his father's voice admonishing him, 'Go down a hill in the same gear you use for going up it.' Overcautious and fatuous advice, he had always thought, until this moment. He took

113

another corner, with the transmission clamouring in protest. This time he did meet another car which, perhaps alerted by the roar of his engine, had almost stopped. He shot past, millimetres away, leaving the other driver honking his horn in rage at the near miss. The gradient steeper now, and the next corner swept out rightwards. He released the clutch, freewheeled into it, then crunched the gear into second. The lurch of deceleration threw him forward against the steering wheel and the back wheels spun and lost their grip. The edge of the precipice appeared below the nose of the car.

'*Porca Madonna!*'

Some cool, dispassionate part of his mind noted with wry amusement what his final oath was likely to be. Meanwhile his hand, seemingly unguided by thought, pulled at the handbrake as if he wanted to rip it from the floor, while his other hand sent the steering wheel into a spin towards the arriving edge, a counterintuitive move that he had learned many years ago at the advanced driving course. He felt the car spin away from the edge, and slide sideways into the opposite lane, and just as he was relishing the idea of stopping, something hit the passenger door, which crumpled inwards.

The car he had hit bore the words *Polizia Provinciale* on the side along with the insignia of the province. He had bounced off the car of the local traffic police. Unexpectedly, he found himself wheezing with laughter. After reasserting some control over himself, he got out of his car and started walking up the hill. He touched his face, neck, the back of his head. Nothing, he was perfectly fine. The driver's door of the car opened, and a *vigile* in his early forties, quite dashing in his pale blue uniform and very white shirt, got out. He was now performing the 'I can't-believe-this-has-happened-to-me-through-no-fault-of-my-own' mime common to all drivers in Italy, with his dented car as his audience.

The *vigile* brought his recital of outrage to an end by crossing his arms and staring at Blume.

'I am a colleague,' said Blume. He did not like saying this for various reasons, one of which was that he felt superior to this man, whose job was to control the parking in a tiny town and occasionally hassle shopkeepers for permits and health certificates. Another reason was that it sounded ingratiating.

'My brakes failed,' he paused, noting the three yellow bars on the *vigile*'s sleeve, and added, '*Sovrintendente*.'

The *vigile* acknowledged the recognition of his rank with a curt nod. 'That's very rare.'

'Well, it happened.'

'Have you been drinking?'

'Absolutely not,' said Blume.

The *vigile* took out a pen, stuck it in his mouth, and sucked thoughtfully as he regarded Blume. 'Since it is too early for you to have been drinking, Commissioner Blume, it must be the medication. Didn't Dr Bernardini tell you not to drive?'

'How do you know about Bernardini? And my name?'

'And why should I not?'

'Could you just check the brake cables?' said Blume.

'You think they were cut? That would be attempted murder. Who is trying to kill you?' The *vigile* took the pen out of his mouth and wrote a note on a pad.

'I misspoke, sorry. It must be the shock.' Even so, an image of Niki sliding under his car and cutting the brake line had come into his mind.

'If it was brake failure, rare though it is,' said the *vigile*, 'the fluid

115

will have drained out from one of the bolts at the master cylinder. That's what happens.'

'You think?' He was not quite ready to drop his mental charges against Niki.

The *vigile* smoked his pen and nodded. 'Definitely. So, you ignored the warning light?'

'There was no warning light,' said Blume, trying to remember.

'No warning light? So the vehicle has faulty electronics, too? Or maybe you weren't paying attention? Let's have a look.'

The two of them walked down to Blume's car. Not one more vehicle had passed them in all this time, Blume reflected bitterly. Just his luck to find the one car and for that one car . . .

'Brakes seem faulty,' said the *vigile* who had sat inside the car and pumped the pedal for a while. 'But I am not excluding reckless driving. Where were you going in such a hurry?'

'Back home to Rome, only I wasn't in such a hurry.'

From behind his back the *sovrintendente* produced Silvana's exercise book. 'I found this on the floor of the car.' He opened up the first page. 'See there? It's written Silvana Greco. What were you doing with her exercise book?'

'I was going to drop it off.'

'How did it come into your possession in the first place? It's hardly proper for a man of your age.'

'I was just going to return it. I was enrolled in that course she was doing.'

'What course?' asked the *vigile*.

'A course on Bach Flowers, herbal medicines, relaxation techniques, all that . . .' His upper arms started itching again, and he took off his jacket to scratch, revealing hoops of sweat beneath his armpits.

The *vigile* was looking at him sceptically.

'It's hot. I have a rash . . .' He took a tube of pills from his jacket and waved it at the man. 'This helps with the rash.' He dropped a pill into his mouth, and chewed. It tasted vile. 'Any water?'

'No.'

'Never mind,' said Blume, swallowing the bitter grains in his mouth. 'Anyhow, as you know, the course had to be cancelled.'

'So I heard. Come on, let's get back for some form filling. You can have some water there.'

'I see,' said Blume. 'So we're reporting this accident in full? Wait a second. You *heard* the course was cancelled?'

'Heard, yes. Why, am I supposed to be, deaf?'

Blume tried to recall his conversation with Silvana. The past 24 hours had been confusing. 'It's just that she said you or one of your colleagues closed her down. She said the ASL declared the accommodation not fit for purpose, and the Provincial Police arrived to enforce the order. That's why she had to close the whole thing down.'

'No. We never did that. Maybe you dreamed it, Commissioner. Come back to the office. Maybe you need to rest a little before you leave us? Also, you now have no car.'

14

BLUME SPENT the next hour filling in forms in the company of the *vigile*, whose name was Fabio, and a thin woman with jet-black hair, black-framed glasses, and small dark eyes who regarded him severely with schoolmarmish disapproval, though she was probably 10 years his junior, and never spoke a friendly word. He could see that Fabio was embarrassed by her hostility, but not yet ready to share a complicit rolling of the eyes with him.

It was agreed that Alfredo the mechanic would rescue his car. Fabio, if not his colleague, had turned a bit friendlier now that Blume was, in theory, accepting responsibility. It was felt his insurance should cover everything. Even poor maintenance might be forgiven, Fabio tentatively suggested, which earned him a look of contempt from the woman who, however, held a lower rank.

Blume glanced at a wall clock behind the desk. It was now past two, as if time were stretching out to make up for the smallness of the place.

Fabio followed his glance. 'Yes, these things take time.'

'Is there a taxi service of some sort?'

'Paolo runs a service.'

His colleague looked up from her paperwork, and said 'Paolo's not available today. He is picking people up at Rome airport. The Commissioner will have to make do without a taxi.'

Fabio slapped his thigh, remembering.

'What about a bus?' asked Blume.

'There is one at 10:20 every day, goes to Rome. So it's gone. And one at 11:00 to Naples. And every weekday, but not today, because it's Saturday, a third one goes to Pescara, though I've never seen anyone use it.'

'Hotels in town?'

Fabio sucked his teeth as if witness to a near miss. 'There *used* to be a hotel. But it closed down before I was born.'

'You'll just have to get someone to collect you, Commissioner,' said the woman.

At half past two, Blume put on his orange sunglasses, left the Provincial Police office, and went to explore the town of Monte-rozzo.

★

The town was built on what was essentially a single massive boulder with a flattish top, which looked like it had been cast down from the heavens, splintering and fracturing in its lower regions when it landed. The streets, steps, alleyways, and paths followed the lines of the clefts in the rock. As the upper section of the rock was less fissured, so the number of streets and available land for building decreased. He imagined that as he moved towards the top the various streets and alleys would begin to converge. The most complex maze-like part of the town was in the middle section, where a large slab of the mountain had broken off leaving room for the town to develop a little. He decided to reach the summit to get a clear idea of the layout. On his way up, he passed by a mechanic's shop, consisting of a garage door set in front of a natural cave. *Autoriparazioni Alfredo De Santis. Fiat e Plurimarche*. It was closed.

Blume felt an uncharacteristic longing for people, filth, and life as he passed empty house after empty house, some of them freshly plastered and clean, others in a state of decorous collapse. He continued walking upwards. This street was inhabited, just. He could tell by the potted plants, the occasional piece of furniture, or even shoes left on the porches and steps. It was like walking through people's private homes.

The few cars around were sitting on cement platforms built to neutralize the steep gradient. Getting a car up here would be hard. The streets widened a little as the rock formed a ledge, leaving space for a few shops, including a greengrocer whose three-wheeled Ape sat outside. Although it was now 3 o'clock, the shop appeared to be open. On an impulse of pity mixed with sudden hunger, Blume went in and bought himself a bag of apples. The old man inside served him without a word, and Blume left feeling disapproved of. When he bit into his apple, it tasted of wax and flour. He bit into a second one. Same story. There were no litter bins to throw them away, though the idea of tipping the bag and watching them roll them down the street was very appealing. No one was around, no one would see. He imagined the apples bouncing up onto the porches, knocking on doors, thumping against the bodywork of the cars, rolling all the way down to the bottom of the –

'Excuse me?'

He was so startled, he let go of the bag of apples, all of which rolled into a side gutter and settled there. He followed them with his eyes, then swore at them before remembering he was in company.

A woman, the height of a child, 90 if she was a day, wearing a crimpy black dress and flesh-coloured gloves was looking up at him, her expression as severe as the tight silver bun into which her hair was gathered. She was so thin that he felt a strong wind might whisk her away.

'Were you looking at the notice?'

'Notice?'

She pointed. A faded blue cardboard notice encased in a plastic envelope that had turned as orange as his sunglass lens was pinned to the wall. He couldn't make out a word.

'It says apartment to let,' she explained. 'Were those Pino's apples?'

He pointed back in the direction he had come, 'I bought them just round the corner.'

'Pino's,' she nodded. 'They belong in the gutter. So were you looking for somewhere?'

'To let? No, no. I'm afraid not.'

'Pity.'

'Yes,' said Blume. 'I'm sorry,' he added

'No need to be sorry. It's not your fault. The room is also available on a daily, weekly, or monthly basis, just so you know. Maybe you'll tell someone about it in Rome.'

'I'll be sure to.'

'Don't treat me like I am a child who needs to be humoured.'

'OK, I will tell no one about it, then,' said Blume, 'even if they ask me.'

She smiled at him. Her teeth were white, straight, small. He noticed she wore no glasses either, and her expression was intelligent. He doubted he would be in such good shape if he ever made it that far in life.

'That's better,' she said. 'No point in lying to a person you'll never see again, is there?'

'How did you know I'm from Rome?'

121

'Your choice of words when you dropped the apples.'

'Oh.' He felt himself blushing as she continued to stare at him.

'I am not shocked. It's quite amusing to hear apples being accused of whoring.'

'Yes, well . . . I need to be getting back.' He pointed at the faint blue smudge on the wall. 'You might want to change that notice. It's completely unreadable now.'

'It doesn't matter. No one comes up this way anyhow. Nowadays, if people can't drive to a place, they don't bother. Apart from the occasional scooter, I never hear any traffic up here. I have a lovely little terraced garden, and all I hear in it is birdsong. Want to see?'

'As I said, I need to be heading back . . .'

'Not that I like the little bastards. The house martins are fine, they eat insects. Blackbirds can sing all they want, but they still eat my seeds. And as for those vile ravens! And now we have these ringed parakeets from that damned garden below. Parakeets! Here in central Italy!' Her voice rose to a shriek. 'Have you heard them?' She shrieked again, and he stepped back. 'Well might you step back, when they make that noise,' she said, then did another imitation. 'And then they worry about lovely young African men coming over here. It's the animal invaders we need to watch out for. I can see you are in a hurry. Don't bother picking up those apples. The crows will fight over them this evening, which will give me something to watch.'

'Well, as I say, I need to go now.'

'Either you want to get away from me or you are in a terrible hurry. Let's be polite and assume the second. In which case, you should go down that way.' She pointed to the right. 'The road ends, but there is a low wall. If you just hop up on that and walk a few metres, you'll find yourself back at the church. It's far quicker. Mind your step, though, the wall is low on this side. On the other it's about 15 metres straight down into an escarpment.'

'I think maybe I'll just walk back the way I came,' said Blume.

15

ALFREDO, THE town mechanic, studied his irredeemably black fingernails before answering. 'I am waiting for a part from Germany.'

'It's an Alfa Romeo.'

The mechanic shook his head sadly. 'The parts still come from Germany.'

'What if I said I don't want it?'

'Too late, I've ordered it already. Three days. Five tops.'

'I don't want it.'

The mechanic dug his hand into his pocket and produced a handkerchief that might once have been red. Its purpose now seemed to be to apply more black grease to his forehead. When he had finished applying his paratrooper's camouflage, he said: 'Hot this afternoon.'

'Did you hear me?' said Blume. 'I do not want it.'

The mechanic took out a crumpled soft-pack of MS cigarettes from the kangaroo pocket in his overalls. The one he extracted looked like a flaccid penis, and he began to stroke it thoughtfully into shape as he considered Blume's outburst. He placed the cigarette in his mouth and took out a lighter. Blume waited, interested to see if the tobacco paper, now grey and impregnated with oil from the rubbing treatment, would flare when lit.

'Want one?'

'No thanks.' Blume was disappointed when it ignited normally. The mechanic took a long drag, then pulled the cigarette out of his mouth with a grimace, and squinted suspiciously at the filter.

'So, are you going to leave me a down payment?'

'I do not authorize you to do this. You were supposed to look at the brake lines, talk to the *vigili*.'

'I did. Then I ordered the spare parts.' The mechanic seemed thoroughly disgusted with his drooping cigarette. He gave it three of four more pulls before flicking it contemptuously into a puddle of oil and spitting next to his shoe. 'I've already put in a new brake line to your front wheels. What we're waiting for from Germany is a master cylinder. Yours half-failed. They only ever half-fail, it's a safety thing, which is why you are alive now.'

'The brake lines were fine then?'

'No. I just told you, I replaced the lines to the front. They were frayed and leaking a bit.'

'But not broken or snapped?'

The mechanic shook his head. 'The master cylinder's your problem.'

'This master cylinder. What's it like?'

The mechanic measured a space of air with his hands, revealing incongruously white palms. 'A thing about this large.'

'Have you got one here?'

'If I had one, would I order it all the way from Germany?'

'Not for my car, an old one. So I can see.'

'*Aho, stronzo, dove ti sei cacciato?*'

A head suddenly bobbed up from the floor a few metres to the right. 'What do you want?' said the head, which had wild tufts of light hair and an oil-flecked face, and was staring at Blume's shoes.

'Get your lazy arse into the back and find me an old master cylinder. Any type, any condition. Go on, you useless fucking halfwit.' The mechanic turned to Blume with a look of considerable pride. 'That's my son, Dario. He's not going back to school next year. He's going take over the business.'

Blume looked about him. The Pirelli calendar was 4 years out of date. There were two cars in the place besides his own, and it looked as if they were using one for spare parts to build the other. The kid climbed out of the pit, which might have been where he lived. There was certainly no car over it that he might have been working on.

A few minutes later he returned, and handed his father a dull metal object that looked like the electric motor of some heavy-duty kitchen mixer. His father made a playful attempt to bash him over the head with it.

'There you go,' he told Blume. 'Want it?'

'Just to look at,' said Blume. It was a welded solid unit. It did not look like the sort of thing a person could easily tamper with, or would tamper with when the hydraulic lines were so simple to find that even he had a rough idea of where they were.

'And this is the part that failed on my car?'

'Yes. Is that all you wanted to see? I'm very busy, you know.'

'So give me my car back,' said Blume.

The mechanic shook his head with the mild obstinacy of a mule. 'I can't do that. You have no brakes. You would kill someone or yourself as soon as you drove out of here and started down that hill. You'd probably drive into Mrs Servillo's kitchen at the first corner.'

'If I demand my car back, you must give it to me.'

'If you get into your car with no brakes in this town, I'm calling the *vigili* and the Carabinieri.'

Blume felt his shoulder skin prickle. 'This isn't finished, you know.'

The mechanic pushed his oily thumb into his nostril. 'I know. Five days. Once the piece arrives from Germany.'

Blume left the shop in a rage, visions of beating the mechanic over the head with one of the outsized spanners hanging on the wall vivid in his head. He popped two of the anti-itch Doxepin pills that he had, in fact, stolen from Caterina's mother. He walked downhill, choosing a random itinerary, and stopped at the first bar he saw with outside tables. He sat down, still angrier than he knew why, and ordered a pastry and coffee from the bar boy who might have been the brother of the boy in the pit. When they arrived what seemed liked several hours later, he gulped back the coffee washing down two Lyrica tablets for his nerves, but abandoned the stale pastry after one bite. Then he sat back in his chair and realized he was in a suntrap, the town was quiet and sleepy, and his rage subsided.

He took out his smartphone and, for the first time in several days, turned it on. Tentatively, and feeling foolish, he gave it a vocal command and watched in fascination as a Google results page popped up. He hit the first result and there was the name of a mechanic in a town 60 kilometres away. He did not bother reading the details. The part that interested him was that they advertised emergency pickup services. He went into the bar and asked for a pen and a scrap of paper.

'What for?' asked the kid who had served him.

'To write with, what the fuck do you think?'

With the same irritating slowness to take offence evinced by the mechanic – surely they were all related in a place like this? – the kid said, 'Sure. All I meant was you don't need it if you need to copy a number from the phone. I'll get you one.'

By the time he had come back, Blume felt more charitable. 'Go on, then, show me how it's done.'

'If you tap, you can copy and then paste it, and if you put it here . . .' The boy's slender fingers danced over the face of the phone as several windows went flashing by, opening and closing. Blume felt like a caveman confronting a spaceship.

'. . . and then if you want to call – do you?'

Blume nodded helplessly. His pride in knowing how to look up the internet on his phone was shaken.

'Ah! If that's the number you want to call now, all you have to do is press it on the screen. See how it's coloured blue?' The boy handed the phone back to him.

'Thanks,' said Blume. 'I'll have another coffee.'

The boy made a strange gesture, bringing his hand to his ear, then pointed at Blume's hand. Blume pointed at his own hand and smiled and nodded pleasantly. A tiny voice was saying something.

'Your phone,' said the boy. 'I think they've answered.'

'Oh, right . . .' He brought his hand up too quickly and slapped himself on the ear. He told the irritated person on the other end of the line that he had bad reception. Then he ordered a pickup truck immediately.

'Where are you?' said the voice.

'Monterozzo.'

There was an inhaling of air, as if worst fears had been confirmed. 'That's pretty far.'

'Emergency breakdown service, that's what you do?'

'Sure. It'll cost you is all.'

'Not a problem,' said Blume.

'So what's the address in Monterozzo?'

Blume went back onto the bar, and asked the kid to give the voice directions to the mechanic's.

'To Alfredo's?'

'Is there another mechanic in this town?'

'No.'

'So, yes: to Alfredo's.'

The kid and the voice on the other end of the line seemed to have a lot to say to each other. Eventually he said, 'He wants to talk to you.'

'Yes?'

'Let me get this straight,' said the voice. 'Your car is in a repair shop, but you want us to come along with a pickup truck and tow it away, and bring it to our repair shop 60 kilometres away?'

'Precisely,' said Blume.

'Right, well, I'm going to need your name, the registration of the car, and its make.'

Blume gave the details.

'And you want an emergency service, as in today?'

'As in as soon as possible.'

'Fine. Someone will be there in a few hours. Don't go anywhere till we get there.'

16

BLUME DECIDED he might as well get a newspaper to while away the time and, in the back of his mind, he knew he was looking also for a notebook and some pens. It was not quite an investigation he had got himself involved in, but, well, he wanted to get a bit of clarity, and writing things down seemed like a good start.

He felt a twinge of regret at the way he was treating the mechanic, but he refused to be made a fool of. He cared nothing about the car itself. In fact, he had been meaning to buy himself a new one (so far he had used his inherited wealth only to buy an apartment whose value had then plummeted as the constructors went bankrupt, but there was plenty left), but had not got round to it. What he needed to do was go into a dealership somewhere in the Parioli quarter of Rome and tell a haughty salesman that he was looking for a car that was quiet. That's what he wanted. A big, fat, smooth, and silent car.

He spent half an hour walking around the stony narrow streets until he found a newsagent. He tried to browse, but each time he picked up a paper to glance at the headline, the proprietor became agitated as might an archive librarian watching precious manuscripts being handled. All the titles had to do with the 'spread' and the crisis of the euro. Blume felt that with his new status as a wealthy man, he should care more about this sort of thing. Responsibly, he bought a copy of *Il Sole 24 Ore*. He had never tried to read a financial newspaper before.

Just off the piazza he was pleasantly surprised to find a stationer's. They were just closing for the afternoon when he slipped in, attracting a look of exasperation from the shopkeeper. He bought himself two hard-backed lined notebooks and five blue and one red pens. He loved pens. He had no nostalgia for fountain pens, and had always disliked biros. The new pens, with their gel ink, were a real pleasure. He especially liked the ones with a thick nib that somehow produced sharp thin lines. Although he might draw imperfect ovals and squares, arrows and messy underlining, he liked his actual script to be neat, almost in block capitals. He hated to misspell, because the correction always looked so messy and spoiled the aesthetics of the page, whereas to leave the misspelling was an assault to the eye and distracted him from everything else. The notebooks in a plastic bag, the pens inside his pocket, he resumed his meandering journey through the narrow alleyways. He could hear the sound of televisions, most of them tuned into the early evening news. Invisible children shouted out names, announcements, and protests. Here I am! Mummy. Paolo? Zia Marina! Noooo! I *didn't*. He heard the percussion of plates, glasses, silverware being laid on tables for early family supper. The smell of slow-frying onions and garlic and the soft wetness of boiling pans filled the air, and he realized with a pang that he was hungry.

Finding nowhere much better than where he had been, he returned to the bar, noting at once two large new arrivals, both of whom were dressed in Adidas tracksuits and sported gold jewellery on their wrists. They were joined by a man in a less blatantly criminal get-up who, he was now certain, had been several steps behind him ever since he had left the stationer's.

He ordered a toasted sandwich and beer from the bar boy, and ostentatiously unfolded his pink newspaper. Several minutes later, he remembered why he had avoided *Il Sole 24 Ore* all his life. It was like trying to understand algebra written in Greek. He rustled the pages for the benefit of the watching men. Four whole pages were dedicated to rows and columns of numbers and abbreviations. How did people read this? He searched for an article containing more words than numbers, and found one; but it was not illuminating. A second article persuaded him he should probably use his wealth to push up food prices, though it did not explain how. After reading it, he felt immoral and hungrier than ever.

The beer, which was slightly against his own rules, though he had been managing his drinking pretty well over the past few months, was deliciously refreshing. Half an hour later, he ordered a second.

How had he managed to get stuck in this place? Come to that, how had he managed to get stuck in Italy? He had money now. If he wanted, he could turn his leave of absence into retirement and go back to the United States. It was all a big mistake his being here. All those years ago, he had left junior high school in Seattle, unaware he would never go back. His parents were taking a two-year sabbatical in Italy to study art history. Then they extended it, though his mother lost her teaching post. And then . . .

The shock of *scuola media* and *liceo* in Italy and the need to fit in had made him fluent in the Roman dialect within a year. But he did not become properly Italian until his parents were killed and the people who were kindest to him were the police. Whether casual or traumatic, none of his life-changing decisions had been his decisions. Only by looking back could he see the vast distance he had travelled.

He finished his second beer and weighed up the pros and cons of challenging the men in tracksuits and their older companion. Niki's men, he was sure of it. They had spent far too much time not looking at him. They might as well have been holding placards with his name on.

He was halfway down his third beer, and feeling pretty relaxed and happy, when a shadow fell across his table. He looked up to see a woman standing in front of him. She wore a soft baby-blue cotton tracksuit with white drawstrings hanging over her thighs. She signalled the young waiter, who had come out with the express purpose of gawking at her, and sat down in the chair opposite Blume. Her hair was light brown with auburn highlights. Her eyebrows had been plucked into two inverted commas, and her eyes seemed to have no colour. Her fleshy lips and crooked nose reminded him incongruously of a boxer, but she was slight and feminine.

'Inspector Blume?'

He was too surprised to hear his name to object to the demotion in rank. His hand reached for his glass and he waved an apologetic arm over the tabletop, which, he now noticed, was covered in bread crumbs and rings of beer. 'Yes, that's me. Can I get you something. A drink?'

She tossed her hair back in what he felt was a contemptuous gesture, and suddenly he felt put out. She was young and though her features were fine, her face was hard, and with her eyes narrowed like that he could imagine her old, ugly. She tossed her hair again.

'Your hair looks like orange marmalade,' he said. 'Maybe you were going for a tiger look? It would be nice tied back, I think.'

'Are you drunk, Inspector?'

'Commissioner. Semi-retired. To whom am I speaking?'

'My name is Nadia Antonescu.'

17

THE MAN who had met Nadia and Alina where the dinghy pilot let them off made it clear by the repetition of the word *polizia* and a mime show in which he fastened his wrists with invisible handcuffs that unless they wanted to be picked up by the police, they were to follow him. Did they have passports? Did they want the police? Prison? None of these things? Well, he crooked a finger, they had better follow him.

Nadia made a beckoning motion across the bar table at Blume. 'He went like that with his finger, and we followed. Like sheep.'

'Because you had no passports?'

'Because we had nowhere else to go, we were frightened, hungry, and tired.'

'Do you have a passport now?' he asked.

'Yes. Would you arrest me if I didn't?'

'Of course not.'

'Are you going to keep interrupting?'

'No.'

She told him how they had followed the man on foot through dirty streets full of vendors and hard faces, getting buzzed by boys on *motorini* until they reached a pizzeria. The man sent them into the empty kitchen and indicated that they should wait there. He made no attempt to explain for what or whom. The money was gone and with it the last of their bargaining power. They were tired, and neither could speak or understand Italian. Waiting was the only option.

After half an hour or so, without anyone disturbing them, Nadia began to search through the kitchen for food. She found plastic boxes full of shredded mozzarella in a fridge, and some crusts of bread. Alina shook her head in disgust.

'It's all there is,' said Nadia. 'There are tins of tomatoes, too, but we can't eat them.'

She ate the mozzarella, which was cold, wet, and rubbery, and gnawed at the hard bread. As long as they were not sent back to Istanbul. They might be deported to Romania, but would that be so bad? Besides, wasn't Romania in the EU now, which meant – she was not sure what it meant for someone without a passport. The important thing was not to be sent back to Turkey. She wondered if an international arrest warrant had been issued for Alina. Would they even report the death to the police? She knew the Russians despised the Turkish police. Either way, getting caught by the Russian mafia or Turkish police was not something she wanted to happen. And she had cast her lot in with Alina when they ran together.

Alina came and sat down beside her again on the dirty kitchen floor. 'If we get caught, Nadia, I'll tell them you had nothing to do with it.'

'Hey.' Nadia hugged her. 'We won't get caught.'

'At least we made it to Italy,' said Alina. She looked around the deserted kitchen with its cold ovens. 'Even if it's not a hair salon in Milan.'

'We might make it yet,' said Nadia.

'Sure. And then maybe we'll go to the Harry Potter University of London.'

Peeking out from behind the door, they could see the man who had brought them here seated in the empty pizzeria playing with his phone. Once he looked up and caught Nadia looking and shouted at her. Italian was a lot like Romanian, but his meaning would have been clear in any language. She retreated into the kitchen again.

Over an hour had passed before they heard voices. Two men had joined the first at the table. They were smoking and chatting, spinning cigarette packets and car keys on the table. Nadia had found an angle from which she could spy without being seen. Occasionally she fancied she could understand some of what they were saying. Twice the man pointed in the direction of the kitchen, but no one came to fetch them.

Another half hour passed and the group was joined by a fourth man. Nadia could see from the way the first three reacted, tensing up and quieting down, that this fourth man was not part of the group. The atmosphere had tightened, as soon as he walked in, even though the first three continued ostentatiously to shout, laugh, smoke, shove each other playfully.

The new arrival, an unprepossessing short man, had brought a sports bag with him. From the tight fit of his shirt and trousers, he looked like the sort who might exercise fanatically to try and compensate for his unimpressive body. He dropped the bag on the table, and the man who had brought them here, the man she was now thinking of as the owner of the pizzeria, unzipped it. He pulled out a wad of banknotes, said something that made everyone laugh, and then pulled out another and another and another. The fourth man, who did not look nervous but seemed to be sweating quite a lot, retrieved his now empty bag. The owner handed out bundles to his companions, and they started counting.

It was at this moment that Alina burst out of the kitchen brandishing a curved grey pizza knife with a dull top and edges too broad to be very dangerous. But what it probably lacked in sharpness, it made up for in size. Nadia stood frozen at the doorway in horror as her friend rushed up to the table, screaming that she would cut her own throat rather than be sent back to Istanbul. One of the three men stood up and pulled a gun, but Alina did not notice. She was now holding the flat top of the blade at her own throat, tears streaming down her face, shouting that she could easily take her own life right then, and that they were to let her friend Nadia go.

All in Romanian.

The men all looked at her, and then each other, and suddenly the pizzeria owner burst out laughing, and said something that, though Nadia could not understand, must have been obscene, because she recognized the style of guffaw it drew from his underlings. The fourth man, the one who had brought the money, smiled but did not laugh. The owner signalled at the one who had drawn the gun, but Alina spun round suddenly and waved the knife at him. Almost casually, he flipped the gun backwards and pistol-whipped her to the ground, and Nadia rushed out to save her, cursing the man in Turkish, Russian, English, and Romanian.

There was a lot of blood streaming from Alina's forehead and a deep gash across the bridge of her beautiful nose, still lightly freckled like the top of her cheeks. Nadia sat down on the floor and cradled her friend's head, stroking her red hair and getting blood all over herself. She felt Alina, who had closed her eyes against the blood, beginning to relax in her arms. The blow had stunned her. Nadia bent her head down as she whispered to Alina not to sleep. Alina murmured something, and relaxed still more.

The men began talking again, with a little more animation, and

Nadia knew it was about them. But then the conversation calmed down again and she was no longer sure. No one ordered her to leave, and no one gave her a rag with which to wipe the blood from Alina's face, now quite serene even as a deep bruise appeared on her forehead. Nadia almost envied her friend the peace.

She might have been sitting there under the table at the feet of the men for 20 minutes or two hours. All she knew was that at one point their meeting was over and they stood up to leave. She simply bent her head down and buried her face in Alina's hair.

Someone tapped her on the shoulder. Quite gently. She looked up to see the small man holding out a white towel. She took it and began to wipe Alina's face, but the blood had dried. The man took back the towel, went into the kitchen, dampened it, and came back. He watched her as she cleaned up Alina's face. Then they got her sitting up on a chair. They were the only three people left behind. The man lifted Alina's eyelid with his thumb with an expert gesture, such as a doctor might make. Then he took out a pale green handkerchief and wiped his brow.

Half an hour later, Nadia was sitting in the back seat of a Range Rover, Alina's head in her lap while their sweaty saviour, if that's what he was, drove at excessive speed down the road leading out of Bari. About every 100 metres stood prostitutes, usually in pairs. She expected him to stop at any moment and tell her to stand at the side of the road like all the others, but he kept driving. As he drove, she felt her eyes beginning to close from tiredness. The man would not stop talking, even though she understood nothing he was saying. After a while, he shut up and put on the radio, and she fell asleep.

'The talkative man with the money in the sports bag was Niki?' asked Blume.

'The man who took us away with him, yes.'

139

'What was that money for?' asked Blume. 'Cocaine? Niki deals, doesn't he?'

Nadia shrugged. 'He has a nightclub that is frequented by rich kids and politicians. They expect things. I told you I saw him give those men money. I never said he took anything from them. Except us.'

'That's illegal, too.'

'If you ask were we trafficked, we will say no.'

'Why?'

'Because we were rescued, not trafficked, by Niki. I have no idea what the money was about. If you force me to testify, I might forget all about it.'

'Why risk telling me all this?'

'For Alina.'

'He rescued you, but you still work for him in his nightclub?'

'I can leave whenever I want.'

'And Alina, she could leave too, whenever?'

'Yes.'

'So maybe that's what she did,' said Blume. 'See, there is a bit missing from your story. Running at a group of armed criminals with a knife, even a blunt one, is an act of desperation. She held it to her own throat, too, and threatened to kill herself. It sounds to me like she was *very* keen not to go back to Turkey, am I right?'

Nadia called over the bar boy and ordered a glass of white wine for herself and looked inquisitively at Blume.

'I'll have another beer,' he said. 'What happened in Turkey?'

Nadia said nothing.

'Is it the sort of thing that if you told me, I, as a public official, might be forced to report it?'

Nadia closed her eyes, and raised her face towards the sun.

'What I am thinking,' Blume spoke to her upturned profile, 'is that whatever happened in Turkey might have finally caught up with her here. Maybe Alina had to run again. Maybe she is destined to spend her life running.'

'It's an intelligent theory,' said Nadia. 'But I don't think that's it.'

'Well, I can't tell unless I know what happened in Turkey.'

'And I would prefer not to say.'

'Which is why I can do nothing to help.'

'If it had anything to do with Turkey, I would have heard about it.'

'Were you involved in whatever it was?' asked Blume.

'No, but they – the people in Turkey – don't know that.'

'Has it ever occurred to you that Niki might have sold you out? Or just Alina?'

The bar boy came over with their drinks, except instead of a glass of wine, he carried a whole bottle and two glasses, as well as the beer ordered by Blume, on a tray. With a flourish, he placed a steel bowl of salted nuts on the table between them. 'It's all been taken care of. The beers, too. The man said to give you a full bottle.'

'Who was this?'

'The ones in the tracksuits,' said the boy.

Blume looked up just in time to catch the man who had followed him, the older one, dressed in cheap grey slacks and a shiny fake leather jacket, openly taking pictures of them from the corner. It was as if he had been waiting for Blume to look up.

Blume made to get up and go over to him, knocking some of his beer over the table. Nadia tugged at his sleeve. 'Sit down. You can't arrest him for photographs, and if you're interested in finding out who he is, that's Hristjian, he works for Niki. Niki always makes sure he has photographs of everyone. It's standard practice for him.'

As she spoke, the group got up and left, the older one directing a wink at Nadia and Blume as he passed their table.

'They paid for my drinks to compromise me; now they're taking a photo of me with you, presumably for the same reason.'

'Yes, if you had a wife, maybe. The bar boy will remember they paid – but it is not much. I am not part of some plot to discredit you. I am here for Alina. Have you made an enemy of Niki?'

'He sent those men and you. I mean, you're his whore, right? How did you even know I was here?'

'It is not a large town. Yes, Niki sent them to watch you, but not me. I found out from them you were here. Niki doesn't know I am talking to you. I have been talking about him to a policeman, a drunk and stupid policeman maybe.'

'I am not drunk. The way you tell the story, Niki sounds like a swell guy. But the way I hear it, he picked you two up on the cheap. Bargain basement whores. Or am I being too hard? You're a *dancer*. That's what you are. Alina, too. Does she dance?'

Nadia sipped her wine and watched him, then nodded as if she had come to a decision. 'I know your type, Blume. People like you prefer getting praised to fucking. It's something you learn quickly as a whore.'

She flicked her wrist, as if tossing the word back across the table at him. 'The fucking itself? About a quarter of the time. The rest is spent telling men how great they are. Even when you men are fucking you need to be reassured, are always saying things like "you like this babe, you want this, you want my cock there, don't you, baby?" Of course I don't. Who would? But you have to tell them it is the best thing ever, because if you say no, they go crazy with rage. I said no once or twice at the beginning, then learned to stop. Even the ones who just roll, slobber, and grunt all over you without a word, will usually ask afterwards if you liked it. The answer, by the way, is always yes. Oh, you loved it. Maybe it's true that men don't like to talk so much, but they sure as hell want you to talk. They want you to ask about their nice suit, their muscles, the size of their cock, their patience, their wealth, their importance, their job, their looks. They have to hear this from you, so you have to talk to them. And that takes up three-quarters of the time, and it's worse than the fucking, because it makes your head tired, no? And you are saying all these things you don't believe, and in Istanbul I had to say them in different languages. It gets into your soul, and you think you are a liar in your soul, because you are.'

She grabbed the bottle and refilled her glass.

'I have had all sorts of requests,' she continued. 'Some you would not believe. But all men want you to suck their cock. You know why that is?'

'Well, it's a nice feeling . . .' Blume felt his voice go small. 'What I mean is . . .'

'I'll tell you why. It's because it's the mouth. They want to control your mouth. That's the most important thing for a man. Alina has a beautiful mouth. In the end, that is not good. Not for what we do. What we did.'

Blume felt a trickle of sweat run down his neck, and the itching was starting up again. He dropped a few pills into his mouth, and drank his beer, which now tasted like floor cleaner, waiting for a break in the conversation into which he might slip some sort of apology. But Nadia was in full flow and no opportunity presented itself.

When she seemed to have finished, he cleared his throat experimentally. 'So you don't do that now? Maybe you can tell me about the arrangement you have with Niki?'

'It is simple. We dance in the club. We attract customers. Sometimes we may go with a man, but only if we like him. It is far better now than ever before. Or I thought it was.'

'Do they pay you?' He intended it as a genuine question, not as an accusation.

Nadia looked at him and burst out laughing. 'What do you think?'

He was still feeling ashamed of how he had treated her a moment ago, and chose his words carefully. 'I think they might pay you. What I meant to ask is if Niki taxes you.'

'Niki gets nothing, also because a lot of the men prefer to pay with presents rather than cash. We pay Niki for the accommodation, but he lets us keep our money and he pays us weekly wages. I like Niki. Unless he killed Alina, which I think he could have. In that case, I hate him.'

'You think he could have killed Alina?' said Blume. 'Yet you say you like him. What is there to like?'

'You should have met the others.' She paused and gave him an appraising look. 'You think you're different from those men I was talking about, don't you?'

'Yes.'

'Hmm.' She tilted her head and seemed to weigh up his body with her eyes, and he felt himself pushing out his chest a little and raising his chin. 'You know who you remind me of?'

Blume had always fancied himself as having a certain resemblance to Harrison Ford, and wondered if she had spotted it. 'No. Who?'

'Niki.'

'Niki who?'

'Niki, Niki. Niki Solito. Who else are we talking about?'

'That's just stupid. I could fit three Nikis into each of my pockets. Not to mention the tan and the plastic surgery.'

Nadia laughed. He decided he didn't like her laugh much. It was throaty, full-bodied, altogether too knowing, and masculine. He found it vulgar.

'I don't mean physically. I mean:' she tapped her head, 'in here.'

'No, wrong again.'

'I know men. Were you listening to what I just said? Good, well, some men need more praise than others, and some, who are quite rare, need praise all the time. It's like a hunger. They can even forget about sex, or, how do you say, they make a sacrifice. All they want is praise. These men make you very tired but they can do some good things. And Niki is such a man.'

'And what about this supposed similarity with me?'

'That's the similarity.'

'I want *you* to praise *me*?' Blume affected a tone of haughty amusement, just to remind her who was the whore here. He could feel the nasty tone of a moment ago creeping back into his voice.

'About how kind and gentle and caring you are, yes. But you also want to hear how big and brave and strong and generous you are. Tough but gentle, no? Powerful or with some power, but kind and just. This is you?'

Blume reached out for the wine.

'You are also lonely, yes? A lonely man. Most clients need to hear that, too. *They* are lonely. Not the girl with no family and no future lying on the bed in a foreign country being fucked by ugly tourists and beaten by psychopathic Russian pimps. No, the girl needs to hear how lonely these men are. They sit there and look for pity from her, and give her none back. Are you lonely?'

'I am fine.'

'Yes, you are. Poor . . . what is your name? Your Christian name?'

'Alec – but . . .'

'Poor, lonely, Alec.'

'That will do. Shut up now.'

To his surprise, she did.

He drank the wine, refilled his glass.

'Sorry,' she said. 'I am upsetting you, even though I am the one who came looking for your help.'

Blume viciously scratched his chest with his fingernails. 'I am not upset. I need to piss. Will you wait?'

'Of course.'

When he came back, she was finishing another glass of wine. They had made short work of the bottle. Her lips glowed attractively.

'I owe you more respect than I gave you earlier,' said Blume.

'Thank you,' she said.

'You're welcome.'

They allowed a few minutes to pass in silence.

'I told you about men and praise?'

'Yes,' said Blume. 'No need to go through all that again. I am sorry – I have been drinking on an empty stomach.'

'No problem. What I said is true, but some men deserve the praise. They still want to hear it, like all men, but a few deserve it. Praise for them is OK. Please, Alec? I express myself badly in many languages.'

'You do just fine.' A warm, forgiving glow had settled over him.

'Niki likes praise. He wants to be thought of as a good and generous man. That is why he rescued us. He bought our freedom. We praise Niki and he deserves it, too, for that.'

'Niki? You're talking about Niki again? As someone who merits admiration?'

'I think Alina really began to love him. And then he began to love her. So when Alina disappeared, he was very unhappy. Sometimes I think he wants her back, and sometimes I think he killed her. But Alina did not just walk away, not without me.'

'Niki was fucking Alina?'

'He was also buying her presents.' Nadia opened her purse and took out a gold chain, a string of pearls, and a golden bangle. 'Look.'

'Those are hers?'

'From Niki. She showed them to me.'

Blume looked at the items with interest. 'Alina would have taken her jewellery with her if she was running away.'

'Niki did not ask me if I had them. You know what I think? I think he cared so much for Alina that he is not even interested.' She dropped them back in her bag and shut it with a snap. 'If he asks, I will give them to him, of course.'

Blume was thinking along other lines. 'Maybe Niki does not want to ask for them, because to do so would prove that he knows Alina did not have them with her. And the only way he could know that is if he was there when she disappeared.'

Nadia's eyes dimmed as the truth of this reasoning dawned.

'In other words,' said Blume, 'if she had not run away because of whatever happened in Turkey, I would say Niki is behind your friend's disappearance. Do you need help, Nadia? I can get you away from here if you want. Before I go after Niki. Right this moment.'

'You? You don't even have a car.'

'I can call in help – how do you know about my car?'

'I heard Niki. He was laughing on the phone to that mechanic. It was about you and your car. But I don't need to run away. I need to know what happened to my best friend.'

'I am not on duty. I don't even have a weapon. You need to report this.'

'But you are a specialist, no? You are very good at your job.'

'Praising me, are you? We men just lap it up.'

Nadia shook her head, impatiently dismissing his attempt to be facetious. 'They are worried about something. The old man,

Domenico, he came round to Niki's place last night, and they talked and afterwards Niki was tense and shouting at everyone. I have never seen the old man there before. So it must be something new, and you're the only new thing here. Please say you'll help.'

18

INDISTINCT SOUNDS of people shouting floated up from somewhere below. Blume glanced enquiringly at Nadia only to catch
her looking at him with the same questioning look.

'That's the most noise I have heard at one time since I came here,'
he told her.

They abandoned their table and went around the corner to see.
A group of around twenty people were standing at the next corner
down, many of them shouting what seemed to be instructions.

'A religious pageant?' wondered Blume, though as he said it he
saw the movement and shape of the crowd was too haphazard for
a procession.

'They are all men,' observed Nadia. 'So it won't be anything
important.'

Whatever the focus of attention was, it was out of sight behind a
sharp corner at the end of the road. Some old men were to be seen
standing at the corner waving their arms, and throwing their hands
to heaven. The bar boy came out and looked wistfully at the fun,
then returned inside to the till.

Without needing to ask each other, he and Nadia walked down to
join the group. Everyone was enjoying himself immensely, none so

much as those pretending to be thoroughly disgusted by the scene, which was of a yellow tow-truck that had become trapped on a hairpin curve on the narrow street.

The driver had manoeuvred his vehicle into a perfect snooker, with the front of the cab touching a wall on one house, the back lodged firmly into the wall of another. To complete the totality of the impasse, the front right wheel had slipped into a rainwater channel running down the side of the road. The cab was empty and the driver, visible in his reflective jacket, was in the middle of the crowd, throwing contemptuous open-palm gestures at the narrow street, at the pointless road sign that warned of a hairpin turn, at the unfair rut in which the wheel of his truck was now stuck. A puttering sound was heard as a man with no helmet on his bald head came travelling downhill on his scooter. He stopped, and by means of extensive use of his squawking horn, let it be universally known that the obstacle was so complete that not even a scooter could pass. From behind the truck came a car whose driver confirmed in oaths that the situation from below was just as bad. A car behind that joined in, and now women appeared at windows to shout *Basta! E mamma mia!* and *Ch'è questo baccano?*

Blume stepped back against the wall as Alfredo the mechanic and his oil-flecked son came down the road. Alfredo glanced at Blume and Nadia standing in the shadows, and gave a friendly nod. When he arrived on the scene, Alfredo, rolling up his wrinkles into the impressive frown of a true expert, examined the front of the truck, and peered for a while at the fender, then, hands on hips, looked at the back of the truck. He cracked his knuckles and kicked the tyres. The *vigili* arrived, Fabio and the unnamed woman with the unfriendly glasses, and parked their car with the flashing light behind the scooter, whose driver had lifted into its kickstand without turning off the engine. Nadia nudged Blume conspiratorially.

'Is this something to do with you?' she asked him.

'What makes you think that?'

'The way you are hanging back, trying to stand in the shadow.'

Blume moved closer and stood in the sunlight.

For a minute or two, the *vigili* created a channel through the crowd, waving their arms and giving instructions, but they, too, saw the impossibility of the situation, and were swallowed up in the general hubbub. They reappeared soon after, busy examining the documents of the driver of the tow-truck. They handed back the papers. Everything, apart from the entire situation, seemed to be in order. The *vigilessa*, showing initiative and taking advantage of her thinness, climbed into the tow-truck cab, then slipped out the narrow gap between the other door and wall, and disappeared. Blume assumed she had gone to calm the motorists below, who, to judge from the noise, had gathered in strength and number. Children, which he had thought were completely lacking from the town, now appeared.

Fabio the *vigile* was now examining a new piece of paper that seemed to contain some quite remarkable information. He handed it back to the driver, then asked for it back, and passed it to Alfredo, who read it and handed it into the crowd for general inspection. Heads began turning in Blume's direction. Straightening his uniform and adopting a stern manner, Fabio, accompanied by the driver and several witnesses, approached him.

Fabio indicated the driver, a deeply tanned man with a crew cut who was staring very hard at Blume, and said, 'This gentleman alleges . . .'

He got no further, for the truck driver took great exception to the word 'alleges', and eventually had to be escorted back into the crowd before he committed an outrage on a public official, or perhaps two, counting Blume. Nadia was openly enjoying herself at his expense now, but Blume felt glad to have her beside him anyhow. Fabio affected not to understand or believe that Blume had really ordered an outside tow-truck to storm his town and make away with a car that was already safe in the shop of his friend Alfredo, an excellent and honest mechanic. Fabio was thin-lipped and regretful of the generous impulse that had prevented him from impounding Blume's car. As the sheer spitefulness of Blume's gambit dawned on him, his manner became increasingly frosty. The informal 'tu' became 'Lei' and he called up Alfredo to witness his chastisement of the arrogant Roman policeman.

'Everyone from around here knows that a vehicle that size cannot make it to the top of the town,' said Fabio. 'Isn't that right, Alfie?'

Alfredo, who seemed not the least put out, nodded.

'Not everyone, apparently,' said Blume nodding at the driver, who now sat in his cab, arms folded, refusing to react to the exhortations of the crowd to make another attempt.

'That's because,' hissed Fabio, 'he is not from around here. You called in people who don't know ANYTHING about Monterozzo.' He glared at Nadia to make sure she knew she belonged to the group of foreign outcasts.

Alfredo, whom, Blume was coming to realize, was a thoroughly decent chap, as slow to take offence as he was to fix a car, touched Fabio's elbow. 'It's OK. I'll get it off the corner.'

Fabio shook his head despairingly. 'This is one of the worst I've seen.'

'It's all right.' Alfredo spoke comfortingly, 'We need to take the air out of the tyres on the left side. Get a wooden ramp, then we use some chains and my car. Same way,' he looked at Blume with the mildest of reproach, 'as we tow anything in this town.'

'I don't think we are much help here,' said Blume, still keen to be associated with Nadia.

'You certainly are not.'

'So we may as well go.' He forgot to inflect his voice, so that what he had intended as a request for permission came out as a statement of defiance. He was about to rectify with an 'if that's all right with you,' but Fabio was too quick for him and had already taken grave offence.

'You can't just walk away! You'll have to settle with the driver and his company for a start.' Fabio reached for his pocketbook. 'You may well be liable for any damage done to those buildings. And I would ask you, Signorina, to stop smirking like that.'

Nadia covered her mouth, but her smile was wider than her hand.

The crowd was drifting away now, because only so much fun can be had looking at a stuck truck, and the noisy drivers blocked behind had either found alternative routes or been cowed into silence by the *vigilessa* with the black glasses.

'As I, too, am a public official and a good citizen,' said Blume, 'I'll report to you in the morning, and we can settle all this. If I have to pay something, then I will.'

Fabio seemed mollified, then suspicious. 'Where are you staying?' His eyes wandered over to Nadia, and he gave Blume an insinuating, accusing look. 'I didn't know you were staying.'

'I have no choice. The road is blocked and my car is in his shop.'

Alfredo interrupted the blackening of another cigarette to confirm. 'Next Tuesday at the latest,' he assured Blume. 'But no sooner,' he warned Fabio. He lit his limp cigarette and wandered off in the direction of the tow-truck.

'There is a place at the very top of the town, an old woman, very thin, black dress, does bird imitations?'

Fabio rubbed his chin. 'You're talking about the princess. I didn't know about the bird imitations.'

'Princess?' asked Blume, but Fabio ignored him. He had other objections to make. 'She doesn't have any authorization, so if anything happens to you there, you won't have insurance.'

'If anything happens?' Blume was only half listening to the *vigile*. Nadia had stepped back a few metres and had cupped her hand to her ear, taking a phone call she wanted to hide from him.

'Like a beam falling on your head or something. Not because Flavia would harm anyone. She's mad but harmless.' Fabio shook his head sadly, then stamped his foot in irritation at the way his natural friendliness kept breaking out and betraying him. 'I could stop you from going there, you know,' he said importantly. 'But I am prepared to turn a blind eye in view of the fact that I think you should stay here to answer for the damages you have caused, and to pay Alfredo.'

'Good,' said Blume. 'If you need me, that's where I'll be. If the driver down there has anything to say, he has my phone number, or someone in his office does. Alfredo has my car and you have my address. Can I go now?'

Fabio looked for faults in the logic and found none. He wanted to say something to or about Nadia, but his attention was being drawn down the road again to where the *vigilessa* had reappeared, and raised voices suggested that the driver did not like Alfredo's plan for his tyres.

19

'I SEE no sign of the heavies,' said Blume. 'Mission accomplished, I suppose.'

'I had nothing to do with that,' said Nadia. 'They must have followed me.'

'And got a few photos of us together.'

'So what? Am I so compromising for your honour, Commissioner?'

'I can't work out what's the deal between you and Niki.'

'Neither can I,' she said.

'What do you mean?'

'Nothing,' she turned away from him. Something in the phone call she had taken a few minutes earlier had changed her attitude, and as she became cooler towards him again, he found himself thinking more lucidly, though he could feel the drinks he had had working against clarity.

Both Niki and Nadia had now asked him for help, and he sensed a trap. He wanted to believe Nadia, wanted to disbelieve Niki, but they were both saying much the same thing: Alina had gone. And thanks to Nadia's story of her arrival, bowdlerized though it may have been, he felt some attachment to Alina. She was more than just a name.

'Let me walk you to your car,' he said. 'You have a car, right?'

'Down there, yes. We have to squeeze past your truck to get to it.'

Blume did not want to walk the gauntlet of the remaining spectators gathered around the truck, which Alfredo had, by some miracle of persistence and geometry, managed to manoeuvre into a position from which escape was, if not imminent, at least conceivable. 'Is there another way?'

'We could walk up the street a bit, then down a different one, and around. It's roundabout, but not too far,' said Nadia, who had already set out with long strides even as she was describing the route.

Blume discovered that his companion was even better than he at blanking people out. She walked through several disapproving stares from the few people they met, moving at an unflagging pace through the streets to the bottom of the town where sensible people parked their cars. He turned round several times to stare back at the people watching them go, but Nadia looked straight ahead and never glanced back. Lot's wife would have been safe with her.

Niki had sent a group of thugs to watch him, and they had been as unsubtle as possible. Was that to distract him from the more subtle spy, Nadia, if that's what she was? Were she and Niki working some angle on him, trying to cover their tracks?

He didn't see it. If she was trying to cover for Niki or herself for something they had done to Alina, would she have spent all that time building up his sympathy for the missing girl? But she had also managed to infiltrate the idea into his mind that Alina was running from people. Maybe it was to make him think they had caught up with her. Or that Alina herself was the sort who got into trouble. Maybe the next chapter in the story would depict Alina as a violent person, deserving of her fate. He had to be wary of taking whatever Nadia said at face value.

'I need to see the nightclub. I also need to see where Alina lived,' Blume told her.

She gave him a grateful smile. It looked absolutely genuine. If Nadia was a liar, she was a good one. Or was he an easy target? He realized he had just committed himself to helping her find her missing friend.

'The club's next to our apartments. She lived in the one next door to mine. I'll take you there.' She looked at her watch, an elegant gold timepiece, with a tiny dial that he would have needed a magnifying glass to read. 'It's half past six now. Niki usually spends the evenings with his fiancée and doesn't get to the club until around 11.'

'It's probably better I don't meet Niki anyhow,' he said. 'Was that him on the phone earlier?'

'No.'

The car turned out to be a bulky and ugly SUV. 'It's a bit of a drive,' said Nadia.

'How far?'

'Half an hour, 40 minutes, I never counted the kilometres.'

'I am taking it that this is Niki's car. One of several.'

'Yes,' said Nadia. 'Get in.'

'Just one thing,' said Blume. 'May I see your driver's licence?'

'What?'

'You heard. Because I was wondering when you might have got it. In Romania? Hardly in Istanbul. So you must have got it here, and yet you arrived without a passport or an identity card. But now you have a licence to drive this beast around.'

'It's not so hard. There are no gears. I have been driving for almost 1 year.'

'Licence?'

157

Her lips became tighter and more defiant, but her face reddened. 'Not yet.'

'In that case,' said Blume, 'with the powers vested in me by the state, I am sequestering this vehicle. Move over. I'll drive you home.'

'Niki will kill me.'

'I thought Niki was a sweetheart.'

'Anyone would kill you if you lost their car. People get attached to their cars.'

'Tell him you got stopped by the police. Go on, move over.'

She did, crossing her arms across her chest and scowling at him.

'If you're worried, I'll drive you somewhere else. All the way to Rome if you want, and save you from your saviour.'

'Just take me home.' She drew the seatbelt across her body and stared out the window, not looking at him.

'I am glad to see you wear a seatbelt, Nadia.'

'That's because I am in a car about to be driven by a drunk,' she said.

'Show me your ID card.'

'Just because I said you're a drunk.'

He snapped his fingers and she opened her bag and from an inside pocket pulled out a brown ID card. It looked legitimate, though nothing was easier to forge.

'And your passport?'

'I don't carry that around.'

'That's not what I meant. Olga and then the Russians took it from you. Or so you said. Do you have one now or not?'

'Niki knows lawyers and people. I filled in a form and got a new one sent.'

'Did Alina get a new passport, too?'

'Yes.'

'And did it disappear when she did?'

'No. She left it behind. That's another reason I don't think she went of her own accord.'

'You didn't think to mention this to me?'

'I didn't want . . . You're still a public official. I didn't want to talk too much about passports and that sort of thing.'

'You think your passport is forged then?'

Nadia shrugged. 'It might be.'

'Where did Alina leave hers?'

'In her apartment. In the top drawer of her bedside table.'

'So you looked? You have a key to her place?'

'Yes. I have a key and yes, I looked through her apartment. I told you, I found her jewels.'

He turned on the engine and the car was filled with a doleful music.

'You like Fabrizio De Andre?' He looked at her in astonishment.

'No. Niki listens to that CD. It comes on by itself like that when you turn on the ignition.'

'That's the 1990 concert. A great album,' said Blume. Niki had unexpectedly risen in his estimation.

'There,' said Nadia, pressing a button. 'I prefer Radio DJ. Oh! I *love* this! Do you?'

But Blume had never heard of Rihanna.

★

A neon sign, still off, announced to the passing world that the pink-painted, flat-roofed warehouse at the side of the road was 'Nikis Niteclub'. The curving 'NN' initials were repeated in pink above the door. A piece of Astroturf grass had been laid over the broken concrete forecourt and a filthy red carpet led up to the door. Blume had not expected luxury, but thought a club frequented by professionals and local politicians might be a bit fancier than this excrescence sitting practically on the hard shoulder of the highway.

'It's bigger than it looks,' said Nadia, as he stopped the car and looked out. Was there a hint of defensiveness in her tone? 'There's parking out the back and a beer garden, and an artificial pond with lights in it and big goldfish, and a fountain with lights that make the water come out in different colours.'

She was definitely bigging it up for his sake. Maybe she had suddenly seen it through his eyes for the squalid little drug-dealing hole it was. A trap for young people, too. It drew them in like moths, filled them with drugs, and sent them out into the night to kill and be killed in their cars.

'My place is down there.' She seemed anxious for him to move on.

Her box-shaped low-ceilinged apartment block dated from the 1950s, a period during which many Italian architects decided that their concrete creations would look better for being painted pea-green. The road passed so close to the front door that you could hitch a lift from the foyer.

She unlocked the front door of the building and led him up a narrow flight of steps. The red plastic on the banister had mostly broken off. A soapy smell came from below. 'The lift's out of order, but it's only the first floor.'

She opened the door. The furnishings were not many but they had a lugubrious effect. A dining table, shiny and dark, looking like it was made from hard plastic and wood, took up most of the immediate space. An L-shaped sofa, tan brown, hemmed in an oversized dresser in the centre of which was a large TV. Red tassels hung from the gold-coloured keys slotted into the drawers of the dresser. Cheap china miniatures filled the spaces where books should have been.

Fresh yellow and red flowers in a green vase on a white doily in the centre of the dustless table told him she was proud of her home.

'This is a . . . it's a lovely apartment.'

'Isn't it!' All her world-weariness and her distress and hardness had gone for a fleeting second. She was immensely proud of what she had done, of where she had made it to.

'You have done it up beautifully,' he specified, remembering that the apartment was rented out by Niki.

'Thank you!' she beamed at him. 'I'll get the key to Alina's apartment next door.'

She vanished for a moment into her bedroom, and Blume half followed her. She kept her room neat, pink and full of trinkets. In the middle of the bed, on which the duvet had been smoothed down and the pillows plumped up, sat a pair of soft toys. A furry blue gorilla he might have seen in some ad once, and a panda bear.

She got what she needed and led the way out into the hallway, unlocked the next door down.

'How many people live here?' asked Blume.

'About six apartments are used. There are three on each floor. The one upstairs belongs to the Montenegrins.'

'The Montenegrins?'

'The heavies who followed me to the bar.'

'Except they were there before you,' said Blume.

'I . . . were they? I don't remember.' She flashed him a smile. 'See? You're observant.'

'So which was it?'

'I was looking for you. They found you first at that bar and called me.'

'They called you?'

'Yes, I know them. What difference does it make?'

'It makes all the difference,' he replied. 'You were working with them. It means Niki is behind all this.'

'OK! Let's say he is. Let's say he knows I wanted to talk to you. But Alina really is missing.'

'Be straight with me.'

'I am. I asked Niki about you. He said you have decided he's your enemy, so any requests were better coming from me.'

'He's a criminal, so he is my enemy.'

'Are all criminals your enemy?'

'Yes.' If Caterina were here she would laugh at his pomposity or, if in one of her less predictable moods, grow angry at his fanaticism.

'If all criminals are really your enemy, then all crime victims must be your responsibility, Commissioner. Including Alina,' said Nadia.

Blume opened his mouth to object to the syllogism, but her reasoning was unassailable.

She opened the door and they walked into an apartment so similar, it was like leaving one motel room for another. She led him into the bedroom, which consisted of a large bed and a small bedside table with a cheap lamp perched on top. The blinds on the window were drawn down, and she switched on the light. To the right was a large white wardrobe with full-length mirrors on the sliding doors but not enough floor space between it and the bed. She pulled open the top drawer of the bedside table, and stood absolutely still, as the colour drained from her face.

'The passport's gone. It was right there. I saw it.'

'And it's not there now?' said Blume. 'Are you absolutely sure you saw it in that drawer?'

'Absolutely.'

'And who has the keys to this apartment besides you?'

'Niki, obviously. He owns them.'

'What about the men upstairs?'

'The Montenegrins,' she shuddered. 'I hope not.'

'All right, Nadia,' he said, 'you're pretty good at logical thinking, aren't you?'

'If you say so.'

'Who is most likely to have taken the passport from the drawer if not the person with keys to this apartment? Niki, in other words. Does that make sense?'

Nadia bit her lip, and Blume, implacable, continued his reasoning. 'It is reasonable to assume that Niki has taken the passport you saw in that drawer. He may not have, but it is very possible he did. What would make him do that?'

'So it would look like Alina went away of her own accord.'

'Exactly. And why would he do that?'

'To hide the fact that she did not.'

'And how would he know she did not?'

Nadia made two fists and pushed them against her head as if trying to rub out the logical deduction.

'Come on, Nadia,' said Blume. 'Why would he hide her passport?'

'Because he knows she didn't . . .'

'We've moved beyond that part, Nadia. Why?'

'Because he killed her!' she shouted, pointing at Blume as if he were the killer in the room. 'That's what you want to hear me say, isn't it?'

'I don't want to make you say anything, Nadia,' said Blume, gentle now that he had won.

'You're right. I was wrong. She's dead.'

Although he was not inclined to exonerate Niki, it felt cruel to insist. She had just lost Alina; no point in emphasizing her lack of judgement in regard to the man she had thought of as a friend. The saviour who was a killer. In an attempt to be kind, he said, 'Maybe Niki did not kill her. But I'd say that at the very least he knows she is dead.' He paused to allow all his logic to sink into her mind.

She sat down on the bed. Tears ran freely down her cheeks, but her head was upright and looking forward, and she made no sound.

'Now, do you want to come with me, Nadia?' said Blume. 'Shall we get away from here?'

To his utter exasperation, she shook her head. 'No. I am going to stay here until I find out. And if they kill me, it won't matter.'

'Of course it will matter,' said Blume, beginning to lose patience.

'You could be wrong,' she told him.

'Yeah? And how might that work?' said Blume.

'You weren't there. You have no way of knowing. You see, Alina and Niki – they really meant it. I thought at first she was just trying to get ahead by fucking the boss and that he was exploiting her. We had a row about it. A big row. Before that, we both lived in my apartment. I think I was right – at first – but something changed. I don't know why he would have killed her after helping her so much. It doesn't make sense.'

'Maybe she learned things about Niki and his business life that he did not want known? Maybe it was some sort of erotic game gone wrong. Maybe she tried to blackmail him. He likes them young, does Niki.'

He had had too much of hypothesizing, he was overtired with thinking. 'What about Silvana's father?' he added, more for the sake of completeness of argument than because he believed it. 'That quiet gardener has quite a bit of history.'

Nadia continued to watch the wall, but the tears were subsiding.

'One more thing, Nadia,' said Blume, beginning to regret the ascendancy of his logic over her hopes, 'That was Niki who phoned you when I was talking to the *vigile*, wasn't it?'

'Yes, it was.'

'Thanks for telling the truth. Now tell me what he said.'

'He wanted to make sure you don't get involved in looking for Alina.'

'*Not* involved,' said Blume. 'Until now you – and he – have been saying the opposite.'

He led her gently back to her apartment, asked her again if she intended to stay. She moved in a trance and barely nodded in response to his questions. She began to shiver and he guided her to the sofa, stepped into the bedroom, whipped the duvet off the bed, and covered her with it.

'I think you should leave,' he told her.

'No. Not yet. Don't you leave either, please? Find out the truth. I'll act with Niki like nothing has happened.'

'Can you manage that?'

'Yes. I'm tough.'

'OK, then.' He knew it was wrong to leave her like this, but the hunt was on. Suddenly his being here made sense. Destiny had put him here. He had been dreading the empty hours in Monterozzo, now he feared he might not have long enough.

He took Nadia's phone number and gave her his. Solicitously, he bent down to pull the duvet over her shoulders, but she pushed it off. 'I'm not cold any more,' she said.

He straightened up and found himself looking at a shelf of photographs of Nadia and a young redhead with a slightly upturned nose, high cheekbones, fleshy lips, and a smile that seemed to be at once shy and knowing. Hello, Alina, he thought to himself. He scanned the shelf for a close-up, and found one next to some Orthodox icon of Mary. In this picture, he could make out the freckles on her cheeks and nose, which definitely had a slight bump along its ridge, presumably from the pistol-whipping but plausibly from any one of the many beatings this child had received at the hands of men throughout her brief life. Without saying anything, he took the photograph and left.

20

Blume parked the SUV back where they had taken it from, and continued on foot through the steep streets of the town, thankful to see no crowd and no blocked tow-truck when he reached the fateful corner. Indeed, he met no one at all outside, though it was only a little after nine.

He varied his route a little, entering twice into cul-de-sacs, but it was hard to get completely lost in a place so small when his destination was simply its highest point. He was breathless by the time he arrived. Like the rest of the town's inhabitants, the old woman had gone indoors, and her house, the size of which was hard to determine from outside owing to the narrowness of the street and the general absence of clear divisions in the stone-faced line of buildings, did not even look inhabited, but the warm scent of slow-frying garlic from somewhere inside it told him it was.

Seeing no intercom or bell, he knocked, softly at first, then harder when no one came. He placed his palm on the heavy wood door, pushed gently, and stepped in as the door swung open, his nose appreciating the delicious smell of cooking food before his eyes adjusted to the darkness.

'*Permesso?*'

He was in a small vestibule filled with the ancient relics of someone who had once led an active life. Cracked leather boots, musty umbrellas, sweaters and coats on hooks. He went through the next door, which led him into a far larger room with unadorned walls, once whitewashed, now greying. To his right was a fusty counter, possibly intended as a reception desk. It was so high that if the old woman had been behind it, she would have been quite invisible. 'Anyone here?' he asked of the desk, relieved when no one stepped out from behind it. To his left a staircase went up to a landing before turning back on itself, to the right a door, and from behind the door the smell of cooking. He called out again. Nothing, but he heard a clink of metal on metal, the sound of a saucepan being placed on the stove. He was ravenous.

How could he open the door without terrifying the elderly woman? He knocked on it.

'Come in.'

He pulled the door open and walked into an unexpectedly large kitchen, with a ceiling as high as three of his apartments stacked on top of each other. The walls were lined with enough copper pans to feed an army, all of them perfectly polished. The lighting was modern, and the work surfaces a mixture of old wood and modern steel. The large kitchen was redolent of unexpected wealth as well as food.

'What's cooking?' he asked hopefully.

'Your dinner. I expect you down in fifteen minutes. We don't usually eat too late in this house,' she said, without taking her eye from the frying pan and steaming pot. The stove was too high for her, and she was standing on a plastic step stool such as children use to reach the toilet. She had put on a white apron over her black dress and had perched glasses, which were hopelessly steamed up, on the end of her nose.

'We?'

'Yes, you and I.' She stood down, took off her glasses, and peered in his direction, as if checking to see if she was talking to the right person. 'Go back through that door, up the steps all the way to the last room. It's open. The sheets are fresh and the blanket is clean, but the bed is not made. You'll have to do that yourself. I don't make beds, and I dismissed the girl.'

'What girl?'

'The one who made the beds and cleaned. That was several years ago. I have been managing perfectly well on my own since then. Now you don't believe me that the linen is fresh, but I brought it up myself an hour ago and placed it on the bed. I hope you like the smell of lavender. The front door key is on top of the sheets. I may not always be in or awake when you come in.'

'You knew I was coming back?'

She showed her pearly teeth. 'Telepathy.'

'Oh. I see.'

'God, don't be so stupid, man. The young *vigile* came up here with your suitcase, which you left in some car, which he wanted to tell me all about for some reason. I had him take it up to your room. Telepathy, really, what do you take me for? I have no truck with superstition. Despite my age, I am not even a religious bigot – or a witch. I do believe in ghosts, mind. That's inevitable when you live in this house. I notice you did not ask the price, which is €45 per night, by the way.'

'They told me you are a princess.'

She mockingly knighted herself with the wooden spatula. 'Princess. Well, it's nice to be appreciated.' She softened the R, as they did up in Piedmont, as in France. It sounded forced to his ear. 'Even if I know they use it to insult me. What else would you expect in miserable Monterozzo?'

Montechwozzo. If not a princess, her accent certainly had aristocratic notes to it.

'Cruel peasant mentality,' she continued. 'If you put crabs in a bucket, none ever escapes because the others pull him down. That is what they are like here. The information I have received is that you are a policeman who has been thrown out of the force as a result of some terrible scandal, and are now wandering about the town, sticking your nose into everyone's business, hanging out with go-go dancers, and trying to seduce the little girl with that ridiculous name . . .'

'Silvana?'

'Exactly!'

'You hear a lot from up here.'

'News travels up, socially and geographically.'

The princess, if that's what she was, giggled like a little girl, and covered her mouth with her left hand, still in a flesh-toned glove, which must have been custom-made because she was missing her ring finger. She saw him notice and waggled her remaining fingers at him reprovingly. 'Hurry up. Just wash your hands and come straight down again. I will not dine on cold pasta for your sake.'

The top floor was six flights up, but Blume, looking forward to dinner and thinking of how he would manage his investigation of Niki, found his energy seemed to be increasing the more he climbed. He could feel his heart thumping away. It was noisy but seemed to be fluttering happily rather than hammering. His chest felt light, his head, too, but crystalline, as if his brain fluid had been replaced by carbonated water.

He was therefore disappointed when he finally reached the top floor to see the long corridor tilt slightly on its axis, like some sort of fairground attraction, and even more surprised to find his knees felt weak, and that the blood pounding in his ears was deafening and painful. A great sense of fatigue shoved away the energy of a few seconds ago. He bent down until the dizziness passed, and, since he often felt he was under some sort of numinous observation and did not want even an imaginary being to see him suddenly so weak, pretended to be interested in the granite and marble composite of the floor, which was dull and old, though he could see how it would shine with a bit of treatment. All the pinks and reds and speckles of green would sparkle.

He took a shot of the migraine nasal spray he kept in his jacket pocket, but even before the medicine had time to work, the pain passed and the elation returned. He walked down the corridor, his legs more cautious than his freedom-loving mind. He searched for a song he might sing, just to check if he was breathless. Something told him he was. He could not think of a song. The corridors tilted back again. It was like walking down a ship's galley in a storm, but without the seasickness.

Blume entered the small room, monastic in its sparseness. The bed, which took up about half the space, was heaped with multicoloured blankets. A religious icon on the whitewashed wall above the bed was the only decoration. A dresser with an oval mirror sat to the left of the window. A tiny bathroom was off to the right. The floor was white tiled and spotless. The clean sheets and blankets on the unmade bed seemed excessive for the time of year, but none of the heat from outside seemed to penetrate, and the rectangle of blue sky visible through the narrow window at the end of the room looked cold. He went over to the window and pressed his forehead against the glass, and was rewarded with a riot of descending rooftops with red and yellow tiles. The walls of the houses were orange in the setting sun, and seemed far warmer than top room in which he now stood.

From his suitcase he retrieved his phone charger and found a socket behind the bed. He washed his hands in the basin, splashed some water on his face, less to wash himself than to prepare for the call he now made.

'Caterina?'

'You! How's your flower-power course going?'

How the hell had she worked that out?

'Great. They make us turn off our phones. It's sort of a detox spiritual thing.'

'You must be the star pupil then, since you never turn it on.'

'You know how it is. Being on call all the time is so much part of the job, it's important to switch off when I'm on leave.'

'When are you coming back?'

'I took indefinite leave, so maybe a few months?'

'I meant when are you coming back to Rome?'

'Oh. I don't know: a day or two. Three? Do you want me to visit when I do?'

'You should know the answer to that.'

Caterina was forever saying things like that to him. Things that were self-evident to her were mysterious to him. Maybe, as she said, he should know, but he didn't; whereas to her it was so obvious as not to merit a response. He wondered whether the right answer was yes or no. Whatever it was, he was not going to walk into the trap of committing himself to either.

'I was just checking in.'

'After three weeks' silence.'

'Is it that long? I think I might have tried to call last week.'

'I think it might have shown up on my phone if you had.'

He peered out over the rooftops. Beyond the last of them the mountain fell away, and below that stretched the garden, part of which would now be completely dark in the shadow of the cliff.

'Alec. Are you OK there? You sound far away. You haven't left the country or something? You'd be capable of that.'

'I'm fine. How's Alessia?'

'There you go changing the subject,' said Caterina, but he heard her voice soften. She was like one of those teachers who knew when their students were trying to distract them from the lesson, but couldn't help themselves all the same. 'Little Miss is behaving very strangely this evening.'

'What's wrong with her?' said Blume.

'Nothing's wrong, she's actually sleeping. That's what's strange.'

'I hope I didn't wake her with my call.'

'Of course not. I am glad you called at last,' she said.

'I am glad I called, too. Actually, now that I think about it, I was wondering if you could do me a favour.'

She had a special way with her silent pauses, which seemed to involve some mysterious slowing down of time. Caterina could create a universe that had a life-cycle of two seconds yet the capacity to hold an infinity of recrimination. When she spoke again, her voice was flat. 'A favour.'

'I'd just like to check out something. Have you got a pen?'

'What do you want?'

Blume gave her Niki's name, address, approximate age. 'I think he's from Molfetta.' He thought for a moment before supplying her also with Domenico Greco's name.

'Are these friends you met among the flowers?'

'You could say that.'

'Friends with criminal records, I am guessing. And, tell me, are they there now with you?'

'No.'

'And I get these files on what grounds?'

'I was thinking about that. Go to Magistrate Alice Saraceno, she likes me.'

'Yes, she does, doesn't she?'

Blume did not rise to the bait. 'Ask her from me, please.'

'She likes you that much?'

'Saraceno used to work with a magistrate called Della Valle, whom she loathed. I remember her mentioning Della Valle was an investigating magistrate in this district. It's a long shot, but you could suggest I may have something that might embarrass him.'

'And this is your idea of relaxation therapy?'

'Please?'

'Alec, do you actually know what "extended leave" means? Do you know how dangerous is it to act on your own? And, do I need to say this, a suspended cop acting without the instruction of a magistrate is about the most effective way of rendering everything he touches inadmissible as evidence in court and getting himself into disciplinary trouble. More to the point, what the hell are you doing?'

'Just passing the time. I got a bit bored with the herbal bliss and stuff.'

'What is this about?'

'Well, if you find out some background, maybe you'll get a good idea and we'll have some common ground on which to start a conversation about these two. Now there is, in fact, another little favour.'

She greeted this, too, with silence.

'They found out I was a policeman, and I promised I'd look into something. Just for appearances, you understand.'

'I don't understand, no. Who are "they" and what is this other favour?'

Blume remembered he was supposed to have gone down to dinner ages ago, and tried to summarize the situation as quickly as he could, but it still took some time.

'So,' said Caterina slowly, when he had finished, 'there is a missing Romanian girl who is connected to this Niki, who you think is a criminal of some sort. And all this has to with Bach herbal remedies how?'

'Niki is a criminal. A minor one, maybe, but pimping is the sort of thing that brings you into contact with serious criminals.'

'You are absolutely sure he is a pimp?'

'I don't like him.'

'Oh, I see. You don't *like* him. That's different then. Maybe you feel he's not nice enough to . . . let me see . . .' She checked, or made a show of checking back in her notes, 'Silvana? The young woman who's teaching you about the birds and the bees or Nadia the dancer? And you want me to do what, exactly, about the disappearance of this Alina Paulescu?'

'You still have contacts in the Department for International Cooperation from back when you worked in Immigration Affairs, right?' He left the room and started making his way down the stairs.

'Call in SCIP for this? It's an interforce agency, Alec. Special favours get noticed. And unlike you, I have limits. Do you expect me to put out an Interpol yellow notice?'

'If you don't want to help me, forget it,' he said.

'I didn't say I wouldn't. Have you found someone, Alec? Part of me won't mind if the answer is yes, but please don't lie.'

'No, I am going to tell you everything when I get back, promise.'

'Are you in love?'

'I don't even know that what's supposed to mean.'

'No, I don't suppose you do. Are you with someone now? A woman?'

'Nothing remotely like that. Look, I really need to go down to dinner, now.'

'Oh god, yes. You mustn't miss dinner,' said Caterina.

★

He entered the kitchen where his hostess sat waiting for him. One plate of no longer steaming pasta sat on the table, and she wore a severe expression on her face.

'I thought it might be nice to have company for once, but I had my dinner alone again.'

'Sorry,' said Blume. 'People just keep phoning at the most inconvenient time.'

'Most inconsiderate of them. One should never phone after half past seven in the evening.'

'Quite,' said Blume. 'People just don't think of others nowadays.'

'Do you always talk in clichés, or is it for my benefit because I am old?'

Blume liked this direct little woman's use of sarcasm. 'Because you're old,' he said.

'I have never heard such insolence. By the way, it takes a lot of effort to cook these red caps. First one side, gills down till all the water is gone, then the other side with some garlic, and finally a splash of white wine. The linguine were perfect too.' She paused for effect. 'Fifteen minutes ago.'

'I'm sorry I was late. Really.'

'I'm sure you had a good reason. Now I get to watch you eat. I hope you're embarrassed at least.'

'I am. Delicious, by the way. And not too cold.' He peeled a strip of pasta and a mushroom off his shirt front and put it back on his plate.

'No one ever taught you table manners?'

'I've lived a lot on my own,' said Blume.

'So have I, but I can still manage not to slobber my food all over myself, even with only these four and a half fingers you have been staring at since we met.'

'I wasn't . . .'

'Yes, you were. And now you're blushing. Go on, eat up, I won't say anything even if you get it in your hair.'

Though ravenous, he did his best not to gobble down the pasta, but it disappeared quickly anyhow. He took a piece of bread from the centre of the table and looked to his dinner companion for permission to use it to mop up the remainders on his plate.

'A *scarpetta* is always acceptable. It is a form of praise for the cook, who in this case is me,' she said.

'Thanks . . . I do not even know your name, Signora.'

'My name is Flavia.'

'Flavia. But your full name?'

'All of it?'

'If you would.'

'Princess Donatella Flavia Orsini-Romanelli. But you may call me Flavia.'

He opened his mouth, then remembered his manners, and allowed a piece of wet bread and mushroom to slither down his throat, which evoked a slight emetic response, so that his surprise seemed overdone. 'Romanelli? As in the Villa?'

'I had assumed you knew that.'

'But now you live here.'

'One hates to say this of one's own family, but no proper aristocrat would ever build his residence *below* the town. No noble family was ever so stupid as to build its fortress below the peasants, or if they did, they won't have lasted long. No, we are jumped-up mercantile class, I'm afraid.'

'But aren't you a princess?'

'In Italy that doesn't mean anything. More princesses here than anywhere. Well, anywhere in Europe. We don't count Saudi Arabia and such places, of course. The Romanellis were social-climbing industrialists who made crystal, glass, and industrial products. Not my great-grandfather, mind. He was a mason, a republican, a spiritualist, and not my uncle, a botanist, a scientist, and an experimenter. But my parents certainly were. My father married into an offshoot of the Orsini family, and they, to be sure, are aristocracy – even if they started out as peasant bandits, but that is the way of things. All the money is gone now, of course, and so is the family line. That's my fault, of course.'

'Your fault?'

'No children from me.'

'You never married.' Blume was about to add something polite about that being a perfectly legitimate lifestyle choice but the princess had not finished.

'Marriage has nothing to do with it. I fucked a lot of men. Hundreds.' She winked at him. 'So after you do that and nothing happens, there is only one conclusion to be made, which is that I am barren and the family dies with me. No great loss.'

Blume concentrated hard on his empty plate, while she poured him some white wine. He would have preferred red. He would also have preferred a slightly less frank princess as a dinner companion.

'I fucked peasants, too. Shopkeepers, you name it. One might think I was desperate to keep the lineage alive, but that was not it. I just enjoyed what I was doing.'

'I see,' said Blume.

'You're a bit of a prude, aren't you, Commissioner? My experience is that prudes prefer them young. Like the girl now inhabiting the gate lodge of my old villa. Taut skin, that's what it is about, really. Am I making you nervous? I ask only because you are drinking quickly.'

He put down his glass. 'You lived in the mansion?'

'I was the last inhabitant of Villa Romanelli. Along with my parents and my uncle, the scientist, of course. I was the last to be born in that ghastly pile. Finally, my father, God rest his black fascist soul, realized it had all been a horrible mistake, and he bought this place. It is not much, but it is the highest building in Monterozzo. No one will ever build above us here. He considered it a defeat; I consider it an elevation.'

'Was it you who sold the villa?'

'I basically gave the place away to the state. I received promises that they would look after it, but I never believed them. The Christian Democrat Italian state keep a promise? Hah! But to be fair to them, the place was irreparable from the moment it was built. The only thing worth preserving was the garden.'

'It is a magnificent garden,' agreed Blume.

'*Col cazzo*,' said the princess. 'It is a place of evil. But it is special. The garden was invading the house by the time I left. It is why my father took me away.'

She fixed him with her eyes, which were pale blue and, as he had noticed before, showed no sign of myopia or age, but the face around it was a tragedy of collapse. He felt a pressure on his leg beneath the table. She was pressing against his ankle. He was working out a strategy for gently withdrawing, when she held up her mutilated hand and increased the pressure.

'See this?'

He nodded, helpless.

'Have some more wine.'

The War had not been good for the Romanelli family. In common with most of the upper bourgeoisie and aristocrats, they had sided with the Fascists. The real problem was not reprisals afterwards, but the economic damage from investing in munitions, chemicals, and other areas of the economy that were nationalized to become Enichem and Agusta, or simply stolen by the Americans. During the War, the house had been neglected, and in 1946, the family's resources were depleted. It was impossible to make repairs to the villa, and her father, busy making friends with the Christian Democrats and Liberal Party, had little time to attend to upkeep. He started closing rooms. Literally closing them and locking them up. Paraffin heaters and open fires were the main sources of warmth. The court-yard was turned into a vegetable plot, most of the staff were laid off.

Her mother, well, the less said about her and the Orsini clan the better, although there was poetic justice in her fate. Before the War, the Romanellis had joined forces with German chemical companies in experimenting in the uses of coal tar, until then a waste material from mining. The scientists had come up with all sorts of uses. Purple dyes, aspirin, and a more stable form of laudanum called heroin. Her mother used to wear her hair iron-flat with a silken red rose on the side of her head, as in the 1920s, when she was young and beautiful, which was also when heroin, produced by Romanelli under licence from Bayer, became popular. Meanwhile the Germans took all the profits, even after losing the War. The family lost its investment.

Flavia's governess was a French girl called Cécile. Cécile soon realized that she was on her own with Flavia. Her mother lay most of the day insensible in bed. The servants and cooks were locals who vanished in the evenings. The master of the house was never in. Even if Flavia had become fluent in French, which was the idea, no one would have noticed. Meanwhile the house became damper and colder. Sometimes they forgot to pay the governess.

Cécile, being French, pretty no doubt, and in a backwater such as Monterozzo, soon had *des beaux*, so to speak, young men who would come trespassing looking for her. Inevitably, Cécile began to leave Flavia to her own devices, placing her on the rocking horse in the nursery and vanishing into one of the many empty rooms, except, of course, the room to which she slipped away was not empty, there being some gallant youth lurking in there, waiting for her.

Cécile was what you might call a naughty girl, said the princess, but not a bad person, and so she left the nursery door open, lest Flavia should fall off the rocking horse or cry out. She was fond of the child, and worried about her, and she probably did not manage to get up to all that much, always having one ear open for the baby.

The nursery door was not the only one left open. The churlish hands and sullen servants, the careless groundskeepers and her distracted mother were forever leaving doors open all over the villa, so that all kinds of vermin could get in and build their nests and dens. In fact, her uncle, a botanist and mycologist became so fed up with the situation that he retreated into the cellars of the villa to conduct his experiments. He had his own special entrance built, his own locks, and equipped his own labs in the fond belief the family's fate could be reversed if only his experiments with the forcing of foods could succeed. Mushroom tunnels, patches of rhubarb, which no one had heard of in Monterozzo, radicchio pits, chicory, asparagus. He also carried out experiments which, he claimed, proved that mushrooms controlled the weather. Mad, of course.

On the evening it happened, Flavia's father was on a rare home visit, though not for the sake of being with her mother. The uncle, as always, was locked in the dark basement, and never heard a thing.

Flavia was old enough not to fall off her rocking horse any more, old enough to toddle about the nursery, old enough to call for Cécile in her own baby version of French. She was used to being alone in the nursery, and unafraid, because it had happened before, and all it took was a few plaintive cries and Cécile, adjusting her dress and stockings, would be there in almost no time.

Flavia's scream on this evening pierced even her mother's dulled consciousness. Her father, who was on the telephone to Einaudi at the time, dropped the receiver, the grounds man, weeding the cabbage patch, dropped his hoe, and Cécile disentangled herself within seconds from the son of the greengrocer who ran for the front door of the villa as everyone else ran towards the nursery, passing Flavia's father on the stairs without stopping. The greengrocers son was never to set foot in the premises again. Cécile was there first, of course, and as she ran down the hallway, something bright orange, as if it had its own source of light, flashed past her and vanished, slipping through a crack in one of the crumbling walls. Cécile, too, was shouting as she entered the nursery, and her voice rose to a pitch equal to that of the child when she saw the two foxes. One had its fangs sunk deep into the soft flesh of the child's thigh, the other had its jaws around the little fingers that had reached out to stroke its nose and was shaking its head to and fro. Cécile threw herself upon the child and the creatures, hissing and snarling to make them let go of their prey.

When the father came in, having mistakenly tried two bedrooms first, so long was it since he had been upstairs in his own home, he saw his daughter white faced and motionless as the governess tried to staunch the flow of blood from the severed finger on the small hand. When her mother arrived, she fainted. The grounds man caught one of the foxes, and kicked it to death on the back stairs.

The princess nudged his calf with her foot, then released him, and picked up his plate.

'A week later, my father closed down the villa and took us here. I never saw my uncle again, and my mother died six months later from an overdose.'

That night, after his usual dose of statins, it took Blume multiple glasses of water, two Lyrica, three drops of Lorazepam, a dose of Alsuma, and some Doxepin to fight off migraine, insomnia, and the feeling that someone was outside his door. When he finally did get to sleep, he dreamed of foxes and of apples cascading through endless streets.

21

W HEN HE awoke the following morning, Blume could tell he had a slight fever. It was, he hoped, the sort of flu that he could put off for a day or two before it overwhelmed him. He took three aspirin and, after measuring his sluggishness, four Provigil pills, which he had originally been prescribed to him for what he referred to as 'obstructive sleep apnoea' and Caterina called 'snoring'.

When he got downstairs, he opened several doors to see if he could find his hostess, but she was out. He walked down to the piazza and across to 'his' bar again for a breakfast consisting of a cappuccino with scalded milk and a pastry so stale it might have been the one he had abandoned the day before.

At nine, Blume walked into the Carabinieri station, located just outside the walls of Monterozzo. He had a number of thoughts on his mind, one of which was that he should have done this earlier. He presented his credentials to the tall handsome *appuntato scelto* behind the desk, who nodded, like a hotel receptionist registering an expected guest. He motioned Blume to follow him, knocked with a military rat-tat-tat on a door, and opened it when the voice behind told him to.

Maresciallo Panfilo Angelozzi of the Carabinieri was, above all else, a tired man. This was the overwhelming impression that Blume got as he entered the office. Even Angelozzi's moustache, a large drooping affair more suited to the leisurely years before the Great War, seemed to ache with a drowsy numbness. He was sitting at the desk with one hand pushing up the fat of his cheek so that it folded around his left eye and closed it. He did not get up, but gave a lethargic wave at the chair in front of him. When Blume sat down, the captain, with an enormous sigh, held out a large, warm, and soft hand. They shook, slowly. Angelozzi fell back into his chair, exhausted.

'I was wondering if you were going to pay a visit.' He yawned.

Blume yawned in sympathy.

The maresciallo smiled and nodded, satisfied to register that Blume, too, found all this getting up and staying awake business a bit too much. 'I heard all about you,' he said, putting an heavy emphasis on 'all', as if receiving so much information in one go had been a very taxing experience. 'But the last thing I heard was that you were going home.'

Blume explained about his accident, and the maresciallo winced sympathetically at the sheer effort of it all. He lifted a leaden arm from the table, held it with his other hand, and contemplated his watch for a while.

'Look, I just need to know one or two things, if you don't mind.'

The maresciallo rested his hand on a pile of papers on the desk. The implication seemed to be that if the answers to Blume's questions were not in the papers, preferably at the top of the pile, it would be very difficult to oblige.

'I don't think you need to look anything up,' Blume assured him.

The maresciallo's expression became friendlier.

'Niki Solito,' said Blume. The babyish face in front of him remained calm, peaceable, and expectant. Clearly, Niki was not a source of much trouble to the maresciallo nor, Blume suspected, was the maresciallo a source of much trouble to Niki or anyone. 'Solito claims he is worried about a Romanian girl.'

'Yes,' agreed the maresciallo. 'And so is the missing girl's friend.' He clasped his hands and stretched his arms luxuriously over his head, cracked his knuckles, and yawned again. 'In whose company you were seen.'

Blume ignored the comment. 'So did Niki Solito report her missing to you?'

The maresciallo sighed, and reluctantly pulled the pile of papers towards him. 'I suppose you want a date?' he asked in the tone of a man tasked beyond all endurance.

He opened the pile near the top with his thumb and peered in. The piece of paper was not immediately available, and he sat back, defeated.

'But he did file a missing person report?'

'No, no. You know he couldn't do that. He is not family, not gone long enough. Alina . . . Paulescu. This was, let me see, two weeks back, no . . . . today is Sunday, minus seven, minus Friday, Thursday, Wednesday, Tuesday.'

Blume realized he was supposed to do the rest of the arithmetic himself. 'That's 20 days ago. But you did not,' here he paused delicately, 'pursue any line of inquiry?'

'I persuaded him not to do a missing person report. Not immediately. Anyhow, he seems to have lost interest now. Maybe he heard from her in Romania.'

'What about Niki himself?'

'Hmm?'

'Niki.'

'Yes. What about him?'

186

'What's he like?' demanded Blume.

Sentenced to the labour of explaining, the maresciallo closed his eyes as he selected his words carefully: 'Complicated.'

Blume slowly learned that Niki predated the maresciallo in the town, and that he had never been in any trouble, apart from the occasional court appearance regarding licensing laws, taxes, and suchlike. 'White collar minor stuff – the business of the Provincial Police, the Finance Police but not us,' he told Blume. The maresciallo's predecessor, however, had singled out Niki and the older man Domenico as potential sources of violence. But he had been quite wrong. The predecessor, an overactive and ambitious zealot, in the maresciallo's opinion, believed Niki and Mimmo were on some sort of scouting expedition for the Sacra Corona Unita. But the years passed and nothing happened. The older man stuck to his garden, the younger to a nightclub that was not even in the maresciallo's jurisdiction.

'It was always unlikely that the Puglia Mafia would invest here.' He waved desolately at the wall of the office. 'In Monterozzo,' he specified, lest Blume had misinterpreted the intended scope of the arm wave.

'Drugs, gambling, prostitution, trafficking – isn't that what Niki's nightclub is all about?'

The maresciallo patted a pillar of air with a pudgy hand to indicate that Blume was running ahead of himself and needed to slow down. 'Have you been to the nightclub?'

'Not inside it,' admitted Blume. 'I imagine it's a typical criminal enterprise. It's also a good place for criminals to meet.'

'Yes, scoundrels meet there. Most of them local administrators and regional politicians, but Monterozzo is not high on their agenda. We don't even get visitors, except in the summer to the gardens below.

What you are failing to see here, I think, is that Niki's club is actually far away. Thirty-five kilometres. And from what I hear . . .'

'You've never been to it?'

The maresciallo pondered the question for a while. When he replied it was with the air of a man weighing his words with great care. He had, in fact, been to the club several times. He was, Blume may not have known this, a single man. He was sure that drugs circulated, but he did not feel there was much he could or should do about it.

Blume had a hard time imagining the maresciallo dancing. Or staying up late.

'I get the feeling the drugs arrive with the VIPs and leave with them, too. As I say, the VIPs are mostly politicians but also the occasional magistrate, a judge or two. They would not appreciate a maresciallo from a small town opening an investigation.'

As for the prostitution thing, the maresciallo felt that while the club might facilitate, it did not seem to be the source, and that, all things considered, it was inadvisable to get bogged down in this very muddy area of the law.

'Niki has money, I assume. He is engaged, Silvana does not seem as revolted by the prospect as she ought to be. Do you have any idea why they don't marry?' asked Blume.

'Some women like to make men wait and wait. Sometimes until it's too late.' This was spoken with some conviction and in the widest-awake tone yet, and Blume understood that some flighty woman had carelessly let drop the catch that was Maresciallo Panfilo Angelozzi.

'The father, Domenico Greco, may have something to do with it, too,' added the maresciallo, his outburst about women causing him inadvertently to volunteer information.

'Yes, what about him?' asked Blume.

To conserve energy for what now threatened to be a long to-and-fro, the maresciallo tried to keep his replies as economical as possible. 'Came up here with Niki years ago. Before my time. All in my predecessor's files. Better source than me, frankly.'

Blume stood up, and shook the maresciallo's hand, a tactical move that had its intended disarming effect.

'That's it? You have no more questions?'

'I think so,' said Blume. 'Thanks very much.'

'You're welcome,' said the maresciallo and, on a generous impulse added some details for free. 'He's from Bari. Domenico, the father, I mean. Niki is from Molfetta originally. They already knew each other when they arrived. It took longer for the people in the town to accept Niki, but people liked the father straight away. The child helped.'

'Silvana.'

'Yes.'

'No mother, you know. The father bringing her up alone, never asking anyone for favours. People felt sorry for him.'

'He lost his wife, obviously.'

A sly look crossed the maresciallo's countenance. 'If only. But the truth of the matter is his wife ran away with a younger man. If she had died, people might not have been so embarrassed. For obvious reasons, Domenico never liked to talk about it. The details of the story were never well known to begin with. People have more or less forgotten now and he's just called the gardener, sometimes "the Botanist", because he knows so much about the trees and flowers and . . . grass.' The maresciallo was winding down again. The daylight, attenuated though it was by the grime on the window, showed up all the lines of age and torpor.

'After I check out Niki's place, I am coming back to ask Domenico Greco a few questions.'

189

'Is that really necessary?'

'Am I disturbing something?' asked Blume.

'I think that is what you want to do.'

'Perhaps if you just cleared up a few of my curiosities, I could just leave things alone.'

'What curiosities?'

'Greco's wife running away, his origins in the south, how he came to be here, his relationship with Niki. His money.'

'Money?'

'Someone financed the refurbishing of part of the house. It might have been Niki, except Silvana tells me he did not approve. So maybe it was the old man. But if he's just a gardener, where did he get the funds?'

The maresciallo stood up, and Blume was surprised to see he was quite a tall man though he walked with a stoop. He went over to an old filing cabinet, and came back with a folder that included, Blume could see, some printouts of newspaper articles and a fading photocopy of an *avviso di garanzia*.

'These have nothing to do with me. My predecessor here was one of those overexcitable conspiracy types who see plots and criminals everywhere.'

'Except here he was literally seeing criminals. Domenico Greco had a criminal record, right?'

The maresciallo looked offended and put the file out of Blume's immediate reach. 'He kept files on everyone.'

'You have not added to them?'

'Good God, no. I have more than enough to do as it is.'

'So that file was never updated?'

'Not since I came here, no.'

'Which is how long?'

'Twelve years.'

'Have even you read it?'

'Maybe, once, a long time ago. But Greco has never been a cause of any trouble, so there has been no need.'

Blume pulled the file towards him, and the maresciallo made no move to stop him. 'I see there is an *avviso di garanzia* in here. What's that about?'

'It was issued by a magistrate in Bari a long time ago. It had to do with the disappearance of his wife.'

'She ran away, that's what you said.'

'Actually, she disappeared. It was finally agreed that she had run away. To Australia, I think. A magistrate opened a case, and had to notify Greco that he was under investigation. So that's the *avviso* you see there. Nothing came of it.'

'A magistrate opened a case?'

'The father of the guy the wife is supposed to have run away with accused Greco of murder. The preliminary court closed it down with a do-not-proceed motion. Or the man withdrew his complaint. I can't remember. It's in there.'

'Can I take this?'

'I'd prefer you didn't.'

'I can see that, but what if I did anyhow?'

The maresciallo looked stricken. 'I was showing some professional solidarity, and now you want to cause me trouble?'

'Not you: Greco.'

'Leave the poor man alone, Commissioner.'

'Did your predecessor keep a file on Niki Solito?'

The maresciallo ponderously shook his head, though whether it was to deny the existence of the file or to indicate that Blume was not getting it was not clear. Blume stood up, folder in hand.

'I'll bring it back, promise.'

'Do as you please.' The maresciallo placed his hands on his desk to indicate that he did not intend to move from where he was. 'Just try not to mention me in connection with any agitation you are stirring up.'

22

As Blume passed the repair shop, Alfredo the mechanic was standing there smoking a flaccid cigarette. He gave Blume a friendly wave. Blume waved back.

'I am sorry to see you must walk everywhere,' said Alfredo.

'It clears the mind,' said Blume. 'And the streets are too narrow to drive.'

'You get used to it. But no vehicle can get up to where you're staying. Except a scooter. Are you going there now?'

'As a matter of fact I am,' said Blume.

'You can borrow my son's scooter,' said Alfredo.

'That's very kind of you, but I prefer to walk,' said Blume.

Alfredo flicked ash in Blume's direction. 'You are a very strange man, Commissioner Blume. I have never seen anyone make so many enemies so quickly. It's a good job you're not planning to settle here.'

'Any news on the spare parts?'

'On their way. I am giving your car absolute priority.'

They parted on the best of terms.

At the alimentari in the piazza, he had them make him up a long baguette with prosciutto and mozzarella. He bought himself a drinking yoghurt, three cans of beer and a packet of Molino Bianca digestives.

He had now had food enough until dinnertime. He hoped the princess would not object to his eating in his room. Too bad if she did. He had a day's work ahead of him.

When he got back to the princess's house, the front door yielded to a gentle push, only this time no smell of cooking greeted him, though the coolness of the air inside the building was pleasant after the heat.

'Hello?' He felt the sweat breaking out under his shirt, as his body adjusted to the sudden drop in temperature.

He called out a few times, deepening and steadying his voice so as not to sound nervous, but no one answered. Rather than go straight up to his room, he went down to the kitchen, and dropped his bag of shopping and the file on Greco on the table where they had eaten the night before. Calling out now and then, telling himself it was so as not to startle the princess but finding comfort in the human sound of his own voice, he began to explore.

A scullery off the kitchen was filled with potatoes, onions, strings of garlic, and bottles of wine and olive oil. Behind it, he found a small toilet and a backyard. He returned to the kitchen, and absent-mindedly pulled out his lunch. Panino in hand, he returned to the entrance hall, and opened one of the two doors that led off it. He found himself in a cool, dark room filled with scrap metal, a heap of keys, and a pile of tarnished silver sitting on a broad table and a wall lined with gold-framed portraits, most of them uniformly black and indistinguishable under the 40-watt bulb whose light barely made it from the high ceiling. One painting, more modern and easier to make out, showed a young woman. It seemed unimaginable that the exterior of these very walls were hot to the touch as they baked in the excess of sunlight.

The second door led into a drawing room that seemed even darker than the first, if only for the completeness with which the light had been excluded from the two large windows. Wooden panel shutters closed them on the inside, and their defence against the light had been shored up with piles of books, which had the added benefit of killing all sounds from outside.

Here was a fantastically ugly chandelier from the 1950s, but it at least had room for five bulbs, three of which were working. Two of the walls were lined with old folios and books, some with broken spines, others intact, all of them well dusted. The room smelled of beeswax and cleaning fluid, and the table in the middle shone like well-polished shoes. Near the window sat a television, as old as some of the books. It was a huge 'Pye' set that must have cost a lot in its day, if only for the wood used in its manufacture. On the wall behind it, the sole painting in the room was a representation of Villa Romanelli in its heyday. The perspective was from the side, and showed two sides of the mansion and some of the box hedges in the garden.

Blume, feeling under observation, finished off his panino, and poked his head back out into the hallway and called out 'Flavia' (he could hardly go round shouting 'Princess', or even 'Signora' since she was, in fact, a princess. The first name option seemed the least embarrassing). The hall had considerable power of amplification. If she had been in, she would surely have heard him. He ducked back into the kitchen and grabbed the drinking yoghurt and a few digestives. He'd have preferred a beer, but he did not want to be caught walking about with a can in his hand. The yoghurt and biscuits were bad enough for, as Caterina had told him more than once, walking and snacking was a vulgar American habit. Her rule exempted ice cream, of course, since that's what Italians did.

Back in the drawing room, or whatever its function was, he

brushed biscuit crumbs off his chest and examined the spines of the books. One entire wall was given over to a collection of the laws of Italian states before Unification, a complete set of the acts of the two Houses of Parliament, what had to be the entire corpus of Piedmontese laws, constitutions, chapters, pragmatic sanctions, decrees, government programmes, customs, parliaments, proclamations, and enactments, commentaries on laws, and studies of the public, private, and canon law. The works on or by Cavour, Crispi, Davideni, Depretis, Garibaldi, La Marmora, Mamiani, Manzoni, Rattazzi, Ricasoli, Sonnino, Tommaseo, and Zanardelli were disposed in a defence-in-depth formation against the last remaining sunbeams that tried to filter through.

More interesting was a section, protected from the dust by a lattice of lead and glass, containing volumes and engravings on top of which a large pile of maps and plans had been heaped, some in better condition than others. Some showed old maps of Abruzzi, Latium, the Marches, Northern Campania, Algidus Mons, the Alban Hills, parts of Tuscany, and Molise. Others were more specifically local to Monterozzo, or 'Mons Rudis'. Here he found plans and elevations of Villa Romanelli.

He took one out and unrolled it on the table, only for it to roll up again. He tried to hold it down with his bottle of yoghurt, and almost spilled the contents all over the plan. He gulped down the yoghurt and shoved the plastic bottle in his pocket. Then he remembered a set of lozenge-shaped weights he had seen on a lower shelf whose purpose had escaped him. It was very satisfying to roll out the plan of the villa and pin it down with a heavy iron bar in each of the four corners. He looked down at it, happy finally to have it all laid out before him like that. It fitted in with his plan for the afternoon, which was to map out an investigation not only into the missing Romanian, but also into Niki Solito and Domenico Greco. The way he saw it, at least two young women, Nadia and Silvana, were in danger, but he was not sure exactly how. This is what he would work out, along with a way of getting the men's past to catch up with them.

The map made him feel more in control, too. He now had a God's-eye-view of the mansion in the garden, which had been looming a bit too large in his imagination. It was not a blueprint but a drawing done after the house was built. The dimensions and functions of the rooms were indicated. There was the nursery, governess quarters, various guest bedrooms, bathroom, laundry room, utility room, billiard room, library, kitchen, drawing room, dining room, second dining room, antechambers, halls, vestibules, music room, reading room, hunting room, and so on. He thought of his own new-build apartment at the edge of the city. If the entire high-rise building were cut into sections, it would fit into the second floor of the villa, with room to spare. Three floors and then the basements, cellars, garages, stables, and so forth, which were not even counted. He examined the plan again and saw it was dated 1932. The basements were generically indicated as *cantina* except, he noticed, a section, located at the back of the house defined as *laboratori, vivaio e serre*. The laboratory and plant house also seemed to be located in the basements, which was odd, except that the princess had mentioned her uncle carrying out underground botany experiments of some sort. Evidently, the uncle had been a long-term resident.

He left the room without putting away the map. He retrieved his shopping bag, which now contained just biscuits and beer, and the Carabinieri file on Greco from the kitchen table and clumped up the stairs as noisily as he could, just in case, in spite of all the calling, someone was in the house after all.

In the bedroom, he cleared room on his small desk, pushed his

197

suitcase under the bed, plugged in his phone, took out pens, the lined notebook, and the file on Greco. He got up and made his bed more neatly, moved the bedside lamp over to the table, and closed the door to the bathroom. He surveyed his workspace with satisfaction. He even had internet on his phone. He had all the tools he needed.

He decided to begin with the least likely source of information: the exercise book Silvana had left behind in the hospital. He had already glanced into it, and saw nothing of interest, and he had always assumed she had simply left it behind by mistake. But what if it contained some sort of coded message? A cry for help?

He opened it again, and studied the girlish handwriting. He noted again how she dotted her 'i's with little flowers. He read an entire short story about a knight in shining armour trying to pick up a bundle of blue flowers for his lady only to be dragged down into the water and dying shouting 'Forget me not!', which, Silvana wrote, is 'how the beautiful little flower got its name.'

She had signed the story, as if it were her own. But he had a dim memory of having heard the tale before, which he was able to confirm with his phone and the internet. There was even a poem. Nothing wrong with retelling the story, he thought, but why bother?

The next story seemed to have talking trees in it, which, having no real beginning, middle, or end, he figured was a complete original. She wrote in a bulbous childish script with no hard edges, which after a while seemed to expand and wobble before his eyes. A few pages listed the names of flowers in English and Italian, and he spotted one or two doubtful translations. Weren't you supposed to use Latin anyhow, since vernacular names were unreliable? It was beginning to dawn on him that Silvana, sweet and enthusiastic though she was, might be a bit . . . dumb seemed harsh, but he had given up looking for any coded messages. There was one more complete story, this one about a rabbit, and he was looking up Beatrix Potter on his smartphone when a text message came through from Caterina.

When you coming by? Call?

Serendipitous. That was exactly what he had planned to do next. He opened his notebook, uncapped a new pen, and was ready to call her. She was often angry with him, but always helped him if he asked. She might kick him out, but she never let him down. He called her. She began by complaining about his unreasonable demands, his cagey refusal to say what he was doing or where he was or who with. He let all this flow by, waiting for her to get to the point. Finally, she said. 'Anyhow, against my better judgement, I got some info on a certain Greco, Domenico, aka Mimmo . . .'

'Nothing on Alina Paulescu, the missing girl?'

'Grateful as ever, aren't you?'

'I only meant . . .'

'Forget it. If I had, I would have told you. No. But you did not give me much to go on. And even if you had, this sort of check can take weeks. So, are you listening?'

'Yes.'

'You're taking notes, too, I can tell.'

'How can you tell that?'

'You're speaking in your writing voice. All serious, no humour. But before I start, are you trying to handle this guy yourself? Basically, what I am asking is if you're trying to get yourself killed?'

'No. Nothing like that. He's old now, and a gardener.'

'So what put you onto him?'

'Well, he seems to have a lot of money for a gardener, and no one here is very curious, so I just thought I'd look into it.'

'I think there is more to it than that. You are holding back.'

'Maybe a bit, but the more you help me, the more you'll know about it,' said Blume.

'That's the only reason I am helping you in the first place. OK, get your pen ready. Domenico Greco, used to be known as "Mimmo il Mimo". It's an old nickname. He got it because when he carried out jewellery heists, he took care never to speak. He would just mime what he wanted using his hands and his gun.'

'Armed robbery? When was this?'

'This was at the end of the 1970s. He got done twice for it, but was suspected of being involved in many more than that. After he came out of jail in 1982, he married, seemed to settle down, and falls off the radar for years. He got a light sentence both times he was caught. Either because he corrupted the judge or because, given the historical period, the authorities were almost sympathetic to anyone who was not a separatist or *brigatista*.'

'What about organized crime or the Sacra Corona Unita?'

'Maybe, but the SCU was just being formed around then. The divisions between ordinary criminals and the SCU back in the 70s were very porous. He could have been part in and part out, in a way Cosa Nostra would never allow.'

'Got it,' said Blume.

'So Mimmo il Mimo, soon to become known as Domenico, spends the 1980s living happily married and running a factoring company. I suppose the source of the capital behind that company is open to question, but basically he seems to have gone legitimate, insofar as a financial company in southern Italy can be legitimate in any way.'

'Which is no way at all,' said Blume.

'True, but if he was involved in money laundering, he kept a low profile and his contacts to a minimum. So, as I say, he stays clean for years, never back in jail, never charged, until he next pops up in 1999. That was the year in which –'

'A magistrate re-opened a file against him based on an accusation that he had killed his wife.'

Silence. One. Two. Three. He should have kept quiet.

'Do you have this information already?'

'Just that part, Caterina. I heard it this morning, promise.'

'You promise. Save your promises for things that count. Well, stop me if you've heard this one: the person who made the accusation . . .'

'. . . was the brother of the man with whom Greco's wife was cheating,' finished Blume in his own head, managing not to blurt it out and annoy her again.

'. . . is a certain Davide Di Cagno. Now it turns out he is the younger brother of a man who is said to have run away with Greco's wife,' said Caterina. 'He did not make the accusation till much later, by which time no one was interested. But, reading between the lines . . .'

'You're enjoying this, too, just a bit, aren't you, Caterina?'

'Reading between the lines,' she repeated more firmly, 'it certainly seems possible that Davide Di Cagno knows his brother never ran away anywhere, but was killed for adultery by Greco. Along with the wife. I am not saying that is what happened,' said Caterina, 'but I don't buy the idea that they ran away together, never to be heard of again.'

'Neither do I!' said Blume.

'Yes, but the difference is, I am happy enough to leave it at that. And so should you.'

'Can you find out where he lives, this brother, what his phone number is, if he's still alive, and send me the details on my phone?'

'Did you just hear what I said about leaving it alone?'

'Come on, Caterina. I can look it up myself if I have to. Save me the effort.'

'I've just sent it to you by email.'

'You are a sweetheart.'

'Alec, this is a stupid and dangerous thing. Do you need help? Apart from mentally, I mean.'

'No. I'm fine.'

'Why don't you just come home?'

'I will, as soon as I finish one last thing here. Thanks, Caterina. I am going to look at that email now.'

He hung up and opened his Gmail. There it was: a message that said, 'I may be the bigger idiot of the two of us for sending you this', was followed by the name Davide Di Cagno, date of birth, address, home phone number, no mobile. Born 1979. Surely that was too young?

At the end of the conversation, Caterina had said he should *come*, not *go* home. He felt buoyant as he opened the Greco file on his desk. When he saw the disappointingly few pages it contained, his smile faded, but slowly.

23

PRINCESS DONATELLA Flavia Orsini-Romanelli did not come home. Occasionally Blume opened the door of his room and listened, thinking he had heard a noise. He went twice to the head of the stairs and called out her name. He was content, however, to return to his room to read undisturbed the Carabinieri file on Greco, eat biscuits, and wash down aspirins with beer to head off a chill he was beginning to feel as the day wore on into early evening. He kept the nasal spray handy, too, since the last thing he wanted was a migraine to break his concentration as he wrote up his notes. He was coming round to the idea that, whatever his feelings about Niki Solito, Domenico Greco was the more interesting person of the two, and perhaps even made a better suspect.

At eight o'clock, taking his notebook with him, he ventured down the six flights of stairs leading from the second to the ground floor then down the few steps into the kitchen. If she returned and found him there, she might take the hint and cook. At 8:30, with no sign of anyone, he helped himself to some cheese and bread and, after a brief hesitation, cut up two onions with an oversized knife, which slipped and sliced the pulp of his middle finger.

With the help of some kitchen roll and a lot of sucking (and cursing) he stanched the flow, though when he bent the finger, the blood oozed out again. Having dealt with his finger crisis, he salted the onions, pink around the edges now where his blood had stained them, and ate them raw. Caterina wouldn't kiss him for days when he did that, but she hadn't kissed him for months anyhow.

Rubbing his stomach and puffing out his cheeks as the onion returned in gaseous form, he wandered out to the hall where the old reception desk was. It occurred to him that unless his host returned, he might leave without paying. He went behind the desk, opened his wallet, and counted out €200, which ought to cover it, and left it on the desk, in a conspicuous position. He also took down his own ID-card details and filled out the register. After all, the law is the law, he thought. She should have done that: the last guest, he saw, had been a German from 1992. Maybe he had been the one with the hiking boots.

He also discovered several sets of keys behind the desk, including one to the front door, which was still open to anyone who might happen to pass. He doubted anyone would come in, but he had just put €200 in cash on the desk, and, since the princess would certainly have keys to her own home, decided to shut the door.

Back in the kitchen, he considered taking a bottle of wine but, at the cost of some willpower, decided against it. As he was lifting up his notebook, the photograph of Alina, which he had put between the pages so as not to bend it, slipped out. Unlike his bedroom, the lights in the kitchen were modern and bright, and he took advantage of them to study the photograph, not because he expected any clues, but because he needed to reignite his sympathy for this girl who was little more than a name to him.

The picture had been taken while Alina was in conversation with someone out of frame. Her face was animated, her mouth slightly open, her chin poised at an angle that suggested she was about to speak. The sea was just visible in the background. He wondered what sea it was, and why she had chosen to print that particular photograph. No one printed photos anymore, so she must have felt she looked particularly beautiful in it, which she did, though like so many young people, she might not have been aware how much of what she considered her particular loveliness was part of the general beauty of youth.

'I'm sorry, there is nothing I can do,' he told her. 'I'm sorry, too, for how you were treated. All that courage and spirit, just to end up dead and no one except Nadia caring enough to look for you. Because you *are* dead, Alina, aren't you?'

He placed the picture on the table. 'Were you getting in the way of Greco's plans?' he asked her. 'Is it really that Niki fell for you? Or did he kill you? Or, did he do both?'

Alina continued to look sideways, away from him, always on the point of speaking and forever mute.

No one in the town was in the slightest bit interested in the disappearance of a Romanian girl. He could not hear their conversations, but he couldn't picture them whispering about it as if it were something that concerned them. Striking though she may have been, they would not have seen much of her. As Nadia said, they slept most of the morning, kept themselves to themselves, and went to the nightclub in the evening where they had dinner. Monday was their day off. He didn't imagine the men from the town who had driven 30 or 40 kilometres to Niki's seedy nightclub would be willing to acknowledge them if they met them in the street. Would they even recognize them in ordinary clothes, in tracksuits and trainers, instead of tiny skirts, sequined black tops, boots, and white knickers?

The women of the town were unlikely to befriend them either.

If Alina's disappearance had even registered, it might well have been with a mixture of relief and vengeful pleasure.

A face like hers should have brought respect, love, veneration, and tenderness. But she had been used like an animal. He opened the notebook to a fresh page, uncapped a pen, and wrote down 'Romania, return?', and then angrily bullet-pointed the reasons for excluding this option. He slipped the photo back into the covers of the notebook and returned upstairs. If he could do nothing about a young woman disappearing in the present, he might be able to do something about one who had disappeared in the past, and maybe there would end up being some connection. He still had work to do.

Back at his desk, he reread his notes, and worried about dates. According to the file, and as confirmed by Caterina, Greco's wife had gone missing in 1993, a year that in some ways might have been yesterday except that, he reflected, Alina and Nadia would have been no more than newborns.

He looked through the Carabinieri papers. Marina. That was Greco's wife's name, and she had been born in 1961. That made her 32 when she disappeared.

He wrote down the date of disappearance: 1993, underlined it, and then started working out some ages, which he entered in a column below: Domenico (Mimmo) Greco 45; his wife Marina Greco, née Loconsole 32, quite a gap, but not too unusual; Giuliano Di Cagno, the young man she was supposed to have run off with, born . . . he checked the papers, 1968, which made him 25 at the time. A 32-year-old woman leaving her 45-year-old husband for a younger man – perfectly plausible, except there was a child in the middle of this, Silvana who, in 1993, would have been about 8. And then there was Niki who was 22 at the time.

That made Niki and him practically contemporaries. Blume stood up and went into the bathroom for a piss, and observed himself in the mirror. He figured he had aged better than Niki. Better angina and migraines than diabetes. Speaking of which, he hunted round for his medicines. He realized he was taking them more or less at random now, eking out those of which he had few, gobbling down those of which he had plenty.

Domenico, born 1949, had been arrested in 1972 for armed robbery. He had been in prison until 1982. That was prehistory. Most of the other people, himself included, were either children or had yet to be born. Blume imagined himself sitting in front of a highly sceptical magistrate, setting out not fact but theories; not evidence but a story, which, somehow, he knew to be true. If he told the story right and got the right sort of magistrate, then the case might be reopened, there being no statute of limitations for premeditated murder – of which he had absolutely no proof. He'd need a youngish ambitious magistrate, and he would need to do all the investigative work for him. He looked at the driving licence photo of the considerably younger Greco. 'You can't just disappear women like that, you bastard.'

He had to spell it out, to sell his version of events, and, above all, he needed a witness. This was going to be his final task this evening. Despite what the princess said about manners, supper times, and calling, it was pure common sense to phone people in the evenings after dinner when they were most likely to be in. At least from a policeman's perspective. It was now 9 o'clock. He'd give it another half hour, then, with the number Caterina had sent him, he would call the brother of the disappeared man. That would be the make or break moment, and, he was not ashamed to admit, he was nervous. Without the corroboration and backing of the younger brother, his investigation into Greco would fail, no matter how convincing his reconstruction of events. He reread what he had written earlier.

On the morning of 19 June 1993, Marina Greco, née Loconsole, received an anguished-sounding call from her lover, Giuliano Di Cagno. In it, he asked her to meet him at the town of Molfetta that afternoon.

He checked on his phone's diary, and added the fact that it was a Saturday.

She would have been surprised at this request, because Giuliano was not from the town, and the last time they had met, taking advantage of the absence of her husband, who was engaged in some of his usual shady deals in Foggia, he had made no mention of it. Giuliano, however, insisted, saying it was an emergency, and told her to take the train.

We may imagine that she wanted to know why, and Giuliano will have replied, 'Just do as I say. Don't use the car. I'll explain when you get here. There is a train that leaves at 2:15 for Foggia. Take that, I'll be waiting for you at the station.'

Or words to that effect.

Since we cannot by any means equate unfaithfulness to a husband with lack of maternal instinct, she will have raised the objection that she had to look after her child. It is interesting to speculate, of course, whether this child, Silvana, was her husband's.

If not, it might explain why poor Silvana's 'father' was so casual about her marrying that freak Niki.

This could be established beyond all doubt, though it might not be germane to the case and would certainly devastate the child, now a woman.

He had had to imagine Marina wondering what to do with the child. Mothers don't often abandon their children. As Marina was ultimately Greco's victim, Blume was disposed to think the best of her.

'Leave her with your sister.' There would have definitely been something wrong with Giuliano's voice as he gave her these instructions, but that would only have served to heighten her sense of urgency. She went round to her sister's with the child. We need to check if she had another car – probably not. Did the magistrate look into this?

Blume had stopped here. He imagined that the unmarried sister and she did not get on very well, but the baby had brought them closer. Marina would perhaps have been surprised at the reserves of tenderness in her elder sister, none of which had been apparent when they were growing up together. This did not stop her sister from asking her sharply enough what was so important that she had to abandon her child for the whole afternoon and evening. But he could not reasonably insert this depth of speculation in his report.

He double-checked the files. Yes, there had been a sister, and even the hint of a custody dispute, which is how he had found the name. He was deeply dissatisfied with his storytelling here. He took out his phone and called Caterina, suddenly appreciative of the power of technology. It seemed wonderful that he could hear her voice in this room. He was on the verge of saying so to her, but she answered with a weary sigh of impatience. Well, if that was her reaction to seeing his name on her phone, then what was the point of telling her he wished she were here with him now in this bare room at the top of an empty house at the top of a hostile town, overlooking a ruined villa and an overripe garden.

'Hi, Caterina. Can you do me a quick favour?' was all he said.

'What else have I been put on earth to do?'

So sarcastic.

'Marina Greco, née Loconsole, 1961, Bari. I forgot to background her family. What I need to know is did she have any brothers or sisters. Also, can you double-check that she absolutely vanished from sight. If she turns up alive and well in some other part of the world, then I have been wasting my time. I can't believe how dull-witted I am being. Can you look that up for me?'

'I am at home, Alec.'

'Right. Call someone, get them to do it, then send me the details in a text. As soon as possible.'

'Is that all?'

'Yeah, no, wait, Alessia's OK?'

'Do you want me to text you the answer to that, too?' She hung up on him.

She'd come through. She always did. He sat back and dreamed up Bari in 1993.

'Greco has sent for me,' said Marina. 'It is urgent. Silvana hates travelling. If you don't want her, I can take her, but I thought I might be doing everyone a favour, including Silvana. She loves you.'

Here he left some blank space. He hoped there would not be too many brothers or sisters that might complicate his narrative. You never could tell with southern Italians. Suffice to say the baby was deposited somewhere safe.

He saw Marina. She was crossing the piazza in front of Bari central train station where she was picked up on CCTV – this fact is established in a police report from 1993. The cameras had just been installed owing to a high crime rate in the area. She was reportedly carrying two suitcases, which, like her, vanished from history.

Blume tried to picture Marina, making sure not to confound her in his mind's eye with Alina. He made her heavier, not as pretty, thicker but perhaps a good deal sexier, standing on a platform waiting for the train to arrive and take her towards what the court decided was irresponsible freedom, but he knew was a bitter death. He put down his pen and left her standing there for a while. He needed to fill in some details about her unfortunate lover, Giuliano, and that brought him closer to making the fateful phone call he was putting off.

A droplet of sweat hit the page and smudged the ink: which was odd, because he was freezing cold. He wiped his brow with his arm, took the blanket from his bed, and wrapped it round himself. The drop of sweat had soaked through two pages, so rather than trying to write around it and risk tearing a hole he skipped two pages, but when confronted with pristine white, he lost track of what he was supposed to be saying. Among other things, this was supposed to be delivered as a persuasive speech. He could not afford to forget himself mid-sentence. Looking back would be cheating. He huddled closer into the blanket. It was almost ten in the evening. Now was the moment to call in his witness.

Outside the corridor, stairs, and house were creaking. If he allowed his imagination free rein, it sounded like people were walking up and down outside his door. He heard whispering, then whispered to himself to compare the sounds. He climbed back into his blanket, and dialled the number Caterina had sent him. It was answered on the third ring.

24

'I AM looking for Davide Di Cagno.'

'Speaking, who is this?' The voice of a suspicious man.

'Alec. That is to say, Police. I am a commissioner with the *squadra mobile* of Rome. My name is Blume.'

'Are you sure you have the right person? I have no connections in Rome. And isn't it a bit late to be calling?'

'It's about your brother, Giuliano.'

'Really?' For a moment the voice seemed hopeful. But the note of caution returned immediately. 'How do you know it's him?'

'Do you think he's alive?' Blume regretted being so brutal with the question, but hope must have died a long time ago in that family.

'No. I expect you are calling about his remains. Have you found them or not?'

'I'm afraid not,' said Blume.

'Then what the fuck is this about?'

'I was hoping to reopen the case of his disappearance.'

'No point in that, unless something has changed. You have not found the body. What is this, some sort of cold case file you have been assigned?'

Not assigned, thought Blume. Not quite a cold case either. Alina made it current. The man was saying something else, and Blume realized he had allowed his mind to wander. He remembered he had some Provigil tablets in his suitcase. They were supposed to help with concentration, and stop daytime sleeping. To be on the safe side, he took two. He needed his wits about him.

'Yes.'

'Well?' demanded the voice.

Blume found he could not swallow the pills. He ran into the bathroom and gulped down mouthfuls of freezing water directly from the tap. The pills went down and his throat felt better. 'Sorry, I missed that.'

'So you are not interested. Then I think that's all we have to say on this. Goodbye.'

'Wait!' He needed to say something. 'Domenico Greco is dead.'

'No, he's not.'

'What?'

'Greco's not dead.' The voice was certain and accusing. 'What game are you playing here?'

'It sounds to me that you would not be sorry to hear if he was,' said Blume.

'Someday it'll be true, won't it?'

'How about we get him in prison from now until then?'

'House arrest, you mean. He's too old for prison. You're supposed to be the cop. What difference would that make to him? He's been happy not to leave his garden all these years.'

Davide had certainly not forgotten.

'Do you mind me asking you how old you were when your brother, Giuliano, allegedly ran away with Signora Greco?'

'I was fourteen.'

'And do you agree with the finding that he left, of his own free will?'

'Look, who did you say you were?'

'I am someone interested in reopening the case.'

'You said you were a policeman? Is that true?'

'Yes, Davide,' said Blume. 'That part is true. Can I call you Davide?'

'What part isn't true then?'

'I am writing out the story.' He grabbed the pen again. 'So, Davide, would Giuliano have done that?'

'Why are you talking in that tone?'

'What tone?' asked Blume.

'I don't know. Like it is really urgent. It's twenty years ago now.'

'It is urgent. This is the last chance we are going to get. You are lucky to get this second chance. Almost no one is allowed to correct the past. You can. So, tell me now, would your brother have upped and left for Australia and never contacted anyone again?'

'Of course not. Neither Australia nor anywhere else.'

'So what do you think happened?'

'None of it matters any more. Everyone who mattered is dead. My parents, too. As for Giuliano and Marina, they both died a long time ago, I am sure of it. My brother wouldn't have left me like that. He wouldn't have left our parents. He knew Dad was sick. Sure, he had some fights with Mamma, but he would never have done that. Even if he had decided to run away – people can do crazy things – he would not have tortured us by remaining silent. Someone killed him. Greco or, more likely, Greco had someone do it.'

'Why did your family accept the disappearance? Why did you not make more of a fuss?'

'Lots of reasons.'

'Will you tell me some of them?'

214

'It's very painful to think back. It's humiliating.'

'I understand your father tried to get a proper inquiry opened, didn't he? Then what happened?'

'He was bullied, scorned, and then he died. That's what happened. Greco had money, we were poor. He had the lawyers, political friends, and other sorts of friends, too. It was made clear to us that he could, if he wanted, get someone to visit and hurt us. The investigating magistrate was in his pocket. Dad was sick and had no energy. Mamma, well, she was so ashamed about the revelation my brother had been fooling around with a married woman that she didn't even want to speak about him. She disowned him – at least at first, though she had more than forgiven him by the time she died.'

'And you?'

'I tried again in 1999. But nothing came of it. My parents were dead, the magistrates had all moved on, and the world had changed.'

'What about now, are you doing something about it again?'

'Is that some sort of accusation?'

'No!' Blume was taken aback.

'It sounded like one. There is still a part of me that imagines him there, happy in Australia or South America or somewhere else in Italy.'

Blume wrapped the blanket around himself. Davide's voice did not sound right to him, but he couldn't say why.

'Silvana,' said Blume. He had nothing to follow it up with. He just threw out the name to see the reaction, and find out if Davide remembered the daughter. After all, he might even be her uncle.

The line went dead.

To keep warm, he dragged himself over to the bed and lay on it without taking off his clothes.

In his dreams, a healthier and fitter, younger and more alert version of himself was to be found walking up and down the corridors of the empty house, making creaking sounds on the floorboards that scared the feverish version of himself in bed. The healthy Alec Blume was able to vault over the box hedge of the garden, walk unscathed across the marshlands, and even ascend without any effort to the second and third floors of the Romanelli mansion, and fly around it, peering into its windows, watching the people inside, floating upwards to view it from above. Stretching out his arms, he found he could fly, back to Rome, even over the ocean, and all the way back home if he wanted. With exhilarating velocity, he pulled up into a rapid ascent as he reached the black cliff face overlooking the garden, but his angle of ascent was too steep and he could hear the stall alarm beeping at him now, warning of an imminent crash to earth. Three beeps, stall, stall.

He reached out his hand and grabbed the beeping phone from the floor, and opened one eye. It was, unbelievably, ten minutes to midnight, and a new message had arrived from Caterina. He forced himself awake to read it, and grabbed his pen and notebook.

Marina Loconsole had only an elder sister called Serena. Their father had died when they were children. Their mother died of cancer on New Year's Eve 1999. In 2000 just after her mother's death, Serena filed a suit against Domenico Greco in which she sought custody of her niece. The suit got nowhere. Serena, unmarried, died in 2003 of an overdose of pain relievers. The coroner ruled accidental death. Don't ask me for more help.

Another woman silently killed. Blume resolved to write her back into existence, but the pen dropped from his hand and rolled under the bed.

25

WHEN HE awoke in the morning, he felt light and thin, as if he had been on a diet for a month. He also felt hungry, thirsty, and dirty. He dealt with the thirst first, and by the time he had finished, water was sloshing about in his stomach and his momentary lightness was gone. He had a shower, which was a miserable trickling and cold experience that required considerable courage when it came to washing his back, but when he put on some clean clothes, he felt better.

He packed his suitcase, carefully separating clean and dirty clothes, took out a small shoulder bag, and put in his notebook, the documents he had got from the maresciallo inside it, along with Silvana's book of children's stories. Both these were going back to their owners this morning. He glanced inside at Silvana's book again. Yes, the chunky handwriting still looked strange. He picked up the key for Niki's car. That, too, would be returned.

He shaved, splashed cologne on his face, and brushed his teeth. His phone was fully charged and showing 7:15. The house remained quiet, quieter than it had seemed at night. Houses did that. They liked to come alive at night, settle down in the morning, and allow the streets outside to make the noise. The rectangle of sky framed in the window was pale blue. The air shone, the roofs outside were a clay red and relaxing yellow, and when he opened the window, the air that came in, cooled by the hours of darkness and the stony buildings of the town, was fresh, though he could already detect hints of pollen, perfumes, and cut grass. It was going to be a hot day. One of those early summer days, that gave respite in the early hours and the evening, but rose to August levels of intensity in the middle. He took off his jacket, and folded it into his suitcase.

At 8 o'clock, he would go down to the Carabinieri and make an official denunciation of Domenico Greco. They would have to take down his statement.

His efforts to reopen an old case would not go unpunished by various superiors, no matter what the outcome, but that was all right. He had made commissioner, which was an honourable position. He was not going any higher anyhow. He had loads of money. He had a blue passport with a big bald fucking eagle on it. He could go wherever he wanted and take Caterina with him, too. Show her a big country.

He unlocked the door and went downstairs, checking once again for signs of the princess, of which there were none. The €200 was still there. Locking the front door, he left the house and walked through the town, now familiar, out past the walls, and to the Carabinieri station, his notebook at the ready. He told the *appuntato* at the desk, a different young man from the other day, that he wanted to file a report.

'Lost something?' The *appuntato* handed him a piece of lined paper. Blume explained that he wanted an official record of statement concerning a crime, and the Carabiniere looked pained. 'I'm the only one here right now . . .'

'When is the maresciallo coming in?'

'In about half an hour?'

'I'll wait,' said Blume. 'I have some work to do anyhow.' He took a seat on a wooden bench, and pulled out his notebook and the file on Greco.

So Marina boarded the train thinking she was going to Molfetta, which is what she in fact did. She never had any plans to stay on the train as far as Foggia where her husband told the police he was waiting.

Greco made a great show of being seen at the Foggia station. He got a taxi to the station and he got a taxi back. Both taxi drivers remembered him and were part of his alibi, and this was one of the reasons given by the preliminary judge for throwing out the case. His car was indeed broken down and at the mechanic's.

The mechanic also testified in Greco's favour, further strengthening his case. While at the station, around the time his wife was supposed to arrive, he made a point of getting into a fight with some stranger.

He underlined the last part of that. It stood out like a sore thumb. Any decent investigator should know when a suspect was overdoing his alibi. The rule was simple: if a suspect went to a great deal of trouble to get himself noticed in one place rather than another, the investigator should go to an even greater deal of trouble to check the exact times.

This behaviour ensured that the stationmaster, other passengers, and, best of all, the railway police all confirmed his presence at the time his wife was supposed to be arriving.

Why was he, Blume, the only person to see this? He felt that this detail merited special note. He took out a red pen, put an asterisk over the word 'supposed', and went to the last page and wrote:

Greco may well have arrived at the station by taxi, but as he himself said in his statement — which needs to be read with greater impartiality — he arrived too early. That is the crucial point. He would have us believe that he stayed at the station patiently waiting for hours until tired and disappointed, not to say humiliated by the non-arrival of his wife, he got into a fracas with a stranger. It is sometimes hard to remember the absence of mobile phones. It used to be that whatever arrangements were made had to be kept until contact could be made again. Can we pull up some records to see whether Greco had one? If so, this fact would help the prosecution case. Public phones were often vandalized or not working, and calling his wife in Bari may have been difficult. Unfortunately for our argument, unless he had a mobile phone, it is quite possible that in 1993, a man might simply choose to wait for the next train and the next and the one after that, until the last one of the evening.

Here, for the benefit of a geographically illiterate magistrate, he drew a few lines showing the relative positions of the towns.

Having ensured his presence was registered in the station, perhaps he also asked the stationmaster or ticket clerk to confirm some train times, he walked out and stepped into a car and drove, or was driven, north to Molfetta, the town to which his wife had been called by her lover. Greco, remember, was claiming to be without a car — an unlikely story for a businessman of his calibre. We can assume another car was parked at the Foggia train station or nearby. It is easy to get one's hands on a car when need be.

I believe he drove alone because he had only one accomplice, Niki Solito, a young man and a native of Molfetta. (Molfetta, as far as I can see, has two main claims to fame: (1) the conductor Riccardo Muti comes from there; (2) it is surrounded by carsic caves, many of them unexplored — and used for illegal toxic-waste dumping by the Sacra Corona Unita, which is precisely the sort of criminal organization with which a man such as Greco would have connections.)

He frowned. There was something a bit rambling about his prose style. He was far less incisive than he thought. He crossed out the bit about Riccardo Muti.

When he called Marina, for the worst betrayal he ever made and the last act of his life, Giuliano will have been a captive, possibly with a gun to his head. His captor, Niki, would need to have been armed, for he is a small man, who is heartless but not tough. It is therefore possible that Niki had help, and the help may even have been Greco's. It may have been Greco himself who originally waylaid Giuliano at some isolated spot, and forced him at gunpoint or knifepoint into a car, then delivered him trussed and tied, perhaps beaten and cowed, too, to Niki to manage. However the moment of capture took place, we must assume that Giuliano was being held hostage by Niki when he made that treacherous phone call to a woman he was meant to love but betrayed out of cowardice. (It would be good not to emphasize this aspect until we have secured strong evidence from Giuliano's brother. But it's impossible to ascribe motives to a dead person. A pistol held against the warm throb of your temple is a terrifying thing. The idea of a bullet ripping though your pulsing brain is unthinkable, and yet it may be about to happen, and when you realize the unthinkable is not only possible but imminent, then you find it is easy to do unthinkable things. I can attest to this from personal experience.)

And so we should be understanding of Giuliano, despite this last act. I see him as a broad-shouldered young man. There is one photo of him in the news clippings of the day. It is a blurry enlargement of his ID card. To my eye, it shows the open face and good-natured eyes of a man who genuinely believed he could eventually win the hand as well as the heart of the married woman with whom he had fallen so desperately in love. I believe that he was hoping the trap for Marina would not be fatal.

That was stupid. You cannot really tell much about people from looking at their faces. Maybe Giuliano was no great shakes after all. But Blume had met Niki, and knew him to be a coward, and glimpsed into the dark mind of Greco, too. He was becoming increasingly convinced now that Silvana was Giuliano's daughter, because it seemed impossible that one such as Greco could generate such a light-hearted and sweet thing as Silvana, even if she might not be much of a writer. Maybe that was what was behind Greco's idea of allowing her to be courted by Niki, who was a sort of adopted son. Blume liked his own thinking, but decided he would not write that bit up. He imagined Niki using threats against Giuliano's family to persuade him to make that call. Niki would have pointed the gun in poor Giuliano's face, and told him that if he did not call Marina the first bullet would be for him, but the next would be for his little brother, his father, and his mother. Blume wrote that part in. More than half an hour had passed. He looked questioningly at the *appuntato*, expecting a shrug, but the young man snapped to attention.

'Something must have delayed the maresciallo.'

'That's fine,' said Blume. 'It's hardly your fault.'

An interesting aspect of the case is that the fact of an affair between Giuliano and Marina was never contested. The evidence was overwhelming. Letters were found in Giuliano's house, phone records showed countless calls from one house to the other, and the call durations were themselves proof. The investigators even found hotel records in which both had signed their own names. The old law by which guests must produce a document of identification had proved its worth once again to the investigators, but would have served no purpose had the information not slipped out in the first place. We can imagine Greco, who had, what, 2 or 3 hours with Giuliano, as they waited for Marina's arrival, sitting there, pen in hand taking down details, nodding in an understanding manner, chatting back to show he was not really that angry but needed details for his own peace of mind. And Giuliano, as proud of having a woman love him so as he was scared of Greco, will have sat there, giving as many details as he could, increasingly convinced that he was pleasing and mollifying his captor.

When the train pulled into the small station of Molfetta, Marina got off, a suitcase in either hand, and looked around. It takes no more than half a minute to establish whether someone is waiting for you or not at such a station. Seeing no one, the sense of confusion and alarm perhaps rising in her chest, she walked through the ticketing hall straight onto the small roundabout. The road at twelve o'clock looks down towards the sea. I have not personally reconnoitred the scene of the alleged crime. These last moments of Marina will have to be reconstructed with particular forensic care under the direction of the magistrate.

Blume sat staring at but not really seeing the Carabiniere, trying to imagine Marina arriving to her execution – maybe even suspecting it? Maybe thinking she might talk her husband out of it? Would she have known Niki? He would have been an unprepossessing young man, half a head smaller than she. She might have recognized him as someone who worked with her husband.

I know you are a friend of my husband's, but I don't remember your name.
    Niki Solito: Allow me. He takes the suitcases.

Does she know now what is happening? She asks about Giuliano at this point.

Giuliano is fine. It's more than he deserves. He's waiting for you.

Then she draws a deep breath, and climbs into the car, preferring the back seat. Niki circles the piazza, and takes a road that leads away from the sea, towards the innumerable inland caves.

The *appuntato* sprang to attention again as the door to the station opened and Maresciallo Panfilo Angelozzi slowly squeezed his way through the gap. Following behind was Domenico Greco.

26

'I SHOULD have guessed this might happen,' said Blume as they took their seats in the office.

Maresciallo Angelozzi bent his head down and rubbed his eyes for a long time with his fists. 'Can we get this over with, please? It is utterly exhausting for everyone.'

Blume pulled the files out of his bag. 'I wanted to return these files on Greco.' He tossed them on to the desk in front of the maresciallo, who seemed reluctant to touch them. The photocopy enlargement of Greco's driving licence slipped out and a younger Greco stared up at them. The maresciallo looked into the dead space between Blume and Greco.

Blume pulled out his notebook, and opened it. 'I have taken down the details that matter, and added a few of my own, and nothing in that file is an original document, apart from a gun licence application. So even if it were to disappear, it would not matter.'

'The gun licence is for shooting foxes and other vermin, Blume,' said Greco, the first words he had spoken. 'Just in case you wondered. So, *Dottore*, or Commissioner, what are you trying to do to me. And why? The maresciallo informs me you were thinking of making an official denunciation.'

The maresciallo made a grunting noise that fell diplomatically between affirmation and denial, but then, energized by a bright idea, sat up almost straight to say, 'Would either of you gentlemen like a coffee?'

Curtly rejected by both his visitors, he folded his arms and lapsed into a sulk that soon took on the appearance of a nap.

'Don't you sometimes think, Signor Greco, that women are more trouble than they're worth? Your wife all those years ago just upped and left you in the lurch. Isn't that how it went?'

Greco glanced at the maresciallo, whose head had fallen a bit to the side.

'Do we have to have this humiliating conversation here?'

'I prefer it,' said Blume. 'Perhaps the maresciallo could prepare a *verbale*?'

The maresciallo bestirred himself and launched a resentful look at Blume. 'A *verbale*? What for?'

'Maybe we should be minuting this meeting,' said Blume.

Maresciallo Angelozzi looked at Greco. 'Is this a meeting? I thought it was a conversation. Do I have to call in the lad Paolo from outside? Then who would look after the desk?'

'You could take my statement,' suggested Blume.

'Me?' the maresciallo began wheezing. He continued wheezing as he bent down and spent some time with his face below the desk, and Blume eventually realized this was laughter. When the maresciallo finally resurfaced, it was with an old Casio tape recorder. 'How about this?' He pressed the button; there was a squeak and some hissing, then the tiny tinny voice of Gianni Morandi singing *Fatti mandare dalla mamma* could be heard. He popped out a brown cassette and frowned at it. 'That's funny . . .'

'Let's be reasonable,' said Greco. 'The maresciallo can be a witness to an informal conversation. If at the end of our conversation he feels that action needs to be taken, I am sure he will perform his duties. I will, if necessary, repeat everything I tell you here because all I have to say is that, for me, my wife, my ex-wife after the divorce *in absentia*, was always worth more than a little trouble.'

'She and her lover took off for Australia?'

'That's what I heard,' said Greco, his eyes unblinking, his jaw straight and unreadable. At least he had the decency not to smirk. 'Of course, there is no telling if it's true.'

'Because Australian immigration has no record of her entering. I found that nugget in the very brief file compiled by the prosecuting magistrate in 1993.'

'Mistakes are made, things were laxer back then. And before you say it, no record of her or Giuliano. I think they changed their names illegally so they would never be found. It can be done, you know.'

'Between her disappearance and your reporting it . . .'

'Ten days elapsed, yes. That seems very suspicious, I agree. I was humiliated. I could not bear it to be known that I was a cuckold. We southerners. . . .' This time there was a hint of a smirk as he continued, 'It is interesting though that *his* family did not report him missing.'

'He was a young man. Ten days without contacting his family is not exceptional – I am sure they would have filed a missing person form eventually,' said Blume, annoyed to find himself having to make up explanations. He should have woven that into the story, been prepared for it.

'But they didn't,' said Greco. 'And I did. The investigators at the time – No, forget it. I don't even know why I am answering these insinuations.'

The maresciallo snuffled to show he was still there, though the expression on his face suggested that he did not want to be.

'Humiliating,' said Blume.

'Yes. Which is why I left. I wanted to leave everything including the way I had been living. Also, I had this idea of a garden being ideal for bringing up a child. That's why I chose it.'

'How did you find it?'

'I heard a place was open. They didn't seem too bothered about whether I knew anything about gardening.'

'Did you?'

'My parents worked the land. And no one else wanted the job. It pays badly and is hard work. Also, I was lucky I made some friends on the town council.' Greco rubbed his finger and thumb together.

The maresciallo smiled wistfully as if visited by a pleasant image in a dream.

'You bribed them?'

'Yes,' said Greco. 'I bribed them to get a low paying job that no one wanted. Are you going to try to do something about that, Blume?'

'No, I'm not. You got rich from – let's ignore your earliest past – factoring. It's one of those terms I've heard all my life and never looked up properly.'

'It's like lending. That's all there is to it.'

'Uh-huh? Maresciallo, are you following this? Do you know about factoring?'

The maresciallo opened a sly eye. 'Has it something to do with farms?'

'Well, Maresciallo,' said Greco, 'let's say you are a company, and you sell a whole load of . . . olive oil centrifuges.'

'See? Farming instruments.' The maresciallo looked pleased.

'Centrifuges, washing machines, fresh pasta,' continued Greco. 'Then you sell your product to customers. These people then owe you money, right?'

'Yes, we get that,' said Blume impatiently.

But the maresciallo was enchanted to be included in so complex a discourse. He even went so far as to say, 'I can see the logic there.'

'But sometimes they take their time in paying. Sometimes it's just the normal 30 days, sometimes three months, sometimes they have genuine problems, often they are cheats. For one reason or another, it takes longer than you can afford. So you go to a factoring company, and you ask them to buy your receivables, and give you the money right away, obviously taking a percentage. So if someone owes you €100, the factoring company may give you €90. Then it is up to the factoring company to get the money from the customer. If the customer never pays, the factoring company loses.'

'Marvellous,' said the maresciallo. 'And you thought of this?' He looked admiringly at Greco.

'Yes, but a factoring company has to have a way of making sure the customer pays,' added Blume. 'How does it do that? Threats?'

'Legal threats, yes. Lots of lawyers in the business,' said Greco. The maresciallo nodded enthusiastically and glared at Blume, defying him to fault the logic.

'So, obviously, the factoring company needs to have a lot of cash. It's sort of like a bank in that way, right?' said Blume.

The maresciallo frowned. Blume had lost him.

'So you moved out of that profitable line of work and became a gardener. That's not something you hear every day,' said Blume.

'St Francis of Assisi renounced his wealth,' said Greco.

The maresciallo tapped his thumbs together in minute applause at the comparison.

'And was Nicola Solito, Niki to his friends, one of the debt collectors?' pursued Blume.

'Niki was the accountant. Hardly a debt collector, him. The size of him.'

'But you worked together and . . .'

In a burst of alertness, the maresciallo suddenly interrupted. '*Niki* as in Niki's the club. *That* Niki? Your daughter's, um, friend? I didn't know he used to work for you, Mimmo. You should have told me that.' The maresciallo looked sorely tempted to pick up a pen and write a note, but settled instead for a severe frown of concentration.

Blume opened his notebook and pretended to be looking for something. The maresciallo was listening properly now.

'Mr Greco,' said Blume, 'On the day your wife ran away, you were in Foggia waiting for her there?'

Greco fingered his upper lip, and stayed silent.

'You waited at the Foggia train station, and she never showed, I believe? And then when they eventually, reluctantly, investigated a bit, they found proof that she had in fact boarded at Bari on the train for Foggia. May I ask what you were doing in Foggia?'

'Work.'

'Fair enough. And back then, it was established that your wife got on the train bound for Foggia from Bari Central Station. How did they do that?'

'Video footage.'

'Damn, we cops are good. They managed to identify her from CCTV?'

'They asked me to look at it, and I saw her. Just her.'

'You saw her get on the train?'

'Yes. I saw her. I can sue you for defamation. The maresciallo is my witness.'

'Give me some more rope to hang myself with, then,' said Blume. 'And forgive me for saying none of this makes sense. If she was going to run away, why would she have gone to get that train? I mean, if she was planning to run off to Australia, or get away from you – I'm sorry if the memory is painful – why not get a flight out of there, a ferry to Greece, a train in the opposite direction?'

'Maybe she meant to come to me, but changed her mind at the last moment.'

'So she got off the train a few stops early? Do you think her lover, Giuliano, was waiting for her between Bari and Foggia?'

'That's a possibility, but the Carabinieri think she may have gone on to Rome, staying on the train longer rather than getting off early.'

'The train went all the way to Rome, then? It was an intercity?'

'I have no idea.'

'Because if not, she would have changed at Foggia where you say you were waiting. Wouldn't you have seen her?'

'One more word out of you, and I am going to denounce you here in this office.'

The maresciallo looked unhappy and made a calming gesture with his hands. 'I am not following all this.'

'Blume here is just trying to plant poisonous seeds of doubt in your mind,' said Greco.

From the maresciallo's face, Blume knew he had succeeded, though it might take ten slow conversations before the maresciallo actually understood anything. By now, it was a direct battle between him and Greco.

'You think you have cracked it all wide open. But you haven't. I loved my wife with all my heart. You can't understand that because you don't love your wife nearly enough.'

Blume felt the chill of the previous night seize hold again. Simply by introducing the idea of a wife, Greco was threatening Caterina. Greco knew Blume had received the message, which had sailed far over the maresciallo's nodding head.

'She's not my wife,' said Blume.

'Exactly. That says everything about you. And your daughter? I had mine learning to walk in the grass beside me, playing in the warmth of the courtyard in the evening outside the lodge, playing hide and seek and *lupo mangia frutta* with her friends, while I stood and watched her grow. Where's your daughter, Blume? What would you do if someone threatened her?'

Fuck. Not even the slumbering maresciallo could have missed that. 'Maresciallo,' said Blume. 'Maresciallo!'

'What? I'm listening.'

'You recognize that for what it was?'

'Mimmo here merely said . . .'

'Never mind. I should have explained it better to you before this. This man wants to sue me for calumny. So let us be clear, then, about what I am saying. I believe Domenico Greco killed his wife and her lover, or got Niki to do it for him, or they did it together. That's the hold Niki has over him. That's why he is allowing his daughter, the one he claims to love so tenderly, to be importuned by that misfit with his discos and his prostitutes, his . . . creams, and tattoos and hairless chest, and plastic surgeon's nose.'

'Maresciallo,' said Greco, 'you do realize the Commissioner is talking about a case that was already closed in 1994?'

It was all too much for Panfilo Angelozzi. He stood up; he sat down; he spoke: 'I suggest you two reach a settlement of some sort and present a coherent version of events. If you cannot come to agreement, then we shall take separate statements from you and pass them on to the office of prosecution.'

The phone on his desk rang. Never was a man more pleased to receive a call, but the pleasure did not last long. 'What? Who? Are they sure? *Santo Dio!* No question that it might be . . . Because people sometimes throw rubbish down there. I see.'

He put down the phone. 'Signori, please leave my office.'

They looked at him, both taken aback by the unexpected sound of real authority in his voice. 'I am afraid something has come up. This –' he waved his hand dismissively at them both, 'can wait for another day.'

'What's happened?' asked Blume.

'I am not at liberty to say.'

'We're colleagues of a sort, remember?' said Blume.

'I believe you are on leave and,' he nodded at Greco, 'a civilian is present.'

'I'm a commissioner of a murder squad, Maresciallo. I recognize the sort of call that you have just received. Where was the body found?'

'You could never have heard . . .' He peered at Blume's ears suspiciously. 'Then you will also recognize that I will not respond to such questions, and that you must leave now.'

27

'GIVE ME a lift into town, Greco?' said Blume, as they left the Carabinieri station.

'*Stramilamurt ca tin, 'mbam*,' snarled Greco. 'We're not finished.' He pushed past Blume and jumped into the old Fiat in which, only days ago, Blume had lain gasping for breath. The memory gave him a momentary pause, since, looked at from a certain angle, Greco might even have saved his life.

'Who's dead, Greco?' he shouted after him.

He asked the same question of the maresciallo, who had assumed a very a dignified mien, and walked with his head up and a look of purpose on his face. Behind him, the *appuntato* was almost jumping with the excitement of it all.

'I have not been informed, Commissioner. The investigating magistrate is on his way.'

'Where?'

'At the bottom of an escarpment on the far side of town.'

'Male or female.'

'First reports speak of a female,' said the maresciallo, practising his television manner. 'No doubt further details will become available as . . . we find further details concerning . . .'

Blume had already started walking. He had parked the SUV just inside the walls, no more than a minute or two away. Nadia had not called him yet, and he was worried. On his way to the car, he called her and it went to voicemail.

He called her twice more, still without response, the second time as he was driving past the clinic out the arched town gate. He hit redial several times during the drive to her apartment. He had not foreseen this.

Thirty minutes later, he jumped out of the car and ran into the ghastly green block, fearing the worst and cursing himself for having left her. If they could kill Alina, they could kill Nadia, especially if they knew she was kicking up a fuss. Whatever about poor Alina, for whom he had always been too late, Nadia was his responsibility.

He smashed open the front door of the building with two sharp kicks, but found himself bathed in sweat and unable to run up the stairs. His fever was mounting again. Each foot fall shuddered up from heel through spine into his brainstem. He started hammering on the door of her apartment. No one came. He kicked it, centring the escutcheon with his heel, but though the door shuddered and the wood in the frame crackled a little, it hardly budged. He tried again, but this time his kick was less accurate. If she were dead in there . . . He needed the right sort of equipment and he had none. He was mulling over the complications of calling in backup, when he heard footsteps, fast and thunderous rushing down the stairs. Coming down the corridor, in arrow formation with the smallest in front and the largest two behind were the three Montenegrins.

'Looking for Nadia?' said Hristjian, the photographer of the day before.

Blume looked at his options. He had the overwhelming sense that they were the only people in the building, and no one would hear him being kicked to death on the ground.

'I am Police,' he said. 'And I need to know where Nadia is.'

'You are an off-duty busybody,' said the Montenegrin in his perfect Italian, which had a hint of Calabrese in it. 'But you're in luck.'

'How so?'

'We're looking for Nadia, too.'

Blume, belatedly realizing she might be cowed inside, placed himself between the men and Nadia's door. 'What do you plan to do with her?'

'Locate her.'

'And then?'

'Ask her if she knows where that fucker Niki has got to.'

'Niki's gone?'

'He never came to the club last night. Neither did Nadia. He owes us money.'

'What for?'

'Wages, what else? He's been putting it off, and breaking his promises for weeks. He said again yesterday that he would pay us, but he has taken off. His car's gone. Not the SUV you're driving obviously. His Range Rover. Then we noticed Nadia wasn't around either.'

Blume stood away from the door, and the oldest of the three nodded at the two behind him who, with a single unified and unexpectedly graceful movement, hit the door simultaneously, one with his shoulder, the other, slightly to his right, with his foot. The wood frame gave way with a short sharp crack and the door jumped open. Politely, Hristjian ushered Blume in first. 'If you don't mind my saying so, you shouldn't be trying to kick in doors in your condition.'

'My condition?'

'You do not look well. It had better not be contagious.'

By way of reply Blume said, 'We're looking for a passport or any indication of where she might have gone.' He walked through the living room, which showed no signs of struggle. He checked the bedroom where the bed was neatly made up. The furry blue gorilla and the panda bear sat exactly where they had been the day before. 'She didn't sleep here,' he said, as much to himself as to the three large Montenegrins stumbling around the apartment, looking for clues and making a nightmare of any forensic work that might have to be done later.

There was nothing in the apartment to indicate where she had gone. The Montenegrins might, he supposed, be playing an elaborate game for his benefit to divert suspicion that they had anything to do with her disappearance, but their imprecations and oaths suggested otherwise. They were seriously pissed off, and, if they were really trying to persuade a policeman that they had nothing to do with any violence that might have been perpetrated against Nadia, then perhaps they would not have repeated so often their plans to kill, burn, strangle, and slit the throat of Niki.

Blume's impression was that this was more than a question of unpaid wages. There was urgency and an edge of fear to the way they were behaving. If so, he was not going to look too deeply into it. He had enough on his plate already. He called over the leader, Hristjian, the photographer, as he thought of him.

'I want to find Nadia. If I find Niki, I'll let you know. This is not an official investigation yet. I don't want bad things – more bad things – to happen to Nadia.'

The man squinted at Blume, then nodded quickly.

'Is Niki in financial difficulty?' asked Blume.

'Not that I know of.'

'Is this the first time he has missed a payment?'

Hristjian frowned. 'Yeah, I guess it is. He has been distracted recently. We thought it was because of Alina running off like that.'

'So you think she ran off?'

'I don't know. She went. Niki was upset. He got distracted, and now there is serious trouble.'

'Did Alina like Niki as much as he seems to have liked her?'

The man scowled at him. 'Girls worry about that sort of shit. Do I look like a girl?'

'No, you can rest assured on that point,' said Blume. 'But they were together?'

A shrug. 'Ownership has its privileges.'

'This has to do with more than just wages, right?'

'What do you mean?'

'Why you're so anxious to find Niki. It's a debt of some sort, which puts you in danger. I'm thinking drugs.'

The man took a menacing step towards him, but Blume stayed put. 'Speaking as a policeman, but one off-duty and not interested in doing you any disservice . . .'

'Yeah?'

'No matter what, you need to front the money. Pay whoever it is with your own money, if you have enough. You can get Niki later. Pay up: I have seen what happens in these cases, and I think you have, too.'

'With our money? Niki's debt?'

'Yes. Because if they don't find Niki, you'll do instead, as an example. You know how it works.'

The man regarded him levelly, then imperceptibly nodded. With that nod, Blume had confirmation that Niki was in the drugs trade.

He hoped Hristjian would follow his advice. He needed his prosecution witnesses to be alive.

Hristjian evidently felt he had been helpful enough. He clicked his fingers and said something in whatever it was they spoke in Montenegro, and the three of them left the apartment with its splintered door.

Ten minutes later, after a quieter and more scientific search of the apartment had yielded nothing, he went outside again. The sun was strong now and he donned his orange Gucci sunglasses. As he was climbing into the SUV, his phone rang. It was an unknown number from a landline with the local area code.

'Alfredo here. The parts have arrived. Your car will be ready tomorrow morning.'

'I don't care . . . No, wait. Listen, there was some sort of accident in the town today. Do you know anything about it?'

'Oh that. The maresciallo is being very secretive. Earlier this morning, Pino – you won't know him, he's an ancient greengrocer uptown, terrible prices and lousy fruit – well, this Pino says he saw a body lying at the bottom of a ravine below his back garden, which is where he gets most of the lousy fruit he sells, by the way. A few other neighbours looked over the wall, and concluded it was just clothes. No one really listens to Pino, you see. Then one of these neighbours fetches a pair of binoculars, and they take turns staring down at these clothes, and it turns out that Pino was probably right. It seems to be a body.'

'Any idea whose?'

'They're not saying if they know – also because they are only getting down there now with their ropes. It's a long drop to the bottom. But word is no one in town is missing, thanks be to God, so it was probably an outsider. Maybe a gypsy thief. It's unlikely to be a tourist, since we don't get any. The fire brigade arrived with ropes, you know, to pull the body up, and had to carry them up the last bit. I expect we'll hear soon enough.'

That had better not be you, down in that ravine, Nadia, Blume thought to himself. And if it is, I am sorry.

28

'ALEC!' SILVANA was delighted to see him. 'I thought you were Niki. Did he lend you that car? He hardly ever uses it. Are you coming in?'

'Is your father about?'

'Somewhere in the garden, as always. Why, do you want to talk to him?'

'Maybe later,' said Blume. Maybe later, after he had delivered his message, she would fall weeping into his arms, fly at him with her fists, or, and this was his objective, leave the house and garden under his protection.

She smelled of pears. Her dark hair was wet and shining and sleek, she must have just showered, and some drops of water had fallen onto her sleeveless top. She was barefoot. Her feet were the same golden colour as the rest of her skin. He thought of his own feet, whiter than the rest of him, cold, flat, waxy, like the feet of a corpse.

As he passed her on the way into the lodge, she laid a reassuring hand lightly on his arm. 'You look terrible, Alec. I'll get you something.' She brushed by him on her way to the kitchen.

He sat there staring at his arm, defying it to lose the tingling sensation it had received when she touched it. She came back with a green liquid in a glass and sat down in a chair opposite.

He looked at it suspiciously. 'What's this, a cabbage smoothie?'

'It's not cabbage, silly.' She aimed a playful kick at him and he moved his leg to make sure she got him. To be polite, he brought it up to his nose.

'Go on! You're like a child, Alec. It's rock rose, impatiens, clematis, star-of-Bethlehem, cherry plum and crab apple. It's absolutely delicious. And it's good for curing trauma.'

'Why is it so green: is that the apple?' He took a very small sip.

She leaned forward. 'Shall I tell you a little secret?'

For a moment, he thought he might let Greco off the hook. After all, it was a long time ago, and Greco had taken him up to the clinic. All he had to do to preserve the happiness of the young woman in front of him, was to keep quiet. But what of afterwards? How could he leave Silvana ignorant of the true nature of her father, and, possibly, in danger from a man her father seemed happy to marry her off to? He had a duty to release this girl, who had now brought a finger up to her lips, as if warning him not to broadcast the great secret she was about to tell.

'I put food colouring in! Isn't that so naughty! It's supposed to be all natural, no adulteration, the vibration of the Bach Flowers, and, sure, I believe in all that, but that green is just such a far-out lovely colour, and then I find out that food colouring, if you buy the right one, is vegetable based! By the way, my secret ingredient is a thing called glucomannan, it's a dietary fibre from the root of the konjac flower, from Asia. It adds body to the drink, and it's really good for you. It's great for the heart, I read that. Or is it the bowel?'

He went for another reluctant sip, and said, casually, 'Seen Niki recently?'

'Dear Niki. He's so busy at work, then rushes over here to be with me as soon as he has a minute. I am often afraid he'll have a car accident.'

'That would be terrible,' said Blume.

She wrinkled her forehead at him then and squeezed a few more drops or water from her hair onto her loose-fitting T-shirt. 'You loathe Niki, don't you? I thought when I saw you get out of his car that there had been some sort of reconciliation. Lending his car is just the sort of generous thing he would do.'

'I have seen the way Niki bosses you about. It is the mark of a bully and a violent man. You know what I'm saying.'

Silvana ran her tongue over her bottom lip, and sighed. 'Niki only does that for show. It was because you were there. When we are on our own, he is the sweetest guy on earth.'

He thought of her chubby, childish handwriting. 'Isn't he a bit old for you? And when I say a bit, I mean a lot?'

'Age can't stop you loving, but loving can stop you ageing,' said Silvana, looking at him earnestly.

'New Age cant. You found that platitude on the internet, probably with a picture of two old wrinklies dressed in white staring at a sunset, holding hands, and figured you should learn it to explain the fact you're throwing yourself away on a creepy little criminal almost twice your age.'

'You would be far more attractive if you were kinder.'

'Kind like Niki who beats you?'

'He does not hit me.'

'I saw it, for God's sake.'

'You never think you might have mis-seen?'

'No.'

'Always clear-headed, are you?'

Blume sat back and let out a long, long breath, releasing a lot of the tension in his chest. This was so frustrating. Why was this woman not responding better to him? 'Just say the word and I can get you out of here.'

'Where would you take me. To your house?'

'No! I mean, there would be room, but no, of course not. Wherever you wanted to go.'

'In Rome? I have been to Rome. I studied there.'

'You should have found someone there and stayed.'

'I did. I found a boyfriend there, too. An older man. Almost drove Niki to distraction. They never met, which is probably a good thing.'

'You like older men?'

'Yes, Commissioner, I do.'

Blume averted his gaze and began looking around the room for something to look at that wasn't her face, legs, bare shoulder, the way the T-shirt fell away when she leaned in.

Everything in the room seemed to be made of wood: the walls, the parquet floor, the cherrywood shelves stocked neatly with dark orange bottles in the style of a ninteenth-century chemist. The bottles had handwritten labels on them identifying their contents. The writing was not a stylized calligraphy but again those bulky, childish letters. The room smelled of pine and vanilla. In the centre, a table contained a pile of articles, the pages black around the edges and in the middle from inexpert photocopying.

Then he remembered the exercise book, which he had left in the car.

'I brought your notebook back, the one with the stories? You left it the other day, and I've been meaning to return it, but what with one thing and another . . . It's in the car. I can fetch it.' He stood up.

'Never mind. You can do that later. Or just leave it in the car, since it's Niki's. Did you read the stories?'

'They are . . .' He wandered across the room to look at the collection of herbal bottles and avoid her questions. 'I don't think I am your target audience.'

'Don't you have children?'

'I do, as a matter of fact.'

'Well, then.' She stood up and skipped over the room to where he was. 'I'm hoping to have them published as soon as I find a decent illustrator.' She brought her hand up to his brow and furrowed her own. 'Are you feeling all right, Alec? Because you don't look well.'

'I may have a touch of the flu,' he admitted, pulling back. 'It's been trying to break through for the past 24 hours.'

'I could give you an elixir or an infusion. Would you like that?'

He nodded, then asked, 'What's the difference?'

'An infusion is made with water, but for the delicate flowers we don't boil the water like when making tea. We leave the flowers suspended in water for several hours in the sun. We do use boiling water for the woodier plants, like hornbeam. And for the tinctures, we use Italian brandy. Tomorrow night is special because there is going to be a super-moon, when the moon is both full and nearest to the earth. It looks huge in the sky and its influence is enhanced. Tomorrow will be an ideal night to make tincture.'

She pointed to the first bottle. 'Remember this yellow one? Agrimony. It's an autochthonous plant. Autochthonous means it is native to Italy.'

'I know what autochthonous means,' said Blume.

'Really? I had to ask Papà to explain. Anyway, not all of them are native. My father grows this in his herb garden. Actually, he's grown all of them except for the tree one, which was already here.' She swept her slender arm through the air to indicate the large outside world.

'And what's it for?'

'It cures people who look cheerful, but are tortured inside. People who fear the unknown. That's not you, though, is it?' She laughed. 'I mean you don't look all that cheerful on the outside either.'

'I am extremely cheerful on the inside.'

She looked at him and bit her lip as if considering this as a real possibility before passing on to the next bottle. 'Now this one here is centaury, or *Centaurea minore* to use the Latin. We prescribe it to people who can't say no to others, people who are a bit weak-willed and get exploited. I have prescribed it to myself, actually.'

'Any improvement?'

'I think so, yes. I feel a good deal stronger than I used to.'

'So you let Niki bully you less?'

She ignored his question. 'This here is chicory, which a lot of people eat anyhow. It's for people who are very possessive and will even hurt others to make sure they stay under their control.'

'Presumably I would have learned about this on the course.'

'Yes. I was going to teach all that. Another time, I suppose.'

Blume leaned against the wall, which was pleasantly cold to the touch, and folded his arms, watching her. 'It is a shame you had to cancel it,' he said. 'What was it again? Some problem with the licences from those bureaucrats at health and safety?'

She nodded.

'And the *vigili* came down and ordered you to close down the wing of the house you had done up, right? And so you sent out the emails cancelling the course, the one I failed to read.'

'Yes, that's what happened.'

'Funny thing, though,' said Blume. 'I happened to bump into Fabio, the *vigile*. Literally bump into him as you may have heard. And, well, he denied doing any such thing. He never executed any order from the ASL to shut you down.'

'Oh, I see.' She stood still for a moment, and her shoulders seemed to tremble. He was torn between the desire to put his arm around them and the wish to push home an advantage that he had not yet turned into an insight.

Silvana took a wicker chair, carried it over, and sat down close to him so he was looming over her as he stood there. He felt like a bully.

'Do you want to know why I told that little white lie?'

'I am interested,' said Blume.

'It's funny, but with you I don't feel so embarrassed; but in front of those people, you know, the others who didn't get their emails, I felt humiliated and stupid. The truth is that Niki, who was never enthusiastic about this whole herbal enterprise of mine, suddenly decided to tell. He told me it was either the course or him.'

'And you chose him?' Blume asked incredulously.

A tear ran down the side of her nose. She flicked it away with her little finger and smiled at him. 'I know you don't understand. You made that perfectly clear in the car park.' She gave a resigned laugh. 'I realize Niki might not seem much, but . . . he is so much part of my life now. He always has been. I don't want him to go away. It would break my father's heart, too. They have known each other for years – but you knew that, didn't you?'

'Yes, I found out.'

'Look . . . The thing is I couldn't bring myself to marry him, even though he wanted me to. I was waiting for Mr Right, except how am I supposed to find Mr Right in this place?'

'Maybe by starting a Bach Flowers course and seeing who'd turn up,' said Blume.

'Exactly! Which is why he put his foot down at the last moment.'

'Is he as faithful to you as you are to him?'

'I know, I know.' She looked at him as if pleading for his understanding, but once again, of Niki, not herself. 'He has that nightclub. He calls it Niki's nightclub. I mean that's its name.'

'A narcissistic name,' said Blume.

'Is that how you see it? I see it as sort of innocent, the sort of name a child would choose. I think it's sweet, really. Look, I know temptation lies in his way, and I know he gives into it now and then, but I believe him when he says the only person he really wants is me. He even offered to close the nightclub down once, as a sign of good faith.'

'And you didn't accept?'

She looked at him uncomprehendingly for a second. 'No! What would Niki do here? It's what he does, and he's good at it.'

'I've seen the nightclub. It's a bit squalid.'

'Exactly. He spends no more on it than he needs to. He takes out of it what he can. He knows it won't last forever, and does not want to invest in it.'

'What does he want to invest in instead?'

'More beautiful things. Perhaps the villa some day. In me. When the time is ripe. But first I want to teach him some tenderness and respect.'

'Is the time almost ripe, do you think?' said Blume. 'I only ask because Niki has fled.'

His comment hit home. She sat back in her chair, mouth slightly open, then recovered her poise. 'Niki, fled? He'll be back.'

'I am not sure that he will, unless he's caught. And if you want us to catch him, then maybe you should consider telling us everything you know.'

'Who is this "us"?'

'The authorities. The police.'

'I thought you and I were getting on better than that.' She stood up, and turned so that the sun streaming in the window lit up her hair with auburn highlights and bathed her in golden light. He still felt an ache of loss in himself and a shudder of regret at images of her and Niki together, her father looking on, nodding his walnut face in satisfied agreement.

'I don't understand why you say Niki has *fled*,' she said, with rather more scorn than he had imagined possible from her. 'All you mean is you cannot find him at this moment.'

'The corpse of a woman has been found in town, at the bottom of a gully.'

'Really?'

He interrupted, 'Do you know Nadia?'

'A Romanian girl, friend of that one who ran off.'

'Nadia has gone missing, too.'

Even in shock, she was elegant. The weakness in her knees caused her to sway sideways, like a dancer executing a flexing exercise. She reached out for the back of the chair, but by the time her hand had arrived, she had already collected herself enough merely to touch it, as if for luck. But her face was still drained of colour. A part of him that he did not like that much felt vindicated and satisfied.

'First Alina, now Nadia. Surely you see some sort of pattern?'

She nodded.

'Not that he necessarily . . .'

'When did Nadia vanish?'

'Last night or early this morning. I have not established exactly when.'

'You have not been asking around town yet? In case someone has seen her. Or Niki, for that matter.'

'I'll be dealing with that later. What I want you to do now is come with me.'

Silvana took his hand. 'Thank you for being so good to me.'

Gently he disengaged his hand from hers. 'I don't think I am being good to you, and I have not finished yet.'

She went back to the shelf and distractedly pulled down a bottle. 'This, is helianthemum, or rock rose. It stops panic attacks.' She took a glass from the shelf below and half filled it. 'You don't mind?' She drank.

She moved on to the next jar. 'This is autumn gentian. It's for people who have lost all hope and feel depressed. And this one here, is an infusion of mimulus, which is also for panic and fear. I am going to mix them.'

'I thought that the other one you just showed me was for panic and fear.'

'Rock rose cures fear of the unknown. Mimulus cures fear of the known. The first is an Alpine flower, but my father manages to cultivate it in the cold garden, the part under the black cliff. The second is not a native to Italy, and so my father grows that, too. I mean, he grows them all, but those two are especially hard for him. Down towards the end of the row there is another tincture of beech. I think maybe you should try some.'

'I try not to drink spirits, and if I start, I don't think it'll be with beech brandy,' said Blume.

'Well, you should. It's a remedy against hypercriticism, arrogance, bullying, and rigidity.' She took another glass and put about two fingers of what looked like ordinary water into it. 'I am adding some mimulus against fear of the unknown, and mustard. It acts against melancholy. Here.'

He sniffed it and wrinkled his nose at the faint stench of water left in a vase full of dying flowers. 'I've just had that green juice.'

'That was to refresh you. This is to cure you.'

'I don't need curing.'

She held out another jar: 'Honeysuckle for nostalgia. Do you want some of this, too?'

'I'm fine, thanks.' Blume drank his concoction. It was not as bad as he thought. Slightly sweet, flowery, the water a tiny bit brackish. He gulped it down and wiped his mouth with the back of his hand.

'Silvana, I have also been filling a notebook with a story you need to read. But I don't want us to do it here.'

'Wait. Have some more of this.'

'I don't need any more, thanks,' said Blume.

'You don't need to drink it.' She took another bottle, uncorked it, and inhaled, then held it out to him. 'Just smell that.'

Blume inhaled. The scent was slightly medicinal, sharp, earthy, and filled him with an unexpected longing for something he could not even identify.

'Like it?'

'Yes.'

'That's heather. There is a tiny patch of it in the cold garden. It cures loneliness.' She inhaled it, too. 'We both need it.'

'Silvana? We need to go. You can help me find Niki.'

'Wait, this concoction here . . .'

'I am not interested in . . .' A slight clink came from the shelf as a light tremor caused two bottles to touch and the wooden floorboards behind him creaked.

He turned round at the same time as Silvana cried out, 'Papà!'

Silvana's father was standing behind them.

29

DOMENICO GRECO held only a trowel in his hand, but he was doing his best to make it look as threatening as a pistol.

'There you are, Greco,' said Blume, surprising even himself at how calm sounded.

Greco turned to his daughter. 'Go up to the town. Fetch the chicken wire I ordered from the hardware store. Stay for lunch. Go up to where the fire brigade are trying to retrieve a body. Talk to people. Be seen.'

'But . . .'

'*Silvana!*'

For a moment she seemed to stand her ground, and he tried a more conciliatory approach. 'It will be all right. Mr Blume and I can go into the orchard, and pick some nice salad ingredients, and maybe some fruit. He looks like a man who could do with some sunshine and good food. Silvana, *dolcezza mia*,' repeated her father, '*ora?*'

Before leaving, she touched him on the arm. 'Thanks for everything you have tried to do, Alec.'

'That's all right. I haven't quite finished yet, I'm afraid.'

'Well, you should. You have done too much already.' She grabbed a straw bag with a red flower from the back of a chair and slung it over her shoulder. 'My shopping bag,' she said, apologetically. 'Natural fibre, reusable, and completely impractical. Bye, Alec.' She gave him a sad smile and left.

Greco laid down the trowel on a bench. 'Let's wait till she's gone, all right?'

'Fine by me,' said Blume. Minutes later, a car engine started up, the gravel crackled, there was a slight swish as the tires found purchase, and then the engine faded. Something about her going was final, and something in her reactions had been wrong. He needed to think about it, but he had Greco to deal with again, and, truth be told, he was feeling very weak. Half his medicine was still in his room. He took out a blister packet from his inside pocket and, without quite checking what it was, popped out a pill.

'Shall we step outside?' said Greco.

'Fine,' said Blume. 'Let me just get some water. I'm suddenly very thirsty.'

'Always thirsty,' said Greco. 'Same as last time.'

Blume walked out of the long room into the antechamber, full of its baskets of dried petals, the sewing machine, the potter's wheel, the potpourris, and its dark corners. He glanced at the old keys hanging on a nail in the wall. Instinctively, he grabbed them.

'What do you want those for?' said Greco. 'Those are Silvana's keys for the villa. We're not going there.'

Blume kept his back to Greco, listening to the rhythm of the footsteps behind him, giving the man plenty of time to make his move. The rhythm changed just before he reached the door. Blume, strangely calm, as if he were controlling the entire scene from above and was almost neutral to the fate of the two characters below, swung round quickly, or as quickly as he could manage, and rushed Greco from the side, just as the old man was pulling a break-action double-barrelled shotgun from below an old wooden barrow laden with sachets of lavender. Blume tossed the keys, grabbed the two barrels, jerked the weapon out of the old man's grasp, and then reversed his movement so that the butt went in hard against Greco's jaw. Greco sat down suddenly on the floor. Blume spun the weapon round, slapping the stock with his hand as he did so. Quickly he shouldered it, then, finger on the trigger, crouched down so that the muzzle was inches from Greco's eye socket. The old man hardly flinched. Blume retrieved the ring of keys.

'Stand up,' ordered Blume.

Greco sat there in defiant silence.

'What were you thinking?' asked Blume.

'I forget how old I am. You're not so snappy either, Commissioner. It's not loaded. I just did it for effect.'

Blume stepped back a few paces and broke open the action. Empty. He threw the gun aside. His finger had started to bleed again.

'Come here.' He patted Greco down. No weapons, no shotgun cartridges even. Blume sucked his finger. 'What was the point of that?'

'People reveal their true natures under the barrel of a gun. I wanted to see what you really want, and I didn't want to waste time. Things are moving fast now. You have already destroyed this world.'

'That was a dangerous way of finding out. Wouldn't it have made more sense for you to have come in with the shotgun already pointing at me?'

'Not in front of my daughter.'

'We can have a frank discussion without either of us pointing a weapon at the other,' said Blume.

'We are already pointing virtual weapons at each other. I can have you killed. I can have your girlfriend killed, estranged or not. I know her name. I can have your baby daughter killed. You were so intent on finding out what sort of man I used to be that it did not occur to you that I might become that sort of man again. I have been speaking to people I would rather not have spoken to again. You made me do that.'

Blume took three quick steps across the floorboards and slapped Greco across the face. He grabbed the old man by the ear and slammed his head against the floor, but his strength was fading, or else his heart was not in it.

'You don't care, do you Blume? I really do not want any of this to happen. Why not just let it all go?'

A wave of light-headedness washed over Blume. It was as if part of his mind had moved to a position somewhere behind him and was now observing the person called Blume with ironic detachment. 'Let's continue the conversation outside,' said Greco. 'I have something to show you.'

'Don't get any ideas,' Blume warned him.

The sun reflected harshly off the white pebble paths. He pulled out his sunglasses, which darkened the green around him to a shade of purple. The air hummed with insects and heat. Things moved in the bushes, and a thin plant of some sort was nodding and twisting all by itself, although there was no wind. The bushes creaked and the grass seemed to sigh. The birdsong from the top of the trees came from what he felt was a cooler and freer place than the one he was trapped in now.

'Sacra Corona Unita,' said Greco. 'It's not much of a mafia compared with the others. I think it's because the ordinary citizens of Apulia have bigger balls than those of Calabria or Sicily, certainly

255

bigger than the people of Campania who allow themselves to be ruled by the Camorra.'

'You're a member?'

'No, and I never was. But I know people who are. And so does Niki.'

'And these are the people who would kill me and Caterina and my child?'

'They might, if I asked. They would if I could present you as a direct threat.'

'Did you murder your wife and her lover, Domenico?'

'I like that, you go back to the intimate first name when you ask me the question. Yes, I did.'

'And did Niki help you?'

'Yes. But he never knew what I had planned. He thought it would be a beating, or a warning. He had no idea.'

'I am not sure I believe that.'

'He didn't know. He has been traumatized since.'

'Poor guy. Did he help you dispose of the bodies?'

'Yes.'

'Where?'

'In a deep underground cave, as I think you had guessed.'

'And why the sudden confession?'

'Because it is all coming to an end anyhow, and because I want to ask you a favour.'

'I am not going to give you any favours. You threatened Caterina and our child.'

'Yes, I did, but you did not back down. So you win. You are willing to sacrifice anyone. Me, I can't do that any more.'

'You just threatened . . .'

'Your Caterina and Alessia are not in any danger. I used my contacts to get their names and addresses, just to intimidate you. Like with the empty shotgun. I would never order a hit on a woman and her daughter. Do you know the story of Cincinnatus, who got total military power, then gave it all up and returned to his farm? I like that story. Cincinnatus fought his last battle against the Aequi not far from where we are standing now.'

'You see yourself as a Roman hero?'

'No. I only said I liked the story. For more than 20 years, I have been trying to make things right. Then along you come. Nemesis in the form of a self-righteous, washed-up . . .'

'What's the deal you want to make?'

'Don't use the past against Niki. Leave something for my daughter. Niki's a good man. He lived with this for my sake, and he has done his best ever since, even if that does mean running coke up from Bari and feeding it to politicians. What else can he do? He has no other skills. If I go, who will look after Silvana? You are ruining her life.'

'No, you did that.'

'Yes, but you are finishing the job.'

They had walked deeper into the garden towards the cliff face.

'Why would I want to do that?'

'Human decency? Maybe if you talk to the people who have known us since that period you have been obsessing about? Look into our lives after the murder. You might see two people trying to do the best . . .'

'Like killing Alina, and now Nadia?'

Greco stopped at a stone bench and sat down. Blume stood in front of him.

'I don't know what's going on there. I asked him. It's complicated.'

'What is?'

'Niki fell for Alina. That much is clear. And I was very angry with him, because his job is to look after Silvana. We discussed it. I tried to work something out, but Niki was beginning to crumble.'

'And so you killed Alina?'

Greco reclined on a stone bench, as if to sleep. Blume reached down and shook him, then drew his hand away. The old man was bathed in sweat.

'Yes, I killed Alina.'

'How?'

'Strangulation.'

'Is that how you killed your wife?'

'Yes,' he let out a long soft groan.

'Where's the body?'

'Deep underground in Puglia. I put her lover in a cave far away, so they couldn't be together even in death.'

'I meant Alina's body,' said Blume.

'Does it matter?'

'Of course it does. I don't believe you killed Alina. Why are you lying to me?'

'Promise me you'll . . .'

'I promise nothing.'

'At least look at Niki without a filter of hate. Then decide. I wanted to show you something, Blume.' Greco stood up, staggered, and almost fell over.

'What's wrong with you?'

'A righteous bully hit me over the face with the stock of a shotgun, remember? Just hold my arm, and I'll take you to her.'

In the garden. He should have guessed. Alina's body was probably fertilizing the lettuces that Silvana was happily eating as part of her vegan . . . it was hard work holding Greco up. It was as if the trembling in the old man was transferring itself into him, as if the weakness was spreading.

'You don't seem that strong either, Blume. Here she is.'

'Alina?' Blume looked around for disturbed ground.

'No. Look at that statue.'

'That piece of grey rock?'

'Come over here, and have a closer look.'

Blume allowed himself to be led across a short lawn edged with starry white sweet-scented flowers.

'Jasmine,' said Blume, proud of his knowledge. 'The smell.'

'Forgive me if I correct you for the sake of precision,' said Greco. 'But that is *Trachelospermum jasminoides*, a false jasmine. There. You don't see an image of the Madonna?'

Blume went up and examined the rock, which gave the illusion of being free-standing, but was simply a protrusion from a large boulder buried in the ground. He saw no resemblance to a Madonna.

'I didn't see it at first either,' said Greco. 'But once you see her face, you'll always see it.' He touched a ridge. 'Lips, see?'

Blume did not.

'There is a great mystery surrounding her.'

'By "her" you mean this rock?'

'She weeps. The legend is that when she cries, her very first tears will cure whoever drinks them.'

'All these weeping, curing Madonnas, you never see them grow back a missing limb on someone, or anything tangible. Always some inner thing, isn't it? Some disease no one can see.'

'You really are not a believer.'

Blume shrugged and leaned against a lemon tree. He broke a leaf and inhaled the tangy scent in an effort to clear his mind, then remembered his nasal spray.

'That's the thing, no one knows when it will happen, and it is very infrequent. The great mystery is that no one knows where the water comes from.'

Blume snorted the taste of the spray into the back of his throat, but the migraine was descending anyhow. 'We are surrounded by marshes, and Silvana told me there are underground rivers.'

'There is no water below that boulder, and no way for it to permeate its way up. The stature rests on a bed of pink peperino.'

'Condensation, obviously.'

'It's more than that. A full stream comes pouring out of the rocks. No one knows where from.'

'When was last time she cried?'

'In 1994,' said Greco. 'I saw it with my own eyes.'

'Did she cure you?'

'I was not the first to drink her tears.'

'Bad luck.'

'It was Niki.'

'So his diabetes is cured?' said Blume.

'He must have asked for something else.'

'This is what you wanted to show me?'

Greco did not answer, he was cutting a diagonal line in the direction of the villa, careless of the flower beds. Twice he staggered. Blume, his own head throbbing now, quickened his pace and caught up. 'What's the matter with you? What has made you change so much since we met in the maresciallo's office?'

'Palm of Christ, angel trumpets, devil's trumpets, and conium.'

'What have you found out?'

'Not what I have found out; I have been found out. How are you feeling by the way, Blume? You seem feverish to me. Go home. I am not going anywhere.'

Blume looked at the old man, and felt a sudden surge of pity. 'Do you want me to call an ambulance?'

'Just finish your work, Blume. I think you need to hurry. I'll wait.'

30

H E BEGAN shaking as he reached the SUV, and had to steady himself before turning on the engine, then remind himself what he needed to do now. Things had taken an unexpected turn, and the investigative plan he had set out with such clarity the night before was no longer of much use. A different idea, a completely different idea, was forming in his mind now.

The first thing to do was find out about the body at the bottom of the ravine, which did not fit in with anything, not even his new theory. He drove cautiously back up to the town, parked Niki's car in its usual place, and began the ascent that would bring him not only to where he understood they had found the body, but to his room, where he would wash, rest, and, above all, drink water, before finishing his work.

Four o'clock. Monterozzo was, as always, empty of people. Maybe there would be a crowd watching the firefighters and Carabinieri retrieve the unfortunate who had fallen off the rock. He had just passed the piazza, and was walking slowly into the steepest and darkest part of the town when his phone rang and Caterina's name flashed up on screen.

Hearing her voice felt almost as good as drinking fresh water.

'Caterina.' His voice came out as a dry croak. He tried to clear his throat and engage some saliva.

'Alec? Are you all right?'

'Fine,' he whispered. 'A bit of a cold.' He passed a fire truck, which had been unable to go any farther, and was now guarded by a lonely youth in an unseasonably heavy brown jacket. He stopped to ask about the operation going on above, and learned that they were only now winching the body up. All the equipment had had to be carried up by hand.

'Alec?'

'Hold on, Caterina.' He cupped his hand over the phone, an automatic gesture, as he turned back to the fireman. 'Any idea who it was?'

'Not yet, and I'm not even from round here, so . . .'

'Old or young?' interrupted Blume.

He didn't know that either, useless youth. 'Sorry Caterina, you were saying?'

'There is someone beside me who would like to talk to you. I am putting you on speakerphone.'

'Hello, Commissioner Blume.'

'Nadia? Nadia!'

'Yes.'

The image of her lying dead at the bottom of the ravine evaporated to be replaced with a surreal image of Nadia and Caterina sitting in the living room, Alessia playing on the carpet before them. None of it made sense.

'I was afraid . . .' he began. 'I thought I had failed you, too. You might have been dead.'

Caterina's voice. 'Are you all right, Alec? She's not dead. She is here with me. We're at the station. It is time to start making this part of an official investigation. She came to me with Niki Solito. He drove.'

'Oh.' This part, too, was beginning to make sense to him.

'He had my address,' said Caterina accusingly. 'He came to my house.'

'That's OK,' said Blume. 'He is not dangerous after all.'

'That's not the point. Nadia rang my doorbell and asked for me by name. How do you think that made me feel?'

'Niki drove me,' offered Nadia. 'He said I would be safe. He stayed downstairs so as not to worry you.' She must have intended this last comment for Caterina.

'All the way to Rome,' said Blume. 'Did he say why?'

He was asking Caterina, but Nadia answered. 'Because of what happened to Alina. He was worried for me.'

'I know who Alina is now, Alec,' said Caterina, her voice amplified and far away at once. 'Nadia has been able to tell me a lot.'

'I may know where Alina is,' he said.

'Alina!' It was Nadia's voice, full of inappropriate hope.

★

He passed right by the cluster of firemen, Carabinieri, and onlookers, relieved he didn't have to bother with them now. He wondered how many people fell off this rock, how many hurled themselves off it. They had brought arc lights and batteries, a winch, stretcher, and ropes. Fabio the *vigile* was there, too. He had come up on a motorbike. The maresciallo was sitting on a doorstep, enjoying a small glass of coffee and a flavoured Toscanello cigar, whose aniseed-scented smoke hung in the still air increasing the relaxed drawing-room atmosphere of the group, in no hurry to drag the battered body of a stranger into their convivial midst. The maresciallo raised his hand in uncertain greeting, and did not call out as it became apparent Blume was not stopping.

Soon after, Blume let himself into the princess's house. The €200 was still on the reception desk. Maybe she had gone out to see the body. It didn't seem like her. Another thought crossed his mind, but he dismissed it.

The coldness of his bedroom was a great relief at first, but soon he found himself shivering, and he climbed fully clothed under the covers, and pulled them over him. An hour and a half, two hours at most, to gather his strength, he told himself. He lay on the bed, closed his eyes, and tried to map out his next moves. It would be better to go down to the garden for the last time before darkness fell.

Only now did it occur to him that Greco had poisoned himself. Or had been poisoned. He had even said it, but Blume was not listening. And then he had said, 'How are you feeling, Blume, you don't look so good?' Or words to that effect. Flu? Unhappiness? Fear of the unknown, yellow flower; nostalgia, blue flower; innocence, white; murder, red; poison, green. All fed to him by Silvana, and he sat there imbibing them, trustful as Alessia. Caterina was looking at him with a puzzled frown, so he went over his explanation again, only to find that his audience had increased, as had the general scepticism about his motives. A room full of women, all of them interested in knowing about the toxicity of the infusions he had drunk. There was his mother, who had something to say about all those pills, too. Alessia, grown up now but recognizable, looked through him as if he wasn't there. Caterina looked as she had when they met a few years ago; Nadia, Alina, Nadia—Alina were poised on the point of saying something. Olga, a large shadow, drank and drank in the corner, and Silvana was laughing and talking to an older man. A knock on the door caused him to lose the thread of his discourse.

265

He got out of bed, surprised it was dark already.

'Your €200,' said the princess, angrily. 'What do I want with that?' He retreated, surprised, then pushed the door closed against her as she tried to force her way into his room. Even with the door closed, he could feel her streaming under the crack below and through the keyhole like a cold wind, which grew in strength until the door burst open again, and he woke up.

Reluctantly abandoning the warmth of his bed, he got up to close it.

There stood the princess, pressing her hands to her temple. She had placed a red rose in her hair.

'Didn't you just . . . ?'

He jerked awake. It was dark in the room. Cautiously, he looked towards the door. It was closed. He waited for the next knock at the door, but none came. So much for getting back before nightfall, he muttered to himself.

He got up and had a shower, turning it to cold towards the end to soothe the hives on his upper arms and lower legs. It set him shivering again, but that passed as he got dressed in the last fresh clothes he had in his suitcase. It would be warmer outside than in.

He decided on a double dosage of Doxepin pills. He did not want to spend the day scratching himself and wincing. In the bathroom mirror, he noticed with detached interest that his pupils seemed very large. It gave him a soft look, and he tried to narrow his eyes into the unsympathetic glare that he had perfected for talking to suspects. He glanced sideways back into his room and froze. The door was open.

His fingers stopped in the process of redoing the button of his shirt, and closed themselves over into a fist. Then, keeping his movements light to compensate for the heavy thumping in his chest, he stepped out of the tiny bathroom into the bedroom. Nobody was there. Bed, unmade, suitcase on the floor, the dresser and the flyspecked oval mirror the colour of dark beer, and – of course! – the window. He had left the fucking window open. The air coming in combined with his pulling open of the bathroom door had created a low pressure wave that sucked open the door.

Even so, he was cautious and regretful of his lack of a weapon as he moved over to the door for what seemed like the third time, then spun round it into the blackness of the corridor. He looked quickly down one side, then the other, towards the stairs – too quickly, perhaps, as a red dot appeared on the periphery of his vision, then floated away.

A click at the back of his head foretold of a migraine. He went back into the bathroom, and fetched some strips of toilet paper. Gently he blew his nose, then shot two sprays of Sumatriptan nasal spray up his nostrils before dropping the bottle, almost finished now, into his jacket pocket. Today was not the day to be blinded by a cluster headache. No day was, but this in particular was one in which he needed clarity of vision. He tilted the mirror upwards on its axis to check his eyes again, bringing the top corner of the room, where wall met the ceiling, into view. He allowed the mirror to fall back into place, and he caught a flash of a red something directly behind him. He did not want to turn round. He would observe it, whatever it was, through the mirror. It was already moving out of his frame of vision, and so he did not so much see as remember that he had just seen a girl in a silver-grey dress, with a rose at the side of her short brown hair.

He breathed out slowly through his nose, and slowly turned around. Nothing and no one, of course, though he caught a grey object flitting on the ceiling, which resolved itself into the shadow of the curtain flapping in the window.

In the corridor outside, as he looked towards the stairs, he saw again the red dot that might have been a rose. Not a rose, a hallucination, he told himself. Just my imagination.

He sang the refrain from the Temptations song. *Just my imagination . . . oooh, ooh yeah, running away with me.* The red carried the suggestion of an outline behind, a glint that suggested eyes but was probably the reflection of the light from his room.

He changed the song to *Papa was a Rolling Stone* and marched towards the stairs, and the red spot receded, as he knew it would. At the top of the stairs, he looked down one flight to the next landing, and saw a shadow slip around the corner. But there was, he remembered, a light switch there. His immediate mission was to reach that and turn it on, before turning round to see what awaited him below. Holding onto the banister, because the risers of these stairs varied slightly in height and there was a danger of tripping, he walked down the nine steps, to where they turned. He followed the gooseneck plunge of the handrail as it turned right and continued down, then executed another turn and stared down the next flight. Again, he sensed someone move out of sight just below him.

Still holding the handrail, with his other hand he swiped at the wall till he found the switch, banging his finger in the process. The light came on, and the next flight below him posed no mystery and held no threat. He affected a nonchalant gait on his way down, but the problem of darkness re-presented itself at the next flight. Once again, the handrail plunged down, into a narrow landing, the stairs reversed direction, and all was dark.

He kept going, talking now, and challenging the figure to make itself known, chiding himself for being so impressionable, laughing a bit even, as he realized he was talking to himself. Finally, he reached the ground floor, where there was more light. He walked down through the hallway, shuffling to keep his footfall quiet.

. . . and when he died
All he left us was alone.

He opened the door to the room with the map. The light switch was by the door, and he flicked it on. Everything was OK. He was just a few hours behind schedule. The plan of the villa, still held in place with the lead weights, lay where he had left it. He went over and tapped the area that interested him before realising his finger was bleeding again, thanks to his frantic scrabbling for light switches in the dark. A drop of blood fell onto the plan in front of him. He tried to clean off the old paper, but merely smudged the mess he had made.

He went into the next room with its mixture of portraits, photos, and junk. A portrait of, possibly, the princess's mother in 1920s clothes, her eyes too lustrous and her lips too full for it to be innocent, stared at him. The small photographs of the princess in the silver frames were mere grey smudges. A deer head looked down at him disdainfully. He lifted up the bunch of keys he had noticed before. They were so tightly packed around the ring that they did not jingle. The weight was surprising, and the heft reassuring: he felt he was at long last carrying a weapon. He was happy to leave the house.

Blume walked slowly, allowing the warm night air to reach his bones and take away the chill of his room, and he felt his step become lighter and his head clearer. The body had evidently been recovered, and all the equipment taken down. Everyone was gone, as if they had never been there. The streets were white and clear under the moon, which shone with unusual intensity. One or two windows had lights on and someone was watching TV with the volume too loud, but Monterozzo was its usual deserted self.

When he reached the car, he opened the boot, pulled at a tab on the floor, and hunted around till he had found the scissor jacks and screw for changing a tyre. He was pleased to find a heavy-duty emergency torch, too. It was one of those with compact fluorescent tubes on the side and a powerful lamp in front. Well done, Niki, for being so prepared, he thought. He dropped them on the passenger seat beside him and drove out of the town. The keys he had taken from Silvana's were also on the passenger seat. The keys from the princess's house sat beside them. The car clock told him it was now 1 in the morning.

He drove carefully down the hill. Nobody and no vehicles were about. The car had halogen headlamps, which cut through the darkness with a fierce blue light. On the first hairpin, the sweep of light caught a rat or a hare, or something that hopped quickly out of sight. On the third hairpin turn, they picked up the white face of a young girl standing by the roadside.

It's OK, it's OK, he told himself. Another hallucination. To be expected. 'It's OK,' he told the girl. 'I know, now.'

31

H E SWITCHED off the headlamps 50 metres before the gate to the villa, leaving the car on the side of the road. He got out, not forgetting the keys and scissor jacks, and flashlight in hand, made the rest of his way on foot.

He slipped in the entrance. No cars, the lodge dark. He kept his footsteps as quiet as possible as he moved across the gravel. Ignoring paths that wanted to him to follow a winding route to the villa, he ploughed his own direct path, which meant he had to push through bushes and trample down flowers. He almost stepped into a pond, so still and covered in fleshy water lilies that, bathed in the strange light of the supermoon, it resembled a patch of lawn. He skirted its edges.

He heard a scream.

He stopped dead, and crouched down. The scream came again, louder and closer, but from a different direction. Whoever was screaming was moving.

Cautiously, he moved onto a white path at the end of which loomed the villa. A streak of red leapt from one side of the path to the other, and he only had time to register what he had seen when the fox or vixen, untroubled by his presence, stepped daintily back the way it had come, and stood its ground no more than 20 paces from where he was standing. A small animal was wedged sideways in her mouth, surely too small to have been the source of the scream? As if to answer him, the vixen emitted a piercing bark that sounded for all the world like a woman in fear. Then she lifted her tail and streaked off towards the villa.

He stepped under the faded piece of red-and-white barricade tape. He swept the beam of the torch along the base of the wall, looking for any basement windows, steps leading down. Nothing, but that did not matter, because he was circling round to the rear to where he had been on that first day, which now seemed so long ago, with Silvana. That would be the place. The night seemed to grow darker, and he looked upwards. A black cloud was rolling across the immense face of the moon.

Death came hurtling down towards his upturned face. An instinctive and efficient part of his brain imparted instructions to his feet, and he had sprung backwards, arching his back like a high jumper clearing the bar, before his mind was able to articulate what was happening. A mass of bricks, rubble, and wood landed at his feet with a thud that sounded all the more weighty and deadly for the way the grass absorbed the noise. He rose from the ground and shone the torch up at the building. An entire ledge and half a lintel had crumbled, taking the shutter with it. The gap looked like a ragged mouth grinning at him. He kept the beam trained on the section of collapsed window, trying to resolve the fleeting image he thought he had spotted as he fell backwards.

He allowed himself a few minutes to recover, then followed the contours of the building from a wider berth until he reached the rear. He passed through the archway into the back courtyard, now containing the overgrown vegetable garden. To his immediate left was an old shed, ruining the symmetry of the enclosing wall. Farther on were Silvana's unused guest quarters.

He turned his attention to the shed, the door of which was secured with a chain linking two hasps, thick enough to look at, but embedded in soft wet wood. It took a single, almost noiseless blow of the scissor jacks to detach the hasp from the wood – almost a waste of effort carting the jack this far. He felt he could have prised the metal anchor out of the rotting wood with his fingers, like pulling a rusty nail from butter.

Using the torch, he looked around. Greco had kept an organized and well-stocked shed. He registered a blue crowbar leaning in the corner, but chose a pair of bolt cutters and a hammer instead.

He pushed the wooden door closed, and walked into the middle of the yard where, in the sunlight, so long ago it now seemed, the killer had pointed him to a herb that tasted of carrot and had almost had the effect of hemlock. The smell of damp was so strong and the soil beneath his feet so soft that he imagined he might be about to step into a swamp. But beneath the soil, he knew, were solid flagstones, and at the far end of the courtyard, as the plan had shown him, would be a narrow staircase leading down to the bowels of the building.

For the last time, he saw a flitting shadow with a reddish halo in front of him, once again, hovering near the steps; she seemed to like steps. His unease was tinged with a growing fondness now, and he almost waved to her. Or it might have been the fox. He walked down a set of seven steps, counting as he went, opening and closing the jaws of the bolt cutter. Part of him felt like whistling, another part felt sad.

When he arrived at the cellar door, he switched on the fluorescent tubes and set the torch on the ground. The door was secured by a heart-shaped padlock that passed through two thick iron hooks, one on the edge of the door, the other on the frame. It seemed as if time had driven them deeper and deeper into the wood, and rust had sealed them there forever. The shackle of the heavy padlock united them and seemed to redouble their strength.

Before trying the keys, he pulled the padlock upwards, cupped it delicately in the palm of his hand, and examined where the shackle curved its way through the hooks. It scraped as he moved it, and a few tiny particles of rust rose into the air. He could not be sure, but it seemed that there might be a little less rust than might be expected, as if it had been opened recently. He took out Silvana's ring of keys, but he could see at a glance that none fitted the padlock. Even so, he tried one or two. He wondered if Silvana had thrown this key away after she removed it from the ring, or whether she kept it on her person.

Now he took out the rusty keys from the princess's house, and started trying in order of likelihood. The fifth one fitted. The padlock fell rather than sprang open. The door pushed outwards so that he had to push it shut with his shoulder to align the hooks and extract the padlock. He knew he was making a mess of potential evidence, but he also knew the door had been opened sometime in the recent past.

He did not want to contaminate the evidence further by placing the padlock on the ground, so he let it hang from the eye of the bolt. He stepped into the darkness behind the door, accidentally kicking in a pebble that resounded inside the dark chamber like an echo waiting to escape.

The smell told him all he needed to know. Automatically, his tonsils seemed to retract and his breathing became narrower, more cautious, and shallower as he tried to keep as much of the funk of rot from filling his lungs. But the body was not there in the small room in front of him, essentially a concrete bunker that looked like it had burst out of the side of the house like a carbuncle.

A gust of wind banged the door shut behind him, but the stab of fear had hardly reached his heart when the wind, just as casually slammed the door open again, then closed, open, and then closed, as if trying to air the room of its stench. Finally, the door and the wind tired of their game.

Blume stood for moment listening to the reassuring whisper and clicking of insects, then picked up the torch from the floor and shone it into the small chamber behind the door. A second door and nothing else. He was in a sort of airlock with a door behind and a door in front. Cement on the walls, floor, and ceiling. Thick black strings of webs in the corner. The door before him had an old-fashioned mortise lock, and above that a brand-new shining padlock holding together two bright new stainless steel clasps, inexpertly hammered into the door and its frame. Now there was premeditation.

He pushed up the iron lip covering the ancient keyhole. It took him several tries, but eventually one of the princess's keys slotted neatly in, and turned, stiffly, but easily. He left the key in the door. Then he bent down and pulled out the bolt cutters. The wind started playing with the door behind him, but he ignored it. He was certain no one was coming, just as he was certain about what was behind the door.

He had seen dead bodies in various states of decomposition, but had never got used to the violence of death's insult to the human form. Even a natural death became as unspeakably gruesome as a multiple homicide. All it took was time and heat.

Here, however, he was disturbed by the rank moisture and over-powering taste not only of death, but of mushrooms. A rotting cadaver he could deal with and almost looked forward to since it usually proved his thesis, but the idea of breathing in millions of tainted spores was making his stomach heave and his nose prickle. His arms and chest started itching, but he knew no pill would make it stop.

He recalled the princess's story of her mad uncle forcing plants in the dark: white chicory, turning radicchio red, plots of rhubarb with poisonous leaves, spikes of pale asparagus. The padlock snapped like gingerbread under the force of the bolt cutters and fell on the ground, and the door swung outwards, releasing a foul breath of vegetable sweat and sick sweet death.

He lifted up the torch and pointed it in. Its diffuse light illuminated a forest of mushrooms, some flat-headed, others puffy, some powdery, others slimy. They were white, black, and brown, gilled, web-throated, stalked and unstalked; and they were everywhere. From zinc pails, washbasins, two ceramic tubs, and what looked like it had once been a wooden lab desk, the mushrooms poked shyly upwards or soared upwards like spongy trees. Some popped as he put his foot on the earthen floor, others leached out juicy liquids, and he had to stop himself from slipping.

It was as if they were all shying away from him, the intruder. They were all pointing, like the tentacles of a sea anemone, towards the deep back of the room. Now his beam picked up a few trails through the foetid broken stems, slimy paths cut through the room, at the far end of which the previous pathmaker, now a black, motionless shape, lay. He gazed down at her. He pulled his shirt up till it covered his mouth and nose.

'Hello, Alina,' he whispered into his own chest.

Her face was bloated, black, and livid, the largest fungus in the room. The body shimmered with insects, though the blowflies seemed to have gone. Her face seemed to glow, and Blume turned off the torch and stood there. Just as he was concluding that the blackness was absolute, he noticed the faintest gleam, there and not there, coming from above the far wall. The remnants of a white moonbeam produced a hint of a dark grey in the blackness. Perhaps when the sun came up, the grey grew a little lighter. It came from some sort of aperture, and possible exit, but not big enough for poor Alina to get through. That's why all the mushroom heads were looking in the same direction, why all the stems seemed to be twisting away from him. They, like Alina, had instinctively leaned towards the feeble light.

32

Perhaps it was the slight change in pressure, a deepening of the surrounding darkness, or a tiny noise, but as he turned round, he heard the clicks of the door close and the key turning.

Taking care not to slip on the slimy floor but being merciless with the fungus in his path, he rushed back to the door and hit it as hard as he could with his shoulder. It would not budge. Just as it had not budged for Alina. The difference was Alina had had no idea, whereas he was guilty of wilful stupidity for leaving the key outside. It had felt heavy in his hand, another encumberance, and he was tired. The heavy torch was as much as he could handle.

He knew she was there. He could not hear her, but he could sense her presence. He suspected she wanted to be addressed before she left and closed the second door and condemned him to the same fate as Alina.

'Silvana! Silvana, I know it's you. Don't do this.'

He fancied he could hear her breathing, though the door was too thick. Had she already left the airlock and closed the second door and returned to the surface?

'Silvana? You're just making it worse.'

'How could it be worse?' Her voice was muffled but distinct, and he sank down on the ground in thankfulness. He might be able to negotiate his way out.

'They know I am down here.'

'Well then, they'll find you, and if you are bluffing, they won't. It's worth the risk.'

'No, it's not.'

'Of course it is. I'd receive a charge of attempted murder on top of one of murder. To me it makes no difference. And who knows you're down here? I don't believe you.'

He pressed his ear to the door. Maybe she had already left him? He needed to keep the conversation going.

'Silvana?'

Nothing.

'Have you seen your father? I think he poisoned himself.'

'That murdering bastard is dead.'

'He poisoned himself,' said Blume.

'If you say so. I found him with a hole in his head, and Niki's stupid little pistol in his hand.'

So Greco had been armed all the while. He had missed the pistol when searching the old man. 'Why did he kill himself, Silvana?'

'You. All because of you, Blume. You see, it never occurred to him that I might know anything about my mother and what happened, and I didn't, not for a long time. But I found out several years ago. Then you arrived and forced him to activate some old contacts to find out who you were and how much you knew. That's when he discovered something about me he didn't know.'

'What?'

'You're the detective, work it out.'

'What was in those drinks you gave me?'

'*Datura stramonium*, a few magic mushrooms. Some acacia seeds, root of pomegranate. Passion fruit, columbine, belladonna, silver berry, nutmeg, morning glory, and yellow hornpoppy. I put a lot of love into it. You must have the constitution of an ox, or you're immune to poisons. You shouldn't even be upright, you oversized bastard. Maybe you feed on poison. You gave me the idea, eating that conium. Back then I had no idea you would be so much trouble. I did fancy you a bit, by the way. Not as much as you fancied me.'

'More than you fancy Niki?'

'Little Niki. Poor little Niki. He's loaded, you know. Even more than you'd think.'

'And Alina? What did she do?'

'She was going to run off with Niki and his money. I had other plans. I still do. But I wouldn't mind knowing where Niki has gone. I don't suppose you have any idea, Alec?'

'I might. But I can't think of one good reason for telling you, Silvana. Unless you're thinking of letting me out of here.'

'I can't do that, sorry,' she said. 'How long do you think you could survive in there?'

'About as long as Alina.'

'I'm worried Niki might say something, you see. He knows, of course. He worked it out the other day. That was the fight you saw.'

Which, thought Blume, is why he took Alina's passport and almost immediately turned against the investigation he had just asked for.

'I can tell you where he is.'

'No, on second thoughts, it doesn't matter now.'

He heard the outside door close and the scrape of the bolt against the brackets.

★

The stool from which Alina had fallen, perhaps mercifully, killing herself with a single blow to the back of the head, was still against the wall, and he climbed up to see what she had been investigating. From above, the stench of the corpse was almost overpowering, but he could not climb, balance, search, and cover his mouth and nose all at once. Alina had been a small girl, and whatever she was looking for, he might be able to reach. He aimed the beam upwards, and realized that there was an aperture high up on the wall. It seemed to be the end of a chute, perhaps used for coal or wood once, or a flue of some sort. But it sloped back and then upwards, and was narrow. His body was never going through there. Perhaps his voice would carry, and someone walking above might hear. But he was not going to start shouting, not yet, not at night, and not while Silvana was still about.

Without warning, without even dimming, the light went out. He lowered his arm carefully, feeling the stood below him wobble. If he fell backwards now, he would land right on top of Alina behind him. He banged the torch against the wall, and the two fluorescent tubes lit up again. At least that was something.

Then they went out again.

It might be possible to construct something long, a stick with a rag, and shove it up until it poked above the ground, and then hope that someone would recognize it for what it was. That is probably what Alina was thinking. He stretched his neck upwards trying to inhale the air coming down rather than the odour rising from below. The scent coming down was powerful, too, off-putting, harsh. Nothing as bad as what was below, but unnerving in a different way. He felt around with his hand, looking for a metal grille or something that might stop an object from being pushed through.

The touch was completely unexpected. A split second afterwards, he realized that it had been preceded by something warm, a wet breath. He yanked his hand out before the warm breath turned into a bite. He dropped the torch, which hit the ground and went off. He was falling backwards, as Alina had fallen backwards, to the same spot where she lay. At the last moment, he managed to push out his legs, and his feet hit the ground, one on either side of the body, before the momentum carried him backwards and crashing through the mush of fungus and stalks. He got up and retrieved the light, shook it. One tube flickered into life. He made his way back to the door, sat down, pulled his knees up, and decided to relax. They would find him eventually. Niki's car would tell them he was here. Unless Silvana was sly enough to remove it, but she would need the keys for that. Would she have the keys to Niki's car? She might. In fact, she would probably drive it away to wherever she was going. He pushed his forehead against his knees, and dismissed the thought.

33

'HEY, THAT'S my car,' said Niki from the back seat. 'There, halfway into the ditch.'

Caterina braked to a halt, and then reversed. The Carabinieri patrol car following them did likewise. 'Take a good look. Are you sure?'

'Of course I am.'

'That's the one that Blume borrowed?'

'Call it borrowing,' said Niki.

Caterina reached over and touched Nadia's knee, seeking confirmation. Nadia nodded.

'Why did he park it there?' said Niki. 'If you can call that parking. He has no respect.'

Caterina swung the car through the gates. A mortuary van, three Carabinieri cars, a white van. Two men from the SIS were chatting as they climbed into their white jumpsuits.

The car following drew up behind and the tired maresciallo who had taken her to the princess's house while Niki and Nadia made their initial statements in the station, clambered out slowly, rubbing his eyes.

'Ispettore Mattiola,' he said. 'Although I do not have men to spare to carry out an extensive search, I will do all . . .' The rest of his words were lost to a long yawn. He stretched and went over to a uniformed officer standing by the gate lodge. They chatted amiably for a while. Beside Caterina, Niki, his skin the colour of a votive candle, shifted from foot to foot. Eventually the maresciallo returned.

'Silvana has gone. No one heard or saw her leave. Personally I don't blame her. What a shock –'

'What about her car?' asked Caterina.

'It's gone too,' said the maresciallo. 'I am worried about her. Your commissioner really brought a lot of trouble here.'

Caterina opened her mouth to say something, but closed it again. She wanted these people on her side and the Carabiniere was right. Blume did carry a lot of trouble around with him. 'Did you know him well?'

'Greco?' said the maresciallo. 'I thought I did, but,' he added philosophically, 'you never know anyone, really.' The maresciallo patted Niki on the shoulder. 'No need for you to be here, then, Niki. Would you like to sit down, perhaps? It's going to be a long day. Longer than yesterday, unbelievably. It never rains but it pours.'

As he said this, the sun cleared the cliff face and bathed the entire scene in soft morning light.

'Sit down?' Niki did not understand.

'In the back of a car, perhaps. With Nadia?'

'You mean like I am under arrest?'

The maresciallo puffed out his cheeks, pursed his lips, and exhaled for some time as he considered this novel idea. 'No, no! But we would all save ourselves a lot of running around trying to find one another. I mean the girl has already disappeared, which is a terrible nuisance. Then when the magistrate comes, he can decide. It's just I can't have you and Nadia trampling around the villa and gardens, when well . . . you know.'

'I thought Greco had confessed to killing Alina,' said Niki. 'So why would I be under suspicion?'

'I didn't say that. It's just . . . It was an incomplete confession, and now,' he waved his hand towards the garden where the crime scene investigators had gone, 'we'll never know.'

'Maresciallo,' said Caterina in her sweetest voice, 'you must be utterly exhausted.'

He shook his big head in sheer amazement at how true this was.

'There is a nice bench over there on the side, by the house, I think you should sit on it.'

He thought so, too. When he was settled there, Caterina sat next to him. 'I'd get you something from the house, but I suppose it would be polluting a crime scene to go in there.'

'Not much of a crime scene. Door open, but no one there. Some signs of a struggle near the door, but nothing else.'

'When was the last time you slept, you poor man?'

'I can't even remember,' said the maresciallo. 'Two deaths in one day. I was on my way back from the first, and I get this phone call. It was 1 in the morning, so I knew at once it was serious.'

'And it was Domenico Greco?'

'He just launched into this mad confession about killing a Romanian girl. He sounded delirious. I thought it was some sort of joke, then, well, I hate to say this, but I thought he might be under threat from your commissioner. None of it made any sense. He said he had poisoned himself, and it hadn't worked properly, and he couldn't bear the cramps any more. It was exhausting trying to keep up. So I told him we should talk in the morning.'

'In the morning,' repeated Caterina.

The maresciallo scowled and folded his arms, crossed his legs, and looked away from her. 'Yes. That's what I said.'

'The public prosecutor is going to be very harsh with you on that point,' said Caterina. 'You know how they get. He'll say things like you received a confession of murder and decided to sleep on it rather than act on it.'

'He can say that, but it wouldn't be true. I came down here, soon afterwards. With the *appuntato* over there. We knocked on the door there, no one in, which is when I began to get suspicious.'

'So you searched the gardens?'

'Yes. The moon was full. It was quite easy to see. We found him lying under a medlar tree, gun in hand, hole in temple. So we called it in and . . . all this.'

'I admire the way you know the name of trees,' said Caterina. 'I wish I could identify them like that.'

The maresciallo made an effort to appear modest. 'The medlar is easy. It's the only tree you'll find in the garden with flowers on it at this time of year. Its white blossoms were really easy to see last night. Also, the medlar is the only fruit I don't like. We had one in our garden when I was a kid.'

'I don't think I have ever eaten one,' said Caterina.

'Don't. The flesh of the fruit has to rot before you can eat it.'

'Sounds revolting. Listen, Maresciallo, while you sit here, why don't I borrow one of your men for a few minutes, walk around?'

'Why?'

'To see if I can find the commissioner.'

'He's here, too? I need to talk to him about some stuff. Where is he?'

'I'm not sure. That's why I want to look.'

'You can have Paolo,' said the maresciallo, pointing at the young *appuntato* still standing stiffly at attention in the distance.

'Thanks.'

'And bring him back here, please.'

'Of course I'll bring him back, I'm hardly going to take him home with me by mistake.'

'I meant Commissioner Blume, if you find him.'

'Oh, I see,' said Caterina.

Niki, complaining and aggrieved, and Nadia, silent and patient, were sitting in the back of a Carabinieri patrol car, which Paolo seemed to be half-guarding. She was about to ask him to accompany her on her search, when a two-toned Smart came at excessive speed through the gates, almost clipping a pillar, then stopped with a whoosh of gravel and spray. A bearded man in his mid-thirties jumped out, as if escaping from a car with a mind of its own, and then grinned at everyone. 'Took the corner too fast. Didn't see it till it was almost too late. Smell that?'

Everyone obligingly sniffed.

'Burning brakes! One hell of a twisty road. Sun in your eyes half the time. Magistrate La Porta at your service. You must be Caterina Mattiola. I know these other bastards already.' He stuck out his hand, and gave her a vigorous pumping. It was hard to imagine this ball of bearded energy and the maresciallo working together.

'Right. Well, first things first. Off to see the body in the garden. Or the bodies!' he winked at Caterina. Catching sight of the maresciallo reclining on the bench, he shouted over: 'Find anything there?', but did not wait for a reply. Instead, he pulled out a piece of crumpled paper from the back of his jeans, and flapped it open under Caterina's face.

'Silvana's phone calls, see? These are the numbers she was calling.'

'She was under suspicion?'

'She was fiancée to the scumbag with the prostitute in the car over there. Of course her calls were being monitored. I got this this morning . . .'

'Niki isn't a complete scumbag,' said Caterina.

'No? That's good to hear. I could have sworn he was.' The magistrate pulled out another sheet, and opened it. 'See this?'

Caterina looked, and her eye fell on her own number, time, date, location. 'That's . . . Blume's phone. You were intercepting his calls, too?'

'Only as of the other day, keeping tabs on the numbers he called. This all began only hours ago, really, after the maresciallo over there contacted me about a peculiar scene that took place in his dormitory – sorry, office – between Blume and Greco, the dead man in the garden. Now here,' he jabbed at a telephone number with a dirty fingernail, 'we have a call made to someone in Bari. And here . . . wait . . .' he swapped the sheets around, 'we have the last phone call made by Silvana a few hours ago, before she realized she should probably get rid of her phone. Interestingly, hers and Blume's go off grid at the same time and in the same place, namely here. And the two of them have called this one person . . . it's all very exciting. I almost went over the precipice on the road up there when the techies called me to mention the match. Any ideas?'

Caterina had none.

'I am waiting for the people at the Tuscolano centre to get back to me. It should only take a few minutes. Want to wait, find out who it is?'

'I'd prefer . . .'

'Of course! Off you go then.' He spun on his heel.

'Ispettore?' It was the young Carabiniere, Paolo, who always seemed to be standing at attention.

'Yes?'

'I think I may have found something.'

'Well, tell me, what is it? And stand at ease, for God's sake.'

'It's just that, well, I might have overstepped my authority, and even if I did the right thing, it might make my maresciallo seem a bit . . . lazy? And I don't want that.'

'Tell me what you found.'

'Well, you know there was a body found at the bottom of an escarpment?'

'Yes and no. The investigating magistrate mentioned it in passing when I was talking to him on the phone earlier, but said it was unconnected. No foul play.'

'The body was of Princess Donatella Flavia Orsini-Romanelli. She probably fell to her death while taking a short cut that involves walking along a narrow ledge. Anyhow, she owns the house at the top to the town, and that is where Commissioner Blume is staying. The idea was to go round there and tell him that his hostess had been found dead, but then the maresciallo got the phone call from Greco, and we came down here, found the body, and well, everything kicked off. We called out two *Carabinieri scelti*, and they secured the area until the crime scene people came, and we went back to the office to get ready for the investigating magistrate, write a report, and so on.'

'Come on, Paolo, get to the point.'

'OK. The maresciallo took a bit of a nap, and I thought I would go up to the house where the commissioner was – it's now five in the morning, and getting bright. On my way, I noticed that a car the commissioner has been using, but belongs to Niki, was gone. I get to the house, knock, call out a bit. Nothing. The front door is locked and I go round the back, because I know the princess always leaves that open – actually, she leaves the front door open too, so I guessed maybe the commissioner had locked it. I know I shouldn't have gone into the house . . .'

'You did fine.'

'I looked in all the rooms. It's creepy as hell in there, by the way. Even with a bit of light in the sky. No sign of the Commissioner. But in one of the front rooms on the ground floor, I found a plan. I put it in the back of the car . . . I'll fetch it.'

'A plan of what?'

'Of the house over there. It was spread out on the table, you see, like someone had just been looking at it.'

The *appuntato* unrolled the plan over the bonnet. From inside the car, Niki and Nadia were straining their necks to see what was going on.

'Hold down those corners. Right. This shows the house over there, right? See this red spot here?'

Caterina bent down to take a look. 'What is that? Blood?'

'That's what I thought, too, which is basically what made me take it with me. Now, see there? That is a partial fingerprint. There was blood, not much, on the person's finger.'

'And he was pointing to that spot there,' said Caterina.

'Which corresponds to an area around the rear of the house.'

'*Appuntato* Paolo?'

'Ma'am?'

'You're wasted here. Come on. Lead the way.'

34

W HEN THEY reached the half-converted stables behind the villa, Paolo noticed the tool shed and thought they should check it out.

'What for?' she asked.

'You never know.' A few seconds later, he reappeared with a crowbar. 'Might come in handy.'

Caterina loved this guy. Stiff and formal, unassuming, polite but with a very sharp mind. If she had been fifteen years younger. Nor did he look smug when they reached the bottom of the steps and were confronted with the first padlocked door, and his crowbar was immediately useful. All he said was 'Shall I?' and with three hard heaves, he had pulled the bolt, hinges, and padlock out of the door. He was first into the airlock, and came straight out again, a look of horror on his face. 'We can't go in there!' He retched. 'What is that?'

'That,' said Caterina, a little disappointed in Paolo now, 'is the smell of death. Give me that crowbar, I'll do the next one.'

He did not need asking twice. He handed it to her, and hovered outside trying to breathe in the air from above. She pushed the crowbar at the bolt, and tried to lever it behind, but it was too wide at the tip.

Someone knocked from the other side of the door, and shouted. A familiar voice, one that made her heart skip a beat for absolutely no reason she could explain.

'Alec?'

'Caterina?'

'Are you all right?'

'I am now.'

The *appuntato* took a deep breath and dived into the airlock. 'Are you talking to someone?'

'Here,' she said, handing him the crowbar. 'This is no good. Get lights – and help. We'll need to break it down.' The young man vanished; she could hear him running up the steps.

She sat down on the ground and put her back to the door; she knew he would be doing the same on the other side.

'You came all this way.' His voice carried well enough through the wood.

'Of course I did.'

'Thank you.'

'Don't *thank* me. Where is your phone, you stupid bastard?'

'In my hand, giving me light now and again. No signal.'

'*Deficiente.* You could have been dead, for all I knew. *Testa di cazzo che non sei altro.*'

'Well, you sound real enough,' said Blume. 'I was beginning to wonder.'

'What is happening to you?'

'I'm not sure. I just sort of found myself in the middle of it all.'

'Just found yourself in it.' She banged the back of her head against the door. 'What's rotting in there?'

'Can't you tell?'

'A corpse. Alina's?'

'Yes.'

How long since Paolo had gone for help? Probably only minutes.

'Caterina, is it bright out yet? I don't know when sunrise is, and I can't see much change in here.'

'Yes, the sun is up.'

'It's easy to lose track of time in here. I knew you would find me.'

'No, you didn't.'

'I did know. Sort of.'

'Because you made it so easy, leaving a dollop of blood on a map in a dead woman's house? Why, who wouldn't follow such an obvious lead?'

'Dead woman?'

'Princess Donatella Something Something Romanelli. Former owner of this pile, turned landlady of what I gather from Paolo is an equally gloomy place that no one in their right mind would want to stay in, so, of course, you did . . . .'

'Who's Paolo?'

'A young Carabiniere you are going to thank profusely. How did you fail to hear about an accidental death in a place like this?'

'I heard about it. I thought for a while the dead person was going to be Nadia.'

'Nadia is here. She came with me.'

She let him digest that for a bit.

'Did she hit her upper right temple in the fall?' asked Blume.

'What? I don't know. How on earth would I? Can't you ask a normal question?'

His silence this time was different. Without being completely aware of it, she had been conscious of the shuffling and scuffling sounds his body had been making, but now his silence was total, as if he were holding his breath.

'Alec? Are you still there?'

'Yes. I am here. Where's Alessia? With your mother?'

'No, I just left her on her own for the day, Alec. She can cope just fine. She's nine months old now.'

'You're the most sarcastic woman I have ever met.'

'You think? She'd make a better job of being alone than you.'

Finally, she heard the sound of approaching voices. 'Here they come now, Alec.'

'I can't hear anything.'

'Well, they're coming.'

'Good, because it's dark in here.'

'You'll be out soon.'

35

C ATERINA HAD never seen him look worse. He managed to leave the cellar calmly enough, shielding his eyes against the light. But 20 minutes later, as the arc lights and the forensics people moved into the dark cellar, he moved to a sunny spot near the front of the house, leaned against the wall, and puked.

She stood a respectful distance away, watching him heave, giving him time and space.

'Why, hi there!'

She was not pleased to be joined by the bearded magistrate, and even less pleased when he stood beside her, folded his arms, and watched the closing convulsions of Blume's spectacle.

'He was in that cellar with a rotting corpse for hours and hours,' she said defensively. 'And he may have been poisoned.'

'Absolutely! Poor bastard. He needs to go to hospital.'

'I agree.' She did not add that he had refused to comply when she had suggested the same thing.

The magistrate dropped his voice as Blume was now walking towards them. 'The local doctor, a chap called Bernardini, is on standby. A toxicologist should be here soon.'

'Right,' said Blume as he walked up. 'Shall we get back in there?'

'What the hell are you talking about?' asked the magistrate.

'The cellar. Where Alina is.'

'I am going in there – unfortunately,' said the magistrate, 'but there is no reason for you to set foot in there again. Haven't you had enough?'

Blume folded his arms, set his feet pointing away from each other, and squared his shoulders. She knew that position, and what it represented.

'That's Alina in there,' he said. 'I have every right.'

'You are not an appointed investigator, you do not operate in this district, you are on leave, you are also, I might say, ill, and I am the investigating magistrate. You are not going back in there.'

'Try and stop me.'

'Alec, please,' said Caterina. 'Don't. Just, for once, don't.'

'Sorry,' he mumbled to a point on the ground halfway between the magistrate and Caterina. 'I haven't been quite myself recently.'

'Not a problem,' said the magistrate. 'Fuck it. After what you've been through. Here, let's talk about something else. I was telling the Ispettore here about a phone number you called, happens to be the last one Silvana called. Now, of course, I know who it belongs to, but for the fun of it, let's see if you know what I am talking about.'

'When did I make this call?'

'Two nights ago.'

Blume thought for a while, then said, 'Yes, that makes sense.'

Caterina wanted to punch him. 'Will you please tell me about this phone call, first? I think the magistrate would like to hear, too.'

'Davide Di Cagno. Am I right, magistrate?'

The magistrate winked and pulled his beard. 'Bull's eye, first shot.'

'I am being slow here,' said Caterina, 'but what's he got to do with it?'

'I phoned Davide and asked him if he was interested in reopening the case about Giuliano, his disappeared brother. His reaction was . . . mixed, I suppose,' said Blume. 'When the magistrate mentioned a call in common with Silvana, it suddenly made sense.'

'She knew him? The younger brother?' asked Caterina.

'Looks like it,' said Blume. 'When she was in Rome, Silvana acquired a mysterious boyfriend, off the map. She had found someone where she was studying. An older man, according to Niki. I didn't pay attention to it, but I think if we look, we're going to find that's who it was.'

'I've looked already,' said the magistrate. 'He teaches economics at Rome Tre Univerity. After one year at Luiss, she transferred there and took his course. I haven't worked out how, where, or when they met yet.'

'I think he probably sought her out,' said Blume.

'So,' said Caterina, 'she became the lover of the younger brother of her mother's lover? That's . . .'

'Fucking creepy,' said the magistrate. 'How did you work this out, Blume?'

'I didn't. I am guessing. But I think this Davide made it his business to contact Silvana and tell her what had really happened to her mother. It's what I would do.'

'You would? Jesus, Alec.' Caterina shook her head. 'So this Davide is the younger brother of her mother's lover . . . Dear God,' said Caterina.

'Possibly her uncle,' added Blume. He waited till they had worked that one out.

'Why would he do that?' said Caterina.

'Not because she had a right to know, but because she does not have a right to happiness. It might be he waited till she was old enough, or maybe he just couldn't take it any more. Certainly, it makes a good way of getting back at Greco and Niki.'

'Spiteful prick, this Davide, if it turns out to be true,' said the magistrate. 'Which it will, given Silvana's last few calls and the direction of travel.'

'She wanted Niki's money, first. Then she was going to leave him.'

'Or kill him?' asked the magistrate.

'Or kill him,' agreed Blume. 'Maybe poison him, but poor Silvana is no Lucrezia Borgia.'

'*Poor* Silvana?' asked Caterina incredulously.

'In a way,' said Blume. 'Davide was an older man. He probably bullied her psychologically. And then Niki and Domenico thought she knew nothing, but she knew everything. That would have fuelled anger, contempt, rage . . . then the accomplice in her mother's murder, her fiancé and sort of older brother, starts getting starry eyed about a Romanian.'

'It's interesting what you are saying about Niki,' said the magistrate. 'I knew you were casting what seemed like wild accusations at Greco about murdering his wife in 1993 – that's when the maresciallo called me in. So you're saying Niki was involved?'

'I –!' Blume snatched his hand out of Caterina's grasp. She had dug her fingernail deep into his knuckle.

'Alec, you are all nerves. We had better get that seen to,' she said, 'you poor man.'

The magistrate fingered his moustache and regarded them. 'You were saying, Commissioner?'

'No, I think I'd finished whatever it was.'

'But you think Niki was an accomplice in the alleged murder of Silvana's mother?'

'I don't know,' said Blume. 'Maybe Niki never had anything to do with it. No way of telling now that Greco is dead.'

Caterina gave him a slow blink of approval.

'If she goes to Davide's,' said the magistrate more to himself than to Blume or Caterina, 'we'll pick her up there, charge her with, well, help me here, Commissioner.'

'Murder of Alina, obviously,' said Blume.

'You're sure?'

'Yes.'

'Almost certainly as you say. Because, hold on . . . *e che palle*, where did I put that fucking . . . here we go. He pulled out a filthy notebook, flicked through what were evidently some children's drawings, found the page he was looking for, and then turned the book upside down for them to read.

She knows, I told her. We need to meet. All 3.

'That was a text message sent,' said the magistrate, 'to Alina's phone.'

'No one thought to check that out until now? She was reported missing, after all,' said Blume.

'You know how these things work or don't work, Commissioner. I am not defending what was done, but, in fact, the phone was registered not to Alina but to Giorgio Moroder.'

'Moroder. What was it he did again?' said Blume.

'*I Feel Love*,' said the magistrate. 'Donna Summer. Hottest fucking sex-kitten ever – oh, excuse me, Ispettore.'

'No problem,' said Caterina.

Blume was staring at the sky, still trying to remember. '*Porco dio*, what's the song I am thinking of?'

'*Together in Electric Dreams*?' suggested Caterina.

'That's it!' said Blume happily.

'No one can accuse Niki of having no sense of humour,' said the magistrate. 'He registered phones under the names Grace Jones, Jean Michel Jarre, Jimmy Sommerville, David Bowie, Michael Jackson, Mr Bee Jee. These phones were distributed to various employees, used by himself – I'll be getting the details later from the DCSA, if they deign to help me. All of which strongly suggests that he knew he was being monitored. I think we can say that Niki is not one of the good guys, right?'

'Absolutely,' said Blume.

'Except,' said Caterina, 'if he knew phones were being monitored, he would not use a text from one to the other to set up a trap.'

That made sense, but it annoyed Blume all the same. What was it about Niki that made women defend him?

'I agree,' said the magistrate. 'I think Silvana will have sent it, using Niki's phone to lure Alina. She would have had access to it. So then we get a message from Alina asking when, and the reply tells her to wait. The next message to Alina's phone is one of those smiley faces. Then at 9 p.m. Alina texts back asking where.'

'*Garden. Use SE entrance.* That's the last message ever to Giorgio Moroder/Alina. She came here, though, and in through the gate, up to the villa. Then it goes off network forever. Not even an IMEI number. So not just switched off, but battery out and phone destroyed. It would be good to know how stupid this Alina was.'

'Not stupid at all,' said Blume. 'Resourceful, bright, brave. All she did, all she went through, only to end up like this.'

'Not the type to go down a dark cellar on her own with an angry fiancée who had just found out? That doesn't seem likely, does it? But Niki, on the other hand, she trusted him. What do you think, Blume? I like Niki as an accomplice here.'

Blume thought about it. At last he said, 'I don't like Niki, but

I don't think I am a good judge of character. It is possible Silvana and her father lay in wait for the girl, or just Silvana.' He paused. 'Silvana can be very persuasive. Deceptive. When you get her in for questioning, I would suggest –'

'Excuse me?' said Caterina. They both looked at her. 'This is your case, Magistrate. It is not the commissioner's. Please stop asking his opinion.'

'I am happy . . .' began Blume before Caterina's look stopped him.

The magistrate stuck out an accusing beard. 'The commissioner is at the centre of all this and his insights . . .'

'Exactly. Question him as a witness. Question him as a suspect, as you stupidly suggested. Do not treat him as an investigator. Can't you see, you'll pollute your own case if you invite him to participate in any investigative work or even speculation?'

The magistrate nodded vigorously. '*Abbestia!* You're right . . .'

'Now wait a minute,' began Blume.

'No, Commissioner, she's right. I need to be directing this investigation without your input, except as a witness. You could lead me in the wrong direction.'

'Deliberately, even,' said Caterina.

The magistrate frowned at Caterina, then shook his head sympathetically at Blume, and shrugged his shoulders. 'Seems like you two have a lot to work out. I need to question you, too, Ispettore. You arrived here with a suspect in your car . . .'

'Not a problem.'

Blume sulked for a good five minutes after the magistrate left. 'By the way,' he told Caterina, 'I forgot to mention that Silvana tried to bury me under a wall.'

'You'll have a chance to tell him that,' said Caterina soothingly. 'Care to expand?'

He brought her round to the side of the villa and pointed to a pile of rubble. 'She pushed that on top of me. I know it was her. She almost got me, too.'

Caterina looked up nervously in case another piece of wall came down.

'Put that in your testimony. Your witness statement.'

'What's the point? I may as well say nothing. It's just a hassle, unless there is some objective evidence.'

'Maybe there is, but it's not your job to find it.'

'What are you doing, Caterina?'

'I am taking you out of this. I am helping you escape.'

He glanced up at the second floor from where the section of wall had broken off. 'There might be proof in that room.'

'Inform the Carabinieri, Blackbeard the magistrate. Don't go up there. And let's get out from under here.'

They walked a short distance, then he looked up again. 'That was the nursery.'

'You really studied that map of the villa well, didn't you?'

'No . . . That's not it. Come over here, OK, now look up there, where the wall has collapsed to floor level. See?'

'That pale thing? What am I looking at?'

'An old rocking horse,' said Blume.

36

A S THEY arrived at the garden lodge, they caught the sight of an ambulance leaving, lights flashing. It turned on its siren as it exited the gates and went wailing into the distance.

'I saw the mortuary vans, the SIS boys in their white suits, didn't I? So who needs an ambulance?'

'You, if anyone,' she said. 'Come on, we can get . . .' She stopped. 'Do you know this man?'

Oh no, thought Blume.

Dr Bernardini was completely *enchanté* to meet Caterina. He tut-tutted upon seeing Blume. 'Get this man some water!' he shouted at no one in particular.

'Dottore!' said Blume, 'we need to keep moving.'

'We do?' said Caterina. 'Where are we going, Alec?'

'Too rushed, *mon Commissaire*. That's one of your problems. Impulsive.' He bent down and messed around in his bag, a proper black doctor's bag, and emerged with a stethoscope.

'How's the heart today?'

'Fine,' said Blume. 'As always.' He avoided looking in Caterina's direction.

'We wouldn't want you spending another night with us.'

'What are you doing here, Doctor?' said Blume.

'I was called out for Niki Solito. He had a hypoglycaemic attack. They should have just called the ambulance, but, well, I did that for them just after they called. I saw him. The girl who he was with, sexy thing, red skirt, zip-up sports top, shouldn't work, but does? She had the wits to run into the lodge and get some fruit juice for him.'

'One of Silvana's concoctions?' said Blume, moving closer to the doctor, trying to get the idiot to move backwards. 'I am not sure that will do him much good . . .'

Caterina interposed herself between them. ' "Another night with us", you said. "How's the heart?" Doctor, I am his wife, and he has told me nothing.'

'He told *me* he wasn't married.'

'I'm not,' said Blume.

'As if anyone has any reason to believe a thing you say,' said Caterina, before leading the doctor out of earshot. When she came back, her expression was grim.

'All right, Alec. The doctor has been telling me some things I should have known about. One of which is that you are taking a medicine that he does not trust. What was its name, Doctor?'

'Lorazepam. I am not against it as such. It may even help a man such as your husband who worries a lot, but I don't think he should drink, too.'

Jesus, thought Blume.

'Is that it? Nothing else?'

'Nothing,' said Blume.

'What about that sinus spray I've seen you use?'

'That just clears my head, stops headaches before they arrive.'

She clicked her fingers impatiently. 'Show it to the doctor.'

Bernardini took the flacon in his hand and shook his head sadly. 'Alsuma. This is Sumatriptan. Who prescribed this?'

'A doctor years ago.'

'And you just kept at it. I asked you if you were on medication.'

'I didn't think it counted.'

'Well, does it relieve the headaches?'

'Not always.' He had nothing left to lose really. 'In which case, I take these and I stop caring.'

'Lyrica,' read the doctor. 'Pregabalin,' he said by way of explanation to Caterina, who nodded as if she knew exactly what this meant.

'Come here, Alec, drink this water,' said Bernardini, not unkindly. 'Tilt your head back, OK,' he started humming, 'follow my finger . . . Very good. *Très bien.* OK, Alec, *t'es pas tout seul, mais arrête tes grimaces, soulève tes cent kilos, fais bouger ta carcasse. . . . Non,* Alec, *t'es pas tout seul, je sais qu't'as le cœur gros* . . . Here, keep this bottle, fill it when it's empty, drink as much as you can.'

'These are my mother's!' Caterina had stuck her hand into his pocket and come out with a light blue box. 'I recognize these. She takes them for that skin irritation. She was complaining about them going missing, and of course I wouldn't even listen to her.'

'I just took a pack because of my hives, or shingles. And they are not hers. I bought those by myself.'

'Without a prescription?' asked Bernardini.

'There's a place in Trastevere,' said Blume. 'They give you the benefit of the doubt if you show you have the medicine already.'

'What hives?' said Caterina. 'You don't have hives.'

'I do now.' He scratched his arm to prove it. 'I think I'm allergic to my new memory-foam bed.'

'*Mon Dieu,* Doxepin, too,' said Bernardini, with something like admiration creeping into his voice.

'And these?' Caterina was holding up a small pillbox. 'That's Provigil,' said Blume. 'It's good for staying up late and focused.'

'You're killing yourself, Alec,' said Caterina.

'Just keeping my head above water, Caterina.'

'And that place you live in . . .'

'Nothing wrong with it,' he said. 'I'm still settling in.'

'Come here.'

He stepped over and she reached her hands behind his back and squeezed him against her. 'You know I am furious with you?'

'Quite right, too.'

'Would you sell that apartment?'

'Tomorrow.'

'No one will buy it.'

'I'll give it away, then.'

★

The centre of gravity had now shifted towards the villa. Any new vehicle that arrived, parked with its nose pointing towards it, people looked towards it as they spoke. The magistrate gazed at its top storeys as he shouted orders into his phone, or whispered to a new group of plain-clothes arrivals. Still on the bench, the maresciallo dozed. No one saw Nadia slip away.

The magistrate was unworried about who was coming or going. He even seemed puzzled as to why Blume felt he had to ask permission to leave.

'You're available whenever, right?'

'I want to go back to Rome.'

'Yeah, like I said, available. Rome's only down the road.'

'It feels farther away.'

The magistrate chewed gum. 'Yeah. When the fuck are they going to get here with food?'

Blume turned to leave.

'Hey, Commissioner. They just picked up Silvana. Bari. Outside Davide's place. I'll let you know.'

Blume tapped his plastic water bottle against his temple by way of acknowledgement.

'Nadia?' said Caterina. 'Where has she got to? Help me find her.'

Caterina felt Nadia might have gone down to the villa in the hope of catching a glimpse of the remains of her friend. 'Not that she'll have been allowed anywhere near. I'll go,' she said. 'You're haunted enough as it is.'

Caterina started off for the villa; Blume into the garden.

He found her sitting with her back to Greco's Madonna, staring at the cliff face. Her legs were drawn up, and she was holding her skirt up against her knees to stop it slipping down her thighs.

He came over and sat down beside her.

'All those men down there,' she said. 'None of them know her. They know nothing. Nothing. I have known her since she was three. They have no idea of the things she did, and then they won't let me go anywhere near her.'

You wouldn't want to see her now, he thought, keeping his opinion to himself. He allowed some silence to settle between them.

'How's Niki?' she asked.

'Niki? No idea.'

'I hope he's OK.' She looked at him, and smiled. 'Niki came back for me. First he took me away, because he was afraid for me. He took me straight to your girlfriend, told me to tell her everything and not worry about incriminating him. I think he was thinking of leaving the country, but when Caterina asked me to call him back,

307

he answered, and came straight back. He put his business and his own freedom second. You never believed he could be good.'

'He's not good,' said Blume.

'Are you?'

'Let's say, I'm not perfect.'

'I am asking you a serious question. Are you a good man? Sure, with faults and weaknesses, but at your core, are you good?'

Blume thought about it. 'I can't answer that.'

'I can,' said Nadia. 'I think you are a good man turning bad, and I think Niki is a bad man trying to be good. I prefer Niki.'

'That makes sense.'

She looked at him. 'You look like a 60-year-old. Someone at the end of his life.'

'Sixty isn't the end of life. And I am nowhere near that age.'

'The number is not important. Someone with no generosity left. Always looking back, always judging. I hope you get to keep Caterina. She's your last chance.'

Blume put down his bottle. 'I don't really wish Niki ill any more. But whatever happens, he's going to be in some trouble.'

'What am I supposed to do now?'

'I don't know. Go back home to Romania, try a fresh start?'

'Idiot,' she said. 'And careful where you put your stupid water bottle. You've just spilled it all over my backside.'

'It was empty.' He could feel water, too, soaking into his trousers.

'Then what's . . . ?' She stood up. 'From the statue? It was dry here when I sat down. *Cazzo*, I hate this garden. What on earth are you doing?'

'Filling my bottle like the doctor said.'

'Don't drink the water if you don't know where it's come from!'

'No, I know about this water. It's famous. It's supposed to be very good for you. Curative. Magic, even. Here,' He held out the bottle. 'Taste.'

'You taste it.'

'Go on. You first. Trust me.'

'Any reason I should ever trust any man again?'

'How about Niki? He came back.'

She smiled. 'A drug-smuggling, diabetic semi-pimp, and a doped-up cop. I heard what the doctor said. At least you kept your promise to find Alina, even if it was too late. What a pair.'

She held out her hand and took the bottle. 'All right, all right, I'll drink. I can't bear to see you look so insulted. Now you look like a disappointed child instead of the old man you are. Are you sure it's safe?'

'Make a wish, Nadia,' said Blume. 'A big one.'

'OK, old policeman. *Noroc.*'

She brought the bottle to her lips and drank.

A NOTE ON THE AUTHOR

Conor Fitzgerald has lived in Ireland, the UK, the United States, and Italy. He has produced a current affairs journal for foreign embassies based in Rome, and founded a successful translation company. *Bitter Remedy* is the fifth in his series of Italian crime novels.

www.conorfitzgerald.net

A NOTE ON THE TYPE

The text of this book is set in Bembo. This type was first used in 1495 by the Venetian printer Aldus Manutius for Cardinal Bembo's *De Aetna*, and was cut for Manutius by Francesco Griffo. It was one of the types used by Claude Garamond (1480–1561) as a model for his Romain de L'Université, and so it was the forerunner of what became standard European type for the following two centuries. Its modern form follows the original types and was designed for Monotype in 1929.